DEAR BOYFRIEND... AND OTHER HIGH SCHOOL DILEMMAS

Dear Boyfriend... and Other High School Dilemmas

An Emma Bishop Story

Rebecca Garner

Also by Rebecca Garner

Why Won't My Boobs Grow... and Other Annoyances (Emma Bishop #1)
Dear Boyfriend... and Other High School Dilemmas (Emma Bishop #2)
We'll Never Be Friends... and Other Girlhood Mishaps (Emma Bishop #3)

For Lucy, who will someday be a teenage girl.
And for anyone who's ever felt left behind.

Contents

I wish a boy would walk three miles to see me.

FRIDAY, SEPTEMBER 17TH

10:01 P.M.

RUBY'S BEDROOM

"Did you make out?"

"Ew, Emma. No one calls it that any more. It's just *hooking up*."

Ruby and I exchange a glance.

"Since when?"

Cher rolls her eyes at me and starts to pull her long blonde hair up into a messy bun. When she's done, she smiles down at her knees, then turns back to us, her eyes glimmering.

"But yeah, we did."

The three of us burst into squeals of delight. We're sitting on a pile of pillows on the floor of Ruby's bedroom. Celsius's new album, *Without You*, is playing quietly from Ruby's laptop. Two minutes ago, Cher climbed through Ruby's window after meeting up with her new boyfriend, Jacob.

"Tell us *everything*!" Ruby says, reaching out to shake Cher's knees.

Cher puts her face in her hands. When she looks up, she's smiling.

"It was amazing. He's so tall, I had to stand on my tippy toes to reach his face. And his lips—" Cher pauses and smiles down at her feet, fumbling with the edge of her socks. "They're so soft."

If it's possible, her smile gets even bigger.

I'm so happy for Cher, but there's also a little pang of jealousy in my chest. She is so giddy and over the moon because of this kiss, and I wish I could feel the same way about someone. My cat, Albus, is the only one who's kissed me recently, and his tongue is very scratchy. And then he bit me a second later.

I snap out of feeling sorry for myself as Cher goes on.

"And Jacob is so sweet, too. He walked *three miles* to come and see me tonight."

Ruby gasps. "I don't think I'd walk three miles even if it meant saving your lives."

"Ruby!" I hit her on the arm. "You're going to let us die?"

Cher shakes her head with a smirk and looks up at the ceiling.

"Ugh fine," Ruby concedes. "I would only do it if it meant I was saving your lives. I definitely wouldn't do it for a boy."

"I think it's so romantic," I say airily. I roll onto my back and gaze up at the ceiling before whining, "I wish a boy would walk three miles to see me."

"I know," Cher says, not unkindly. "I feel like... like... I don't even know. Like my chest is going to burst, and I'm all warm and fuzzy inside, and..." She sighs wistfully, hugging a pillow to her chest. "All I want to do is kiss him again.

"I feel like I'm in a romantic comedy. Like, Jacob's best friend's locker happened to be next to mine? And Jacob happened to beat Henry to his locker on the first day of school? We locked eyes, and I knew it immediately. My heart started racing, but I couldn't look away. I knew we were going to fall in love—"

"Wait. Are you *in love* with him?" Ruby asks skeptically.

"I don't know." Cher touches the blonde bun on top of her head absent-mindedly. "Maybe not yet, but it's definitely a big like. And it's only been a couple weeks. So, obviously, we'll be in love eventually. I can feel it."

Ruby nods without saying anything and glances over at me. I turn my attention back to the faded star stickers on Ruby's ceiling.

"When can we meet him?" I ask Cher. I sit up and try to tame my wavy brown hair as it falls in my face.

"I don't know." Cher pauses and frowns slightly. "I can't believe we don't all go to school together anymore. It's so unfair." Ruby sighs, and I nod in agreement.

All three of us went to St. Lucy's until eighth grade, and now Ruby and I go to the public high school, Oak Ridge. But Cher's parents are divorced and live in two different towns. St. Lucy's was in the middle of the two, which is how she ended up there. Now she goes to the private school in the next town over.

"Does he have any cute friends?" I ask hopefully. That would be convenient.

"I don't know. I haven't really met any of his friends yet, except Henry. And Henry is really nice and all, but I don't think either of you would be into him." Cher says it nonchalantly, but I feel like maybe she's not telling the whole truth. She bites her lip before continuing.

"What about at Oak Ridge? Are there any cute boys you've met there?"

"No," Ruby says automatically. She sits up and leans against the disheveled bed behind her. She had a growth spurt over the summer, so her long legs stretch out in front of her. Her box braids transition to a light purple at the bottom, which makes her look so sophisticated and cool. Her dark brown eyes lock on mine, and she shrugs with a smile.

I smirk back. "Yes there are!" There are so many boys. Way more than at St. Lucy's. Every time I walk down the hallway, I feel like I see a cute boy I hadn't seen before. Oak Ridge is approximately four times the size of St. Lucy's.

"Have you talked to any of them, Emma?" Cher asks, raising her eyebrows.

My mind briefly flits to the cute boy I sit next to in my biology class.

"Not really," I admit. "But they're fun to look at!" We all burst into giggles again.

10:40 P.M.

Ruby made us some popcorn, and we're snuggling down to watch the original *Mean Girls*—a classic, according to Ruby's mom, Georgia.

My arm brushes my boob as I reach for a handful of popcorn.

"I think my boobs are getting bigger," I announce proudly.

Cher's eyes go to my chest, but she doesn't say anything.

"What makes you say that?" Ruby asks. She crawls over and pulls my arms out, so she can examine my boob area. "Let me get a good look at you."

I push Ruby's arms off and sit up to pull my shirt tight across my chest. "I don't know. I can kind of feel them now I guess. What do you think?" I swivel my body to the side, so they can examine my profile.

"Hm, maybe," Cher says, noncommittal, as she tosses a piece of popcorn into her mouth.

"I mean, they're definitely bigger than they were at the start of last year," Ruby says, looking closely at my bits.

I let go of my shirt and cup my hands around them. "Definitely. I didn't even have anything to cup last year," I say with a giggle.

"I'm happy for you, Em," Ruby says, giving me a hug. "And your boobies."

We all laugh as Ruby crawls back to her spot on the other side of Cher.

I cup my boobs again. Small as they may be, I can jiggle them just slightly. I definitely couldn't do that last year.

I smile as Ruby presses play.

Chapter 2

No, thanks.

SUNDAY, SEPTEMBER 19TH

3:07 P.M.

MY BEDROOM

My little sister, Marie, pokes her head in my room. "Emma?"

"Ever heard of knocking?" I say, shutting my laptop. I wasn't doing anything except avoiding my English homework, but still. I hate when my family thinks they can walk in my room without any warning.

"Sorry," Marie says, not sounding sorry at all. She's nine, going on *annoying.* "Can you help me with something?" She has a hair brush in her hand.

"What is it?" I narrow my eyes at her.

"Can you show me how to do a messy bun?" She holds up the brush in her left hand and a scrunchie in her right. Her long auburn hair is down and slightly tousled.

I roll my eyes. "Not right now." I open my laptop again. "I'm doing homework." Okay, fine. I'm not, but I don't feel like helping her.

"But—" she starts to plead, her brown eyes widening.

"I'm busy," I snap before she can finish.

She turns in a huff and slams my door shut.

I go back to reading about the Celsius documentary coming out next month. I need to text Ruby and Cher about watching it together.

3:20 P.M.

I close my laptop again. I'm bored. I text Ruby.

> **Me:** What are you doing? Want to hang out? We can watch Celsius music videos to prepare for the documentary!

> **Ruby:** Ughhh, wish I could, but I'm actually supposed to meet Alejandra at the mall later.

> **Me:** Oh. Ok. Text me later.

> **Ruby:** Will do!! *Twelve heart emojis.*

I sigh, only slightly annoyed that Ruby didn't invite me to go to the mall with her and Alejandra. I'm the whole reason they even started hanging out.

Alejandra sat behind me in our English class last year, and we would talk occasionally. We ended up hanging out with her when we went ice skating once in the spring, and she and Ruby realized they had a lot in common and hit it off. They texted a bit over the summer, but now that school has started, they have a few classes together and have been hanging out.

I text Cher.

> **Me:** Want to do something today?

Cher: Can't. Out with Jacob.

She sends a selfie of the two of them mini golfing. Her blue eyes are shining as she presses her face against his.

Me: Aw cute.

Cher: *Winky face and heart eyes emojis.*

I lie back on my bed and sigh again. All alone. Maybe I should have helped Marie.

3:34 P.M.

I knock on Marie's bedroom door, like the courteous sister I am. She opens it and pokes her head out. She eyes me suspiciously.

"What?" she says, not opening the door any further.

"What are you doing? Why are you being so weird?" I try to push the door open, but she blocks it with her body.

"What do you want?" she repeats.

Why is she being so evasive? She was the one who wanted my help in the first place. I roll my eyes.

"I was going to offer to help you with your hair if you wanted." I put my hands on my hips and let out a sigh.

"No, thanks," Marie says quickly. Then she shuts the door.

I stand there for a second, shocked. I let out another loud sigh before turning on my heel back to my bedroom.

9:01 P.M.

What a boring day. I feel like such a loser. My friends didn't want to hang out with me. Even my sister didn't want to hang out with me.

9:03 P.M.

And I can't stop thinking about Ruby. It didn't really bug me at first, but then when I had nothing to do all day, it started getting to me. Why didn't she invite me to go with her and Alejandra to the mall?

Am I so uncool that she doesn't want to be seen with me?

9:06 P.M.

Ruby wore her gym pants on her head as a makeshift hat as we walked home last week. She can't be embarrassed by me.

9:29 P.M.

Does Alejandra not like me? We were sort-of-friends first!

But she's always really nice when I see her. And she invited me to her birthday party over the summer.

9:33 P.M.

I wonder if Cher has let Jacob feel her up.

I'll have to ask her tomorrow.

9:36 P.M.

I cup my boobs. I jiggle them slightly.

I guess I'm starting to understand why boys want to touch them. It is kind of fun to jiggle them.

Is this weird? Do other people jiggle their own boobs? Probably not.

CHAPTER 3

He's so cute.

THURSDAY, SEPTEMBER 23RD

12:37 P.M.

RUBY'S LOCKER

"I have news," I tell Ruby as she puts her books in her locker.

She turns to face me and claps her hands quickly. "Ooh! Tell me! Tell me!"

"I like someone." I smile coyly and put my chin down on my pile of books.

Ruby gasps, putting her hands on the side of her face. "What? Who? How is this the first I'm hearing of it?"

"You've been very busy. I've barely seen you this week!"

"I know, I know. I'm sorry." Ruby shakes her head and closes her locker.

I hip-bump her as we start walking to the gym. "Plus, I wasn't sure if I actually like-liked him, or if he was just fun to look at until this week."

"Ooh, okay. So, who is it?"

I scan the area around us to make sure there's no one eavesdropping. "His name is Andy. We sit together in biology." I pause, smiling to myself.

"Ahhh!" Ruby squeals.

"I know," I reply. "He's so cute. He has blond hair and blue eyes." I swoon internally, thinking about gazing into Andy's eyes at the end of biology today. That's what I noticed about him on the first day of school: his deep blue eyes. I thought he was cute immediately.

"Okay, okay, what about his personality?" Ruby asks. "What's he like? Why do you like him, besides his perfect white-boy good looks?"

I laugh. "Well, they definitely don't hurt." I think for a second. "He's nice. He offered me a piece of gum before class started. And he's funny. We were partners for the activity today, and he kept making me laugh." My cheeks warm thinking about it now.

Earlier this week, Andy noticed the Celsius sticker on my notebook and said, "James or Stephen?"

"What?" I asked.

"James or Stephen—who's your favorite? Personally, I prefer Stephen because he plays the guitar too. Multi-talented, you know?"

"Wait." I put my hands up. "Do you like Celsius?" I asked in disbelief.

Andy shrugged. "Don't tell my friends," he said with a smile.

That was when I decided I liked him.

Ruby's voice snaps me back to attention. "This is so exciting! Do you have any other classes with him?" Her eyes are bright.

I sigh. "No, only biology. So, I'll have to wait until tomorrow to talk to him again."

"What a bummer," Ruby agrees. She turns her head and calls out, "Alejandra! Hey!"

Alejandra catches up to us as we turn the corner for the locker rooms. She pushes her square frame glasses up on her nose. Her long, raven-colored hair is in a ponytail, and she's wearing a red-and-black plaid shirt and jeans. She smiles broadly at Ruby and then leans forward to say hi to me.

"What's going on?" Alejandra asks.

"Oh, not much. Emma's in love," Ruby tells her swiftly.

I stop in my tracks. "Ruby!"

Ruby turns back to me, laughing. "What? Emma, come on. Alejandra isn't going to tell anyone. Are you?" She turns to Alejandra and raises her eyebrows.

Alejandra mimes zipping her mouth shut.

I'm a little annoyed. I barely decide I like Andy, and Ruby is already telling Alejandra? A small ember burns in my chest.

Ruby and Alejandra start walking again, and I speed walk to catch up to them.

"Yeah, so I think I'm going to try out for the solo," Alejandra says.

"You're totally going to get it," Ruby tells her.

"Solo for what?" I ask.

"Band," they say in unison. They both giggle, and Ruby hip-bumps her. That ember in my chest burns a little brighter. Ruby and Alejandra have three classes together: English, PE (with me), and band. I am not a musical person, so my second elective for this year was art. But Ruby and Alejandra are both really into music. I mean, so am I, but only the listening part. They're into listening to it *and* playing it. Ruby plays the clarinet, and Alejandra plays the trumpet.

"Oh, cool," is all I say. The two of them continue talking about the fall concert as we get changed for class. I curse myself for not being musically talented.

3:17 P.M.
MY LOCKER

"Heyyyy," Ruby says as she comes bounding up to my locker.

"Hey, Rubs." I'm relieved she's alone. My locker is across from the band room, so sometimes Alejandra will come with Ruby to my locker at the end of the day.

Ruby starts telling me some gossip about a junior who plays clarinet and her boyfriend who plays the drums. (Apparently, the boyfriend was getting a little too flirty with Clarinet Girl's best friend when they all hung out last weekend, and they haven't spoken in almost four days. People are taking bets on how long it will take for one of them to give in and break up with the other.)

As I grab my sweater off the hook, I hear a boy's voice. I jerk my head out of my locker, curious who's saying hi to Ruby.

It's not someone saying hi to *Ruby*, but she does have a small smile playing on her lips.

It's Andy.

My heart starts beating faster, but somehow I don't feel any warmth in my cheeks. I'm impressed with myself.

"Hey," I say confidently. I even casually smile over my shoulder.

Andy smiles back at me.

"Hi!" Ruby takes a step closer. "I'm Ruby. Emma's best friend in the world." She puts her hand out. Andy looks at it, confused for a second, but then smiles and shakes it.

"Andy," he says. He's so cute. Those eyes. They're so blue I could get lost in them. He turns back to me, and I tear my attention away from his eyes and focus on his mouth because it's talking to me.

"I have PE last, and you said your locker was down here, so I thought I'd come say hi."

I can't help but blush a little. How sweet is that? What do I say?

"Oh, cool," I manage to spit out. "Thanks."

Andy smiles again. "Are you going to the football game tomorrow night?" he asks.

I turn to Ruby, and her brown eyes shoot over to the band room across the hall. She'll be there, but she'll be playing with the band.

"Maybe," I say slowly. I move to push my hair behind my ears, but when I don't feel any, I remember that all of my wavy brown hair is in a bun on top of my head today. My cheeks flush deeper, and I casually move my hand up to the bun, like that was my intention the whole time.

"You should come," Andy says. It appears he didn't notice the hand-bun incident. He runs his hand up and down his arm. "A bunch of us are going. You could sit with us."

I can't go by myself. Who would I talk to? What if Andy is busy talking to his friends? Plus, Mom would never let me go alone to meet a boy. Maybe I can see if Cher wants to come with me.

"Maybe," I say again.

"Oh." Andy's smile falters, and it hurts my heart.

"It's just that Ruby is in band, and I don't want to go alone. I'll see if my other friend wants to come. It sounds like fun," I assure him.

"Oh," he says again, brighter this time. "Okay. Yeah, let me know." He pulls his phone out of his pocket and glances at the screen. "I've got to run—soccer practice. See you tomorrow?"

I nod, smiling, as he jogs down the hall.

Ruby hip-bumps me. "So that's Bio Boy, huh?"

I giggle, turning to grab my backpack and close my locker. "Mmhm. What do you think?"

"He seems like a little sweetie," Ruby says. "I wish I could go with you to the game." She sighs dramatically. "It sucks that I'm stuck up there all night. I don't even get to sit by Alejandra because we play different instruments."

I know it's not cool, but I get a small amount of satisfaction out of this.

8:09 P.M.
BEDROOM

Why is math so boring? And why do teachers assign only even or odd problems for homework? I mean, I appreciate not having to do any more, trust me. But it's weird right? Why don't the textbook people put fewer problems in the book?

I can't figure out the one I'm working on. Every time I do it, my answer doesn't match the answer in the back, and I have no idea what I'm doing wrong.

I give up and text our group chat.

Me: Cher. Do you want to go to the football game with me tomorrow night?

Cher: At Oak Ridge?

Ruby: Yeah. The boy Emma likes wants her to go!!!

Me: His name is Andy.

Me: And Ruby can't hang out with me because she's in band. I need some support. I can't go by myself!!!

Cher: I'm going to the game at Woodlands. Jacob is playing, and I have to go cheer him on. Girlfriend duties, you know? Sorry…

I roll my eyes, but at the same time wish I had girlfriend duties.

But I'll never get to have girlfriend duties if I can't hang out with Andy!

Me: Ugh, lame.

I send another text immediately.

Me: But also, like, so cute.

Ruby: SO. CUTE.

Cher: *Three in love emojis.*

I lie back on my bed, staring up at the ceiling. What am I going to do? I can't miss this opportunity to hang out with Andy. But I have no one to go with.

Ugggghhhh.

9:34 P.M.
IN BED

Cher is so lucky she has a boyfriend.

My cat, Albus, climbs out from under my bed and hops up next to me.

"How long have you been under there?" I ask him, stroking the top of his little gray head. "I want a boyfriend," I tell him, then correct myself. "I want *Andy* to be my boyfriend."

The disappointment of not being able to go to the game tomorrow overwhelms me. It's stupid, but a tear rolls down my cheek. I feel like I'm missing out on a huge moment of my life.

9:58 P.M.

What if Andy thinks I don't like him because I'm not going to the game? What if another girl starts talking to him, and since I'm not there, he thinks I don't like him, and so he decides to ask her out? And then they fall in love and date for the rest of high school, and go to college together, and then get married and have, like, six babies.

And I'll be over here. Alone. In my bed. With my cat.

CHAPTER 4

Are you going to go to the game tonight?

FRIDAY, SEPTEMBER 24TH

12:35 P.M.
BIOLOGY

Andy slides into his seat next to me right as the bell rings. My heart does a little flip-flop.

"Phew," he sighs. "I made it." He looks over at me sideways, a half-smile playing on his lips.

I giggle and push my hair behind my ear, but our teacher, Mr. Milo, starts talking before I can say anything back. We both turn to the front of the room.

I glance at Andy one more time, and he's staring back at me. I avert my eyes to the slides Mr. Milo is pulling up as my heart does another tumble.

I think Andy likes me. Ahhh!!!!

1:25 P.M.

The bell rings. I couldn't tell you what Mr. Milo was talking about in class today. I took the notes but did not actually listen to anything he was saying. I was too busy thinking about and glancing at Andy. We made eye contact at least three times.

"So..." Andy starts as we both stand up. He rubs the back of his neck.

I avoid looking at his armpit. I don't know why, but boys' armpits make me feel weird. I don't want to see his armpit hair. If he has any. I don't know. When do boys get armpit hair? I shave my armpits. So he probably has hair in his, right? I realize I'm fixating and shake it off.

Andy hasn't said anything else, so I say, "So...?" We didn't get to talk much in class because it was a notes day.

"Are you going to go to the game tonight?"

My heart sinks.

"Um..." I stare down at my shoes. I'm honestly afraid I might cry, and that is so dumb and embarrassing.

"That doesn't sound good," he says quietly.

"My friend Cher can't go with me." I pause. "And my mom won't let me go alone," I admit, even though it's embarrassing. I didn't even ask Mom, but I know better. There's no way.

"That sucks," he says quietly. His shoulders are drooped, and the corners of his mouth are turned down. He offers me a weak smile. And even though I'm so bummed about this I thought I might cry ten seconds ago, my heart lifts slightly because he definitely likes me. He wouldn't be so disappointed if he didn't.

We walk together to the door. As we're about to turn in our opposite directions, Andy says, "Hey, um, do you think I could have your number? Maybe then we could at least talk during the game?"

His cheeks are pink, and it is the cutest thing I've ever seen in my life. And that includes Albus's ear hair as a kitten.

I nod. Andy's face breaks into a wide smile, and my heart soars. He pulls his phone out of his pocket.

I plug my number in, and feeling brave, I add a smiley face emoji next to my name. Then I hit call so I have his number.

I try to contain my giddiness as I hand his phone back to him. I bite my lips together but can't hide the smile breaking through.

"Cool," Andy says, his ocean-blue eyes locked on my sea glass-green ones.

"Cool," I say back. We both smile, and my heart does another flip-flop.

"I'll text you later then?" he says.

"You better." Oh my gosh. Who do I think I am? I am so cool.

With another genuine smile, he turns and walks down the hallway.

3:20 P.M.
MY LOCKER

Ruby and I are chatting away at my locker at the end of the day when my phone buzzes.

> **Andy:** Just wanted to say hi. Wish you were coming to the game tonight.

I show Ruby the screen. Her jaw drops.

"Wow! Girl, he is smitten!" She does a little shimmy for emphasis.

I giggle and bite my bottom lip.

"What should I say back?"

"I don't think it matters. He's going to love you either way," Ruby says with a smirk. She tosses her braids over her shoulder, and her eyes wander to the band room across the hall.

I hold the phone against my chest for a second, taking in this moment. Despite the fact that I can't go to the football game, excitement and happiness still swirl in my chest.

> **Me:** Me too. Don't have too much fun without me, k?

He responds right away.

> **Andy:** No way.

Ruby hip bumps me, reading over my shoulder.
"Smi-tten," she says in a sing-song voice.

7:10 P.M.
BEDROOM

I wonder what Andy is doing. The game should have started ten minutes ago. I text Ruby.

> **Me:** Any Andy sightings?

> **Ruby:** I was JUST about to text you!! He and a bunch of other guys are up in the bleachers.

> **Ruby:** He's looking at his phone now.

> **Ruby:** Maybe he's texting you!!!

I respond with a bunch of nervous smile emojis.

7:12 P.M.

My phone buzzes. I smile at the screen, and a band of butterflies starts flapping in my chest.

Andy: Hey. Whatcha up to?

Me: Feeling like a loser watching TV at home on a Friday night. *Upside-down smiley face.*

Andy: You're not a loser.

Andy: It would be more fun if you were here, though…

The butterflies pick up their pace. I like that Andy isn't trying to be coy. Like, he's making it pretty clear he's into me.

And I'm into that.

8:30 P.M.

I've been texting with Andy for over an hour. He just sent a Celsius gif. I can't stop smiling.

He's said probably three or four times that he wishes I was at the game, or that it would be more fun if I was there. It's sweet, but like, I get it. I'm not there.

I send Ruby a screenshot of the last few messages with Andy. He asked when we're going to hang out.

> **Ruby:** SMITTEN AS A KITTEN. *Thirty cat emojis.*

> **Ruby:** Every time I look over there, his friends are all talking and messing around, and he's sitting in front of them, staring at his phone.

Oh. I don't know how that makes me feel. On one hand, I like that he's paying attention to me. But, on the other hand, I don't want him to *not* hang out with his friends. I also don't want them to think I'm the reason he's not hanging out with them.

Before I respond to Ruby, I send Andy another message.

> **Me:** Not that I don't like talking to you, but aren't you supposed to be having fun with your friends?

He responds immediately.

> **Andy:** Yeah I guess… but I'm having more fun talking to you.

It makes me smile, but I can't fully ignore the little ball of worry in the pit of my stomach.

> **Me:** Me too. But I'm gonna go watch a movie with my little sister. She's been begging me for like an hour now.

It's not a total lie. Marie asked if I wanted to watch a movie earlier, but I walked past her room, ignoring the request.

Andy: Ok, sounds good. Can I text you tomorrow?

Me: I'd like that.

I lie on my bed quietly for a minute, my face pleasantly warm from the conversation with Andy. I still wish I could have gone to the game and hung out with him tonight, but this wasn't a horrible turn of events.

I think about his beautiful, crisp blue eyes, and my heart does a little jump. My imaginary focus moves to his mouth, and the warmth spreads down into my chest. I would like to kiss that mouth.

8:42 P.M.

I decide not to make a liar out of myself and see if Marie still wants to watch a movie. I meander down the hall and tap on her door. I walk in without waiting for a response.

She's reading a book in her bed and drops it dramatically when I come in.

"Ever heard of knocking?" she demands.

"I did knock."

"But you didn't wait. What if I was naked?" She sits up and gestures down her body.

"Thank God you're not. You never knock when you come into my room."

Marie narrows her round brown eyes but doesn't acknowledge that fact. "What do you want?"

"Do you want to watch a movie now?" I ask.

Marie picks her book up and settles back on the pillows propped up behind her. There's like six of them.

"Not really," she says, turning the page of her book. Her eyes aren't actually moving, though.

I stand there and give her another second to change her mind.

"You can go now," she says without looking up from the page she's pretending to read.

I roll my eyes and turn to leave. Whatever, I'll watch something by myself then.

"Where are your friends anyway? Why aren't you hanging out with *them*?" Marie says as I reach the doorway.

It's my turn not to acknowledge her, and I head back to my own bedroom.

9:02 P.M.

I can't get Marie's comment out of my head.

Where are my friends? They're busy, Marie, okay? Ugh.

I was trying to be nice and watch a movie with her, and now she doesn't even want to? She's so annoying.

9:16 P.M.

The football game is probably over by now. I text Ruby.

Me: Hey! What are you up to?

9:32 P.M.

No response. My chest feels tight.

10:04 P.M.

Finally, I get an answer.

Ruby: Sorry, just got home. Alejandra and I went to Dunkin after the game.

Me: Cool. Thanks for the invite…

Ruby: Oh, sorry. I didn't think you'd want to come out this late.

She's probably right, but my chest still feels tight.

Me: K.

Ruby: Oh come on, Emma. Don't be crabby at me. It's not my fault you didn't go to the game.

Me: It sort of is. If you weren't in band, we could have gone together.

I know I shouldn't have sent it the second I did.

Ruby doesn't respond.

10:10 P.M.

Me: I'm sorry. That was stupid of me to say.

No response.

10:12 P.M.

Me: RUBY!!!!!! PLEASE!!!!!!!

Me: I'M SORRY!!!!!!!!!

Me: Don't you want to hear how my conversation with Andy went??

10:15 P.M.

Ruby: LOL I was making a snack.

Me: Oh my Godddd.

Ruby: But, still, pretty lame.

Me: I know. I'm sorry. I know you love band and music and stuff. I guess I'm a little jelly is all. I miss you.

Ruby: It's ok. I still love you. Always.

Me: Always.

Phew. What a relief. I can't stand to lose my best friend right now.

Me: Want to hang out tomorrow and dissect my conversation with Andy?

Ruby: OBV.

I send a gif of a dancing lady and put my phone on my nightstand. I take a deep breath and sink into my pillow. I stare up at the ceiling, feeling both exhausted and hyped up at the same time.

10:22 P.M.

I keep replaying my conversation with Andy in my mind. Every time I run through it, my chest warms pleasantly. I can't wait to see him again at school. Which I guess means I can't wait to go back to school. Weird.

10:47 P.M.

I wonder what Andy is doing now. Is he thinking about me?

CHAPTER 5

I have a date!!!!

MONDAY, SEPTEMBER 27TH

1:26 P.M.

BIOLOGY

"What do you have next?" Andy asks as we gather our books after the bell rings.

"PE," I tell him.

"Cool," he says a little too confidently. His voice is a notch or two louder than normal. I think he realizes it since the next thing that comes out of his mouth is a normal decibel. "Can I walk you there?"

"All the way to the gym? Won't you be late for your next class?"

Andy shrugs. "Maybe. But I can walk fast." He smiles down at me. I never really noticed before, but he's pretty tall.

I smile back and bite my bottom lip.

"I'm actually walking to Ruby's locker first, so we can walk down together."

"Oh, can I walk you to Ruby's locker then?"

Mr. Milo interrupts our conversation, causing both Andy and me to jump. "You two better get moving if you don't want to be late for your next class."

He's right. We make our way out the door, hesitating as we enter the hallway.

"Ruby's locker is this way." I nod to the right.

Andy's sapphire eyes light up. "Let's go then."

We walk in silence for a couple seconds, and then Andy clears his throat.

"So, um…" he starts. Andy is looking straight ahead, and his cheeks are a little pink. (Relatable.)

My heart starts thumping in my chest. What's he going to say?

"The uh… homecoming dance is coming up…" His eyes dart over to me and then back to the hallway ahead of him.

Now it's my turn to blush. I don't know what to do. My heart is still thumping, my cheeks are warm, and my arms feel sort of numb. Andy still hasn't said anything else, and we're almost to Ruby's locker. It's just around the corner now.

"Mm-hm," I say, hoping it encourages Andy to keep going.

"Uh, I was wondering, um…" We stop walking at the end of the hall. I glance to the right and see Ruby waiting for me. The warning bell rings.

"Shoot," Andy mutters. Then, finally, he says. "I was wondering if you wanted to go to the dance with me?" He rubs the back of his neck, which is also pink, and looks down the hall to his left, avoiding eye contact.

He's adorable. I can't believe this is happening. I hug my books tight to my chest and try to hide the smile exploding across my face.

"Yeah. Yes."

Andy turns back to me, his eyes wide with surprise.

"Really?"

"Of course." I gently push him on the arm.

Andy and I take another second to smile at each other before our moment is ruined by Ruby shouting my name. "Emma! We're going to be late!"

"I've got to go," I apologize.

"I'll text you later?" he says.

I smile back at him and nod.

I have a date!!!!

1:31 P.M.
LOCKER ROOM

Ruby and I had to sprint halfway across the school to make it to class on time. We're both huffing and puffing as we change into our PE uniforms.

"So," Ruby says after a deep breath. "What were you talking to Bio Boy about? You were both pink and kind of twirly. Are you guys in love?"

"No!" I throw my T-shirt at her. "We're not in love. What is with you asking people that all the time?"

She smirks and shrugs before pulling her PE shirt over her gigantic boobs. My own little mounds sit hidden beneath my shirt.

"You should give me some of your boobs," I tell her.

Ruby clicks her tongue and looks down at her chest with pursed lips. "I'd love to," she says. She shakes her head slightly before turning her attention back to me. "Come on! What was it?" she demands, putting her hands on her hips.

Heat creeps onto my cheeks again, and my heart does its signature flip-flop.

"Andy asked me to Homecoming," I say quietly.

Ruby's jaw drops. "Oh my God! Emma! Ahhh!" She runs over and hugs me, squeezing as tight as she can. "A real date!" she squeals.

I hug her back, laughing. "I know! Can you believe it?"

Ruby takes a step back, her arms outstretched, hands still on my shoulders. "Of course I can. You're a babe, Em. He's lucky to have snagged you."

She's my best friend, so she has to say that, but I almost believe her.

CHAPTER 6

That explains the colonial pony.

MONDAY, SEPTEMBER 27TH

5:37 P.M.

DINNER

"Let's play High-Low," Marie announces as soon as we start eating dinner. She looks around at Mom, Dad, and me expectantly. For the first time, I notice her hair is in a weird colonial man-style ponytail, parted down the middle and secured at the nape of her neck. I smirk but don't say anything.

"Great idea, sweetie," Mom says before taking a sip of water. "Do you want to go first?"

"I'd love to," Marie says. She purposefully places her fork down on the table next to her plate and folds her hands before she starts. "High: I did my hair all on my own this morning." She puts her hand up to her face and turns her head, so we can admire her work. That explains the colonial pony.

Mom nods and gives Marie an encouraging smile. Her eyes dart to me for a second, probably to make sure I'm not going to make a comment, but I'm not *that* mean. She's clearly proud of herself. I won't spoil the moment.

"Impressive," Dad says as he takes a bite of his potatoes. He adds a thumbs up as he chews. He has no idea what hair is supposed to look like. He barely has any of his own left.

Marie continues. "Low..." She pauses, glancing down at her plate. I'm expecting her usual, *No low indicated*, but instead, she picks her head up with a defiant stare and says, "Ally told me my hair looked stupid."

Mom puts her fork down and focuses all her attention on Marie. "Oh, honey, I'm so sorry. That was not a nice thing to say at all." Her eyes are wide as she turns to Dad.

Dad halts the chicken making its way to his mouth when he catches Mom's pointed look. His eyes seem to say, *I don't know what to do here.*

It's silent for a second too long as Mom and Dad continue staring at each other, so I jump in.

"Did you tell your teacher?" I ask.

"No," Marie says quickly.

"Why not?"

"Because I don't care what Ally thinks." She says this with an air of confidence, looking me right in the eyes, but I also hear a slight waver in her voice.

A fire bursts into flame in my chest. No one is allowed to make fun of my little sister except me.

"Who's Ally anyway?" I say, narrowing my eyes.

"She's new. Everyone thinks she's so cool, but I don't. She's a faker," Marie explains.

"Don't listen to her," I tell Marie. "She sounds like she doesn't know what she's talking about. Your hair is cool," I lie.

Marie doesn't say anything, but she purses her lips and nods, like I've said the wisest thing she's ever heard.

Mom is staring at me with watery eyes and a small smile. It makes me feel squirmy, so I turn back to my plate and take a bite of some green beans.

"You should be proud of yourself, Marie," Mom says.

Dad adds an enthusiastic, "Mmhm," across from her.

Marie nods some more, staring off into the distance. "I am," she says after a second.

"I'll go next," I volunteer. "High: I have a date for the homecoming dance." I press my lips together, waiting for my parents' response.

Mom's eyes go wide again. "You do?" she squeals. "Oh, Emma, how exciting! We'll have to go dress shopping. And maybe I can make you and Ruby appointments at the makeup counter for the day of the dance!"

My own excitement bubbles up and over.

"Who's the boy?" Dad asks with fake sternness. "Or girl?" he adds, raising his eyebrows and pointing his fork at me. He glances at Mom again, this time his eyes saying, *Did you see that? That was good, right?*

I giggle. "His name is Andy. I sit next to him in biology," I share. I wasn't planning to spill all the details to my family, but I'm feeling pretty giddy. Part of me even wants to tell them about his ocean-blue eyes.

"Are you in loooove?" Marie teases.

Why is everyone always asking that?

I roll my eyes. "No." Again, my giddiness encourages me to share more than I normally would. "But he is *really* cute."

"Ah!" Mom squeals again, throwing her hands up in the air. We all turn to her. "I'm sorry. I'm just so excited!" Then she sighs. "My baby is really growing up."

I roll my eyes again. "Yeah, yeah." The giddiness is starting to pass, so I'm ready to move the conversation on.

"Anyways, my low is that I have to do a self-portrait in my art class, and it is *not* going well."

"I bet," Marie says with a snicker. The tenderness I felt toward her two minutes ago is gone.

"What's that supposed to mean?" I demand.

"Nothing," she says, shoveling potatoes into her mouth. Dad throws his balled-up napkin at her. She giggles and throws it back.

I turn to Mom, who's giving me gooey mom-eyes again. She shrugs.

I give Marie the evil eye as Dad starts talking about his high (the ice cream he's going to eat after dinner). She sticks her tongue out in response.

8:17 P.M.
BEDROOM

My phone buzzes while I'm attempting to do my biology homework.

> **Cher:** Helllooooo? I haven't heard from either of you in days! What's going on?

> **Ruby:** HELLLLLLOOOOOOO CHERRRRR!!!

> **Ruby:** I miss you!!!

> **Me:** I miss you, too, Cher! It totally sucks not seeing you every day.

> **Cher:** It does. I feel like I don't even know what's going on with you anymore. *Frowning emoji.*

It's hard when one of your best friends goes to a different school. There are so many small things that happen throughout the day that I would normally tell her, but now it seems silly to try to explain Mr. Milo's weird new haircut to her when she doesn't even know who he is.

Part of me also wants to point out that she might know more about what was going on if she'd gone with me to the football game last Friday. Or hung out with Ruby and me on Saturday night. But it doesn't really feel worth the sass I'd probably get back. Instead, I send only a crying emoji.

Ruby: Emma has NEWS!

My heart races, thinking about my news. I smile as I type out my response.

Me: I have a ~date~ to Homecoming!!!

Cher sends back a dancing cat gif, which I know she did for me because Cher doesn't like cats. Even Albus. One time she tried to pet his belly when he was lounging on my bed. It did not go well. In Cher's defense, she didn't know that when a cat is lying like that, it is definitely *not* an invitation to pet them.

Cher: OMG!!!! EMMA!! That's awesome!!!! Who is it?!

Me: Andy, from my bio class.

Ruby: Bio Boy.

Cher: The one you were supposed to meet up with at the football game?

Me: Yep!!

Who you could have met if we went, I think to myself but don't send.

Ruby sends a bunch of heart-eye and party horn emojis. All this excitement over my date makes my heart swell. I feel happy. I feel important. I feel special. I smile to myself as another text comes from Cher.

Cher: This is so exciting! When is your homecoming again?

Me: October 9th.

Cher: OMG that's going to be here so soon.

Cher: Do you have a date yet, Ruby?

Ruby: Nah. I don't need one. *Winky face emoji.*

I wish I was as cool and confident as Ruby. She would genuinely not be bothered by showing up at the dance with no date, tagging along with Andy and me.

Me: You're going to come, too, right?

Ruby: YOU can be my date!

Since Cher doesn't go to Oak Ridge, she'll need to register as the date of someone who does, in order to come to the dance.

Cher: Um… I'm going to try.

That doesn't sound very convincing. I can't be bothered by her evasiveness right now, though. I change the subject slightly.

Me: What color dress do you think I should get?

Ruby and Cher respond at almost the same time.

Ruby: Yellow!!!

Cher: Black. You can't go wrong with black.

Me: Yellow?! I don't think I've ever worn anything yellow in my entire life.

Ruby: And maybe now is the time to try!

Cher: I'm gonna vote no on the yellow...

9:40 P.M.
IN BED

I think I want to get a strapless dress for the dance. Now that I have at least some boobs, I could look super cute.

I've always wanted to wear something strapless, but Mom never lets me buy any shirts like that.

9:52 P.M.

I wonder if Andy will like my strapless dress.

9:59 P.M.

I wonder if Andy has noticed my small boobs.

Probably. Don't boys always look at girls' boobs?

I do.

Is that weird? It's not like in an I-want-to-touch-them kind of way, but in a how-big-are-they-and-am-I-jealous kind of way.

10:12 P.M.

Should I help Marie with her hair tomorrow? I saw her practicing in the bathroom before bed.

Nah. She won't learn if I do it for her.

10:14 P.M.

I miss seeing Cher every day. But she seems happy at Woodlands. Especially since she's dating Jacob, and I think she's made some friends. She mentioned someone named Lyla today.

And I'm happy at Oak Ridge.

10:20 P.M.

I'm so glad I don't have to wear a uniform anymore.

Tomorrow, I'm going to wear an army green T-shirt with a jean skirt. I want to look super cute so Andy doesn't second-guess asking me to the dance.

10:24 P.M.

I wonder if Andy is a good kisser.

My first kiss was... unpleasant. Connor (the boy I kissed) put his tongue in my mouth, and it just sat there. Honestly, it was disgusting. Oh, and he called it *French kissing*, which also grossed me out.

I hope that if (when?) I kiss Andy, it's better.

I bet it will be. A warmth in my chest spreads all the way to my toes as I think about kissing Andy. He has a nice mouth. His lips are full, like little pillows on his face.

Pillows on his face? That was weird.

I should go to sleep.

10:30 P.M.

I stare at the ceiling and cringe at how things went with Connor. He moved over the summer. We never spoke again after the incident last spring where I ran off after he tried to touch my (nonexistent) boobs. Which I was fine with. He did give me a small smile on the last day of school as everyone was walking out the doors, and I returned it. It closed that chapter of my life—my Connor chapter, my first kiss chapter.

At least, that's what Mom said when I told her about it.

Now I'm in high school. I (sort of) have boobs. I'm (a little) more confident. It's time to move on. With Andy.

10:42 P.M.

Should I wear my khaki sweater with my outfit tomorrow? Or would black be better?

CHAPTER 7

Who's Jeremiah?

WEDNESDAY, SEPTEMBER 29TH

1:27 P.M.

HALLWAY

"Ruby!" I run up to her locker.

She turns and raises her eyebrows slightly. "Why are you running?"

"I have news!"

Alejandra walks up behind Ruby from the other side.

"Hey," Alejandra says, leaning up against the locker next to Ruby's.

"Hey," Ruby and I say in unison.

Ruby and I giggle. Alejandra smirks and lightly shakes her head as she adjusts her pile of books on her hip.

"Anyways, I was talking to Andy at the end of biology—"

"Bio Boy," Ruby interrupts.

"Why do you insist on calling him that?"

Ruby turns to Alejandra and giggles. "I don't know—it makes me laugh."

I roll my eyes and continue. "He was telling me his friend Jeremiah doesn't have a date to the dance. So I told him you didn't have a date either, and he suggested we double date and go together!" I bounce on my toes with excitement. "Isn't that great?"

Ruby isn't as excited as I'd hoped. She glances at Alejandra, who shrugs her shoulders. Why does Alejandra's opinion matter? She's already going to the dance with Jimmy Sherwood from her Honors Geometry class.

"Who's Jeremiah?" Ruby asks, shutting her locker. The three of us start to make our way to the gym for PE.

"He's Andy's friend. I haven't met him, but he plays soccer, and I asked Andy if he was cute. He said that he is, and that he's tall!" I hip-bump Ruby. "Come on. I thought you would be way more excited about this. We can go to Homecoming together! Now we have to find a date to bring Cher. I'll have to ask Andy if he has any other friends who are free. He's mentioned this kid, Matt, a couple times, but I think he might have a girlfriend."

"Yeah… okay, I guess." Ruby gives in as we open the locker room doors. "But let's hang out with them first. I want to make sure he's not a doofus."

"Totally. I'll text Andy after class. Maybe we can go get ice cream tonight!" I'm getting excited again.

"Alejandra and I are studying for our English quiz tonight," Ruby says.

"Oh, okay. Tomorrow then!"

"Sure. But I'm paying for my own ice cream. Independent lady and all that," Ruby says, pursing her lips.

I laugh. "Whatever you say, Rubs."

THURSDAY, SEPTEMBER 30TH

5:27 P.M.
FRED'S FROZEN TREATS PARKING LOT

"Is this a date?" Mom asks. We're waiting in the car until 5:29. We're supposed to meet Andy and Jeremiah at 5:30, and I don't want to be too early.

"Definitely not, Mrs. Bishop," Ruby says, examining her smooth brown skin in her phone camera. She turns it off and leans into the front seat. "I'm only meeting this guy for the first time." She pauses, sitting back. "But I guess it might be a date for Emma."

"Ruby!" I hiss. I turn and give her the evil eye. She smiles back smugly.

"Hm, as I suspected," Mom says. I hold my breath, waiting for the *Boys will come and go, it's okay to say no, you come first,* speech, but it doesn't come.

Mom's sea glass green eyes lock on my own. She smiles but stays quiet. She nods at the dashboard, and I swallow as I see the numbers: 5:29.

"It is time," Ruby says in a low, gravelly voice. She reaches around the seat and tries to tickle my armpit. "Let's do this."

I swat her hand away with a giggle and get out of the car. My heart is thumping in my chest. Why am I so nervous? I don't think this is a real date. I'm so glad I have Ruby with me. I loop my arm through hers as we walk to the door.

I turn back, and Mom is watching us with a soft smile on her lips. She gives a little wave before putting the car in drive. As she pulls out of the parking lot, I feel a weird sensation in the pit of my stomach. It's not nerves. It's something different. A little sad maybe? Why? Why would I feel sad watching Mom drive away? I'm about to go on a date. Well, maybe.

Ruby hip-bumps me, and I realize we've been standing in front of the door for a little too long. I turn to Ruby and hip-bump her back. We both shake our hair behind our shoulders, my wavy brown hair next to her black and purple braids. I take one last, deep breath before reaching for the door.

43

CHAPTER 8

You're cute when you blush.

THURSDAY, SEPTEMBER 30TH

5:49 P.M.

EATING ICE CREAM

Fred's Frozen Treats is my family's favorite place to go for ice cream. It feels kind of old-timey inside, with fluorescent lighting, sticky tables, and all the workers wearing those weird paper hats that kind of remind me of boats. Usually Fred himself is there, too, busying himself behind the counter or talking to people at the tables.

Everyone loves Fred. He's very old but very cute. Not in a weird way that I think old men are cute, but in the same way I think a baby is cute. He's talking to an older couple at the table behind us now, asking about their daughter who went off to college this year.

At our table, things could not be going better. Jeremiah *is* cute. He's Black, with skin a bit lighter than Ruby's. His hair is short and curly and fades down the sides. He's a few inches taller than Andy and has a wide, contagious smile.

The boys are sitting across from us and laughing at some inside joke from soccer. I turn to check on Ruby. She has a small smile on her face as she scoops another bite of her chocolate fudge ice cream.

She turns toward me, and I raise my eyebrows at her, subtly pointing to Jeremiah in a way that clearly means, *So, what do you think?*

Ruby gives a small shrug, which I take as a good sign because it's not a no.

My heart soars. How fun would it be for Ruby and me to date two friends? We could go on double dates and hang out together all the time. Then if we married them, we could have babies at the same time. I'm so excited, I wiggle a little in my seat.

"Do you need to pee?" Ruby asks.

I laugh and shake my head no.

5:55 P.M.

"So, how long have you two been friends?" Jeremiah asks. A shy smile plays on his lips, and he swirls the spoon in his sundae, his attention focused on Ruby.

"Forever," we reply in unison.

Ruby and I burst into laughter, and Andy and Jeremiah stare at us wide-eyed before joining in.

"That was impressive," Andy says.

"We have many talents, Bio Boy," Ruby says.

"Bio Boy?" Andy jerks his head back, his eyebrows knitting together.

My cheeks flush, and I cover my face with my hands. "Oh my God," I say into them.

"That's been your name ever since Emma started talking about you," Ruby explains.

I bravely lift my head from my hands. Andy's face smooths out, and he grins, pink creeping up his neck.

"Oh, I see," he says slowly. "So, you've been talking about me, Emma?"

I must be so red—I feel like my face and neck are on fire. I bite my lip.

"Maybe," I say with much more bravado than I actually feel. The pink on Andy's neck becomes more of a red. At least I'm not the only one. Andy levels his gaze on me, his eyes piercing mine. I don't know what to do, so I break eye contact first and giggle awkwardly.

I bump Ruby's shoulder with my own. "Thanks, Rubs," I say sarcastically.

"You're welcome," she retorts, lifting the corner of her mouth into a smirk.

Then Jeremiah asks Ruby what kind of stuff she's into, and she starts a tangent about music and her stuffed animal and poster collections. Jeremiah nods along like he's genuinely interested in what she's saying, which I'm impressed by. I've heard the story of Ruby's acquisition of the bikini-clad lady next to the red sports car poster so many times I could tell it myself. (She won it on a school field trip to one of those arcade places. It cost her 2,000 tickets.)

My phone buzzes in my purse, and I take it out as Ruby explains the difference between the clarinet and the oboe.

There's a text from Andy. Confused, I look over at him, which he was clearly waiting for. He smiles before turning to his sundae. I open the message.

Andy: You're cute when you blush.

My cheeks warm all over again, and my heart rate, which has barely slowed since we got here, ticks up a few notches.

Me: So are you.

I'm too nervous to watch Andy's reaction to my bold text, so instead I focus very intently on digging out a large chocolate chunk in my mint chocolate chip ice cream.

My phone buzzes again.

Andy: I like you. You know that, right??

I'm afraid I'm going to melt right then and there onto the sticky table. My heart is pounding in my chest. I stare at the message for a few seconds before replying.

Me: I like you, too.

I don't want people to think I'm staring at my crotch, so I force my attention back to the table. Andy's neck is teetering on magenta, but he's smiling. His eyes are bright as they bore into mine. I try to keep it cool and give a coy, close-lipped smile, but I can't stop it from spreading across my face.

"What are you two doing?" Ruby breaks into our bubble of smiles.

"Nothing," I reply quickly, shoveling a large bite of ice cream into my mouth.

"Mm-hmm," she says. She turns to Jeremiah and raises her eyebrows as if to say, *Are you seeing this?*

Jeremiah guffaws before throwing his arm around Andy's shoulder. "He can't help it. This guy is a romantic."

"C'mon, man!" Andy shoves Jeremiah's arm off, but he's laughing.

Ruby bumps her shoulder against mine, and once again, I'm grinning like I've won the lottery. My cheeks may now be permanently pink, but I'm not sure I've ever been happier.

8:45 P.M.
BEDROOM

My head is still fuzzy from our date with Andy and Jeremiah. (Yes, okay, I'm calling it a date now. Andy said he likes me. I'm pretty sure that makes it a date.)

I text Ruby and Cher to recap.

Me: Soooooooo Ruby… What did you think of Jeremiah?

Cher: Who's Jeremiah?

Me: Ruby's future boyfriend.

Ruby: Not my future boyfriend. He was ok. Nice.

Cher: *Shifty eyes emoji.*

Me: What??!! But it seemed like you were having a great time! You don't like him??

Ruby: I did have fun. But you were there, too.

Ruby: Idk.

Ruby: I don't think I can decide to like a boy after spending an hour eating ice cream with him. My brain doesn't work that way I guess.

Me: BUT WHAT ABOUT YOUR HEART????

Ruby: *Three shrug emoji girls.*

Ugh. This is such a bummer. I really thought Ruby and Jeremiah were hitting it off. I mean, I guess I was pretty focused on Andy most of the time. And there was that long silence when Andy went to the bathroom. But, Ruby also laughed at Jeremiah's jokes, and they both love breakfast food. I'm not giving up yet.

Me: Ok… do you want to go to the dance with him?

Ruby doesn't respond right away.
Cher emphasizes the question with the exclamation point reaction.

Ruby: I guess…

My heart soars. "Yes!" I say out loud, pumping my fists in the air. Marie walks by my door right at that moment, once again wearing her colonial pony. She raises an eyebrow at me but keeps walking

Me: YAYYYYY!!!!

Ruby: *Six laughing cat emojis.*

Ruby: I knew that would make you happy.

Me: Who knows?! Maybe after you two spend some time together at the dance, you might actually start to like him!!

Ruby: Yeah… maybe…

I ignore Ruby's hesitation and send a gif of a lady dancing horribly.

Me: All that's left is to find you a date, Cher!

Me: I asked Andy about his friend Matt, but apparently he has a girlfriend, so that's not going to work.

Cher: About that...

I let out an exasperated sigh and lay my head back against my pillow. What now?

I don't reply. Maybe if we don't say anything, she won't say whatever this bad news is.

Cher: I'm not gonna go to your homecoming. It would be weird for me to go with a date that isn't my boyfriend, ya know? Like it wouldn't be fair to Jacob.

Ruby: Is this your opinion or Jacob's?

Cher: Mine, Ruby. I didn't even tell Jacob.

Ruby: Ok.

Cher: I'm sorry. I know you were both excited, but even the idea of it makes me queasy.

Cher: Let's have a sleepover Saturday, though! We can look at dresses and makeup inspo, and you can tell me everything about these new boys!!

My mood lifts a little at the prospect of a night with my two best friends.

Me: That sounds perfect.

Ruby: I am IN!!!!!

Cher: Awesome. I can't wait to see you guys. I miss you so much!!

Ruby: *Ten kissy face emojis.*

9:10 P.M.

What a range of emotions today included.

1. Nervous (Andy)

2. Excited (Andy)

3. Weird, sad-ish (Mom)

4. Giddy (Andy)

5. Excited again (Ruby + Jeremiah)

6. Disappointed (Ruby + Jeremiah)

7. Excited x3 (Ruby + Jeremiah)

8. Totally bummed (Cher)

9. Happy (Sleepover)

And that's only since like 5:30. Ugh.

Now I feel like these emotions have been put into the blender that is my brain, and they're all mixed together.

9:14 P.M.

My phone buzzes on my nightstand. I reach over, and Andy's name is on the screen. My heart does a flip-flop.

> **Andy:** I had fun tonight. I like hanging out with you. We should do it more.

I close my eyes and hold my phone to my chest. I needed this. This is the perfect way to end my night.

> **Me:** I agree. Even if you don't like cherries.

> **Andy:** They're gross, and you can't convince me otherwise.

> **Me:** Hahahaha

> **Andy:** Anyways, good night, Emma. I can't wait to see your beautiful eyes tomorrow.

Oh my God, swoon! Jeremiah was right, Andy *is* a romantic.

> **Me:** Good night, Andy.

I send the floating pink hearts so he knows that I like what he said.

Wow. What a day.

CHAPTER 9

I love Ruby's confidence.

SATURDAY, OCTOBER 2ND

8:08 P.M.

CHER'S BEDROOM

"What kind of style are you thinking?" Cher asks. She's sitting cross-legged on her bed as she swipes through some dresses on her iPad. The soft pink, somewhat lacy comforter is fluffy under her knees.

Unlike Ruby's room, which is covered in posters, Cher's walls have almost nothing on them. Cher's bedroom reminds me of a grown-up's. The walls are cream, it's always tidy, the closet doors are closed, and the bed is made. There are no shoes or clothes strewn across the floor. She doesn't even have any stuffed animals on her bed. It feels fancy to me.

She has a bulletin board above her desk, filled with pictures. My favorite is a photo booth strip of the three of us at the mall from last year. It was right after we'd made up after our big fight over Cher ditching us for the mean girl in our class, Audrey. That makes Cher sound bad, but it was more complicated than that. I also wasn't being a very good friend to her but was too caught up in my own stuff to see it.

I don't think we'd ever had as much fun, or laughed as hard, or hugged as often as we did that day at the mall, just happy to all be together. I smile now at the memory.

"Emma?" Cher says, waving at me.

"Sorry," I say. "Strapless, definitely." Cher doesn't say anything, her eyes darting quickly to me. She nods and starts typing something on the iPad. I can't tell if the nod was a *whatever-you-say* kind of nod or a *yep-you're-right-that-will-totally-look-cute* kind of nod. I cross my arms over my chest and hope it's the latter.

"What about you, Rubs?" Cher says.

Ruby tosses a cheese ball into the air and tries to catch it in her mouth. She does not succeed.

"Damn," she says, reaching down from Cher's desk chair to grab it off the floor and pop it in her mouth.

Cher wrinkles her nose.

"What?" Ruby says. "Five-second rule!"

I nod in agreement. Can't let cheese balls go to waste.

Cher shakes her head, but she's smiling. "I missed you weirdos."

Ruby gets up and sits next to Cher on the bed. She waits a second, then catapults herself onto Cher, trapping her in a tight bear hug.

"I missed you, too," she says into Cher's hair.

"Okay, okay, I get it," Cher says, disentangling herself from Ruby's arms. Ruby doesn't go back to her spot, staying put right next to Cher. Cher scooches over a little. Ruby scooches, too.

"Ruby! Can I have some space?"

"No. I want to be close to you," Ruby says. She tilts her head down and gives Cher a creepy closed-mouth smile.

"I take it back," Cher announces, getting off the bed. "I did not miss you." She settles herself into the desk chair with a huff.

"I know you don't mean that," Ruby says. She stands up to grab the container of cheese balls, then flops back onto the bed.

"Don't get cheese dust on my new comforter," Cher says. Ruby rolls her eyes in response. She tosses another cheese ball into the air and catches it this time. She springs up, her arms raised in victory.

I cheer and clap. Cher smiles before turning back to the iPad.

"Okay, Emma, I pulled up some dresses for you. What do you think?"

9:14 P.M.

After about an hour browsing dresses, we narrow my options down to three.

"I think all of these are great," Cher says. She screenshots each one to send to me. Mom and I are going dress shopping tomorrow, so this session was perfect timing.

"My favorite is the black one with the rose," Ruby says.

"Same," I say. It's an all-black strapless dress with ruching on the side and a small rose pin at the top. *Simple but chic*, is what Cher said.

"Okay, Ruby." Cher turns her attention to our friend sprawled on her belly on the bed. "What are you thinking? Any ideas?"

Ruby rolls onto her back and stares at the ceiling for a second. "Hmmmmm…" She's dragging it out for far longer than necessary. Cher and I exchange a look but wait patiently.

Finally, Ruby rolls again, this time onto her side, propping her head up with her hand. "Maybe something green?" she says.

Cher nods and immediately starts typing on the iPad. "You would be *so* gorgeous in, like, an emerald green, Ruby. With your dark complexion, ooh, and some lighter, glittery eye makeup…"

Cher doesn't finish the sentence, but she does a little wiggle in her seat. Ruby and I giggle. Cher loves this kind of stuff, and she's so good at it. She's thinking about either going to cosmetology school or trying to do some sort of fashion program after high school.

"Style preferences?" Cher asks without looking up from the iPad.

"*Not* strapless." She sits up and points down at her boobs. "Too much going on here for that." She shakes her head glumly.

"You're perfect," I tell her.

"I know," she replies nonchalantly. "And I also know what I can and can't wear with these girls."

I nod. I love Ruby's confidence. Cher's too. They both seem totally okay with exactly how their bodies are. I, on the other hand, spend so much time wishing my body looked different. Mom says having bigger boobs won't make me any happier, but I really think she's wrong. I'm so gangly, especially compared to my two best friends, who both have these incredible curves already.

I sigh but then remind myself I'm the one with a real date for this dance. With a boy who actually likes me. And thinks I have beautiful eyes.

I wonder what Andy's doing. He said he was probably going to play video games with Jeremiah and his other friend Matt tonight. Should I text him?

Nah. I'd rather shop for dresses with Ruby and Cher.

"Ruby," Cher gasps, bringing me back from my thoughts. She turns the iPad for Ruby to see. "I found the *perfect* outfit for you!" There's a sparkle in Cher's eye, and she's smiling like it's Christmas morning.

Ruby's face also breaks into a smile. "It's perfect," she whispers.

"Let me see, let me see!" I whine. I run over and plop onto the bed next to Ruby. My jaw drops when I see the screen. It is Ruby to a T.

But it's not a dress. It's a stunning emerald green jumpsuit. The top has pleated, crossover straps that meet in a V in the back. It has a high waist cinch and wide-leg pants. And it is *so* Ruby. I've never seen anything so Ruby in my life.

Cher smiles a satisfied grin, pleased with herself. "I knew you'd love it."

Ruby is still staring at the screen. She lifts her head slowly. "I am going to look so hot in this," she announces.

"Jeremiah is going to love it!" I say, bumping her shoulder.

"Who cares what Jeremiah thinks? *I* love it!" Ruby replies. She stands and walks over to the mirror on the back of Cher's door. She runs her hands along her sides, then turns to examine her booty. She smiles at her reflection, then turns back to us.

"Mission accomplished, ladies. I'm done."

"You better order it tomorrow," Cher tells her. "It's only available online, and the dance is a week away."

Ruby digs her phone out of her backpack. Her face lights up, and her mouth curves into a sly smile as her eyes dance across the screen, but she just says, "AirDrop me the link. I'm going to send it to my mom right now."

CHAPTER 10

It's just boobs.

SATURDAY, OCTOBER 2ND

9:40 P.M.

CHER'S BEDROOM

While we wait for Cher to make popcorn, Ruby taps away on her phone, texting. I scroll on mine to see if Andy has posted anything tonight. I tap on his profile, and a video of two boys fighting over the last slice of pizza starts playing. One is Jeremiah, and the other is a boy I've never seen before. That must be Matt. He's got brown hair, a tan complexion, and kind of muscular arms.

My heart inexplicably tumbles into my stomach. I tap back and watch the video again. Andy laughs in the background, and I immediately feel guilty. Why am I so distracted by this Matt kid?

Because he's hot. My heart picks up its pace slightly.

But I like Andy, remember? Andy, the romantic. Andy, with the sapphire eyes. Andy, who makes me laugh in biology.

Cher comes in with two big bowls of popcorn, pushing the door shut with her butt.

"Sorry that took so long," she says, handing one of the bowls to Ruby and the other to me. "My mom was interrogating me about Jacob, again." She rolls her eyes.

"Why?" Ruby asks before shoveling a handful of popcorn into her mouth.

"He's coming over tomorrow," Cher says. I can't believe it, but her face is flushed.

Ruby sits up straighter. "Cher! You're blushing!" She puts the popcorn bowl down and pats the ground in front of where she and I are sitting together in our nest of blankets and pillows.

Cher covers her cheeks with her hands, but she's still smiling. "Stop, don't make this a big deal."

"But it *is* a big deal!" I say, scooching closer to her. She's the first one of us to have a real boyfriend. I don't want to miss a detail.

"Things must be getting pretty serious," Ruby says, raising her eyebrows.

Cher turns her attention to the fuzzy blanket on the floor, fiddling with the end of it. She's *still* smiling.

"Yeah, I guess so," she finally says, glancing up at us with her big, blue eyes. They're sparkling again, and her flush lingers. "I really, *really* like him."

"Okay, *now* do you love him?" Ruby demands.

Cher turns back to the fuzzy blanket. She shrugs. "Maybe," she says quietly.

"Oh my God!" Ruby and I shout in unison.

"Everything okay in there, girls?" Cher's mom calls from the living room.

"Yes, Mom. Everything is fine," Cher calls back over her shoulder. She turns to Ruby and me, pointing her finger at us. "Cool it, you two."

"Has he touched your boobs?" I ask eagerly.

"Why are you so obsessed with boobs, Emma?" Cher asks.

I shrug. "I don't know. Probably because I still barely have any." I cup my small boobs in my hands for emphasis. "Now answer the question," I demand.

With a sigh, she finally gives me the answer I'm looking for. "Yes, he's touched my boobs."

I squeal. "How was it? Did you like it? I'm sure it's much better than when Connor tried to touch my flat chest last year."

"Was it a gentle fondling or an aggressive pinching?" Ruby adds.

"Pinching?" I recoil and put my hand on my chest. "There was no pinching, was there?" I ask Cher.

"I can assure you there was no pinching," Cher says with a grimace. "I don't know. I didn't think too much about it. We were watching a movie in his basement and making out, and it just sort of happened. It was fine. I wouldn't say it, like, rocked my world or anything, but there was definitely no pinching, and I was comfortable with it."

"Wow," I say quietly. I wonder if Andy wants to touch my boobs. I suppose we'll have to kiss first, though. I wonder if Matt likes to touch boobs.

Woah. What's he doing in my brain? I shake him out of there.

"I can understand the appeal of boob fondling," Ruby says. I nod, even though I don't fully understand it.

"I guess," Cher says. We all look down at our chests.

"Should we... try it?" I venture.

"I am not touching either of your boobs," Cher says, crossing her arms over her own chest.

I turn to Ruby. She shrugs.

"I'm just curious," I explain.

"Me too," Ruby says. "Let's do it."

We turn to face each other, sitting cross-legged. Cher is still sitting in front of us.

"You two are so weird," she says, holding up her phone.

"Do not post this, Cher!" I shout at her.

She rolls her eyes. "I'm not. It's for the memories. I feel like this is a moment we'll remember forever."

"Okay," I agree cautiously. "But if you ever do, I'll post that photo of you drooling in your sleep," I warn her. Cher nods solemnly, and I turn back to Ruby.

"Should we do it one at a time, or together?"

Ruby thinks for a second. "I guess at the same time, so then we can adjust based on what the other person is doing."

"Good idea."

Cher snorts. Ruby and I both turn. "Sorry," she says quickly.

"Okay," Ruby announces. "Let's do this."

I put my hands out in front of me, and Ruby does the same. We both lean forward. I reach her first. I don't really know what to do with my hands. My palms are sweaty, and my heart is racing. Why am I nervous? It's Ruby.

My hands hover above Ruby's chest. I glance up at her, and she blinks a few times before taking a deep breath and nodding. She takes the plunge first and gently cups my bits from underneath.

Her brown eyes search mine to see if it's okay. I nod and lean forward, doing the same thing. We sit there for a few seconds, each cupping each other's boobs. I've cupped my own boobs plenty of times, but hers are so much bigger. They're heavier than I expected, too.

We lock eyes again and burst into giggles.

Ruby takes a deep breath. "Okay, be serious. It's just boobs."

I nod in agreement.

Ruby moves her hands on top of my boobs and gives a little squeeze. It's kind of like Cher said—it's fine, but not blowing my mind.

Once again, I follow Ruby's lead and turn my hands and squeeze.

"Ow, Emma, geez!" Ruby pulls back and puts her hands over her boobs protectively. "You need to be gentle!"

"I'm sorry! I didn't mean to hurt you. Did I squeeze too hard?" I put my hand over my own boob and try to squeeze as hard as I did on Ruby, but it's hard because my boobs are so much smaller.

Cher snickers. "This is so weird."

I feel the laugh in my belly before it starts, and once it does, it keeps building, until all three of us are laughing, and we can't stop. Ruby's bent in half, her hands still on her boobs. Cher tried to stand up but is leaning on the edge of her bed for support. I fall back onto the pillows behind me, clutching my stomach.

10:37 P.M.

After we recover from our laughing fit, Ruby says, "That was interesting."

"You have no idea," Cher says. She hands Ruby her phone, and I lean over to see. Cher took a video of our boob encounter.

Ruby and I are both concentrating so hard, staring at each other's chests, occasionally flicking our eyes up at each other. Finally, I squeeze Ruby's boob, and from the outside perspective, I can see how hard I actually squeezed it.

The laughter starts all over again.

Ruby gasps for air as she says, "Never... do... that... again."

10:52 P.M.

It takes a long time, but we finally move on from our intermittent boob jokes and laughing fits, and we calm down enough to watch the movie we made popcorn for over an hour ago.

The three of us snuggle down together in our nest of blankets and pillows, Ruby in between Cher and me.

"Don't even think about trying to feel me up, Cher," Ruby says as the movie starts.

"We are in no danger of that," Cher deadpans.

I'm tired now, but I giggle and throw my hand over Ruby's chest, reaching for Cher.

"I'm going to pretend this isn't happening," Cher says.

Ruby wiggles her arms underneath Cher and me. "This is the best night I've had in a long time," she says, pulling us in for a makeshift hug.

"Me too," I agree.

"Me three," Cher says. "Now, how long until Ruby's snoring?"

"Ten minutes, tops," I say confidently.

"Not even," Ruby says, pulling her arms back with a yawn. She wiggles lower on her pillow. "Night, beauties."

CHAPTER 11

She didn't want my help.

SUNDAY, OCTOBER 3RD

1:10 P.M.

BENNIGAN'S GRILL

Mom was a little disappointed that I had a dress already picked out when we came shopping today. I did try on a few others, but the black one Cher found was still my favorite.

Mom really wanted me to get a green one with a ruched top (it *did* make my boobs look bigger), but Ruby already has dibs on green.

Plus, the black one is *so* cute. It's tight around my top and then flares out just above my knees for a fun, flirty vibe. Then we found the perfect shoes. They're silver heels with a thin strap around the ankle and a rhinestone bow across the toe.

Mom says I have to practice walking in them every day. "You don't want to be one of those girls wobbling around on her heels. You'll feel much more confident knowing you can walk in them." I can't wait to get home and practice.

Now we're having lunch to celebrate our successful shopping trip. The restaurant is busy. The table next to us also had a successful day, their spare chair piled with their shopping bags. Another table has a family celebrating a birthday and a little girl perched on her grandma's lap while she reads a card. There's a booth filled with a group of older girls, laughing and sharing a giant platter of nachos.

"Cheers, sweetie," Mom says, lifting her lemonade to clink with mine. "Thanks for letting me take you shopping. It means a lot to me." Her eyes are shining as she takes a sip of her drink.

"Thanks, Mom. It was fun." I take my own sip, hoping to avoid any more mushy stuff. It seems like half the conversations I have with Mom lately are about how I'm growing up so fast, can time slow down, blah, blah, blah.

Mom stares at me with a soft smile playing on her lips for a couple seconds. Then she says, "So, tell me more about your date with Andy."

She's trying to be casual, perusing the menu as she asks, but the way her eyes keep darting up to mine tells me she's eager to hear more.

I nod. "He's nice."

"That's it? He's nice?" Mom says, dropping the menu on the table.

I can't help the smile twisting onto my face. I sigh and continue. "Okay... he's cute, too. He has blue eyes."

Mom interrupts me. "You like a blue-eyed boy it seems." She raises an eyebrow.

I shrug. "I guess so." Andy's friend Matt pops into my head. I don't think his eyes are blue. I shake my head to get him out. Andy. Blue eyes. My date.

"We sit next to each other in biology."

"Does he do his homework?" Mom asks.

"What?" I furrow my brow. "Yeah. That's a weird question, Mom."

Mom shrugs now, picking her menu back up. "You'd be surprised how much you can learn about a person by their school habits."

I guess that's true. Andy always gets A's on his assignments. I'm more of a consistent B gal, but anything we've worked on together, I've gotten an A.

1:22 P.M.

After we order our appetizer (mozzarella sticks, obviously) and meals (soup and turkey club sandwich for Mom and a cheese flatbread pizza for me), Mom asks a little too casually, "Has Marie asked you to help her with her hair lately?"

I groan inwardly. Where is she going with this?

"Um, yeah, once or twice," I say.

"Did you help her?"

I hesitate, and Mom's gaze sharpens on me. She tilts her chin down but waits for me to speak. "I tried, but it was, like, after she'd asked me."

Mom still isn't saying anything.

"So, she said she didn't want my help." I adjust myself slightly on the maroon pleather seat topper on my chair and glance around the restaurant, hoping for a change of subject. "Wow, look at that old lady's hair." I giggle, but Mom is still staring at me.

"What?" I throw my hands up. "She didn't want my help."

"Yeah, after you'd already turned her down," Mom says. She's not yelling at me. Her voice is level, but the line between her eyebrows is very deep.

My heart lurches slightly, thinking about Marie doing her colonial pony by herself in the bathroom.

"Maybe you could offer to help her before school tomorrow," Mom says gently. I stare at her but don't say anything. "Don't blink at me, Emma."

I sigh. "Okay."

"She's the only sister you have. Maybe you need to think a little bit more about the way you treat her."

Heat creeps up onto my cheeks. Ugh, what's with the sister speech? Did Marie tattle on me for not helping her?

Mom takes a sip of her lemonade. Her eyes dart around the restaurant, and then she turns back to me and says conspiratorially, "Plus, you've seen the ponytail she's doing."

I smirk. "She looks like a colonial man."

Mom almost spits out her lemonade. "Oh my God. You're right!" We both burst into laughter.

"You need to help her, Emma," Mom says after a minute. "That's what big sisters are for."

I swirl my straw in my cup, feeling guilty for not helping Marie before. I look up at Mom, my own eyes staring back at me. I nod solemnly.

"I will."

"Good," Mom says. "Now, how was your sleepover last night? How's Cher? I barely see her anymore."

MONDAY, OCTOBER 4TH

7:20 A.M.
HALLWAY

Marie is brushing her hair in the bathroom as I head to my room after breakfast. I'm about to keep walking—I want to put mascara on today—but pause a few steps past the doorway. Mom's voice runs through my head. *That's what big sisters are for.*

I back up and linger in the door of the bathroom.

"What?" Marie says without looking at me.

"Nothing," I snap without thinking. I clear my throat and adjust my tone. "Um, do you want some help with your hair?"

Marie slowly turns her head, eyes narrowed, arm still lifted with the hairbrush over her head. She stares at me for a few seconds. Annoyance immediately starts swirling in my chest.

"If you're not going to say anything, I'm going to finish getting ready. I need to leave in like—"

"Sure," Marie interrupts me. She lowers the arm with the hairbrush and passes it to me. Casually, she continues. "I guess I could switch it up today." She flips her hair over her shoulder as I come to stand behind her.

I start brushing her hair. There are still some tangles in it.

"Ow," Marie complains, touching the side of her head. "Be careful."

I have to consciously tell myself not to call her a baby. Instead, I say, "What do you want to do with it?"

Marie immediately says, "Ballerina bun."

7:26 A.M.

It took a few tries because Marie's hair is much thinner than mine and requires more bobby pins, but she's happy with her bun.

"Thanks, Emma," she says as she walks to her room.

I smile, pleased with myself for being so helpful.

CHAPTER 12

The boys are here.

SATURDAY, OCTOBER 9TH
7:12 A.M.

I wake up with a start. Today is Homecoming!!!!

I stare at the ceiling for a few minutes, anticipation swirling in my belly. I review the plan for the day:

1. A nice, long shower. Don't forget to shave my legs.

2. Get my hair done. I think I'm going to do beachy waves and pin some of it back. Mom wanted me to do an updo, but that seems a little too, I don't know, bridesmaid-at-a-wedding for me.

3. Ruby and her mom come over. Ruby's mom, Georgia, is going to do our makeup for the dance.

4. Finish getting ready with Ruby. Dress, shoes, and jewelry.

5. Pictures at my house before the dance with Andy and Jeremiah. And their parents, probably.

6. Go time!

My heart leaps when I think about Andy. He asked me earlier in the week what color my dress was. He said his mom told him to ask so he could get a corsage that matches. He looked confused when I told him the dress was black but relieved when I told him there was a little red, too.

Will he think I look pretty?

I hope so.

7:30 A.M.

My phone buzzes on the nightstand. I roll over to grab it. It's Ruby, of course. Who else would be texting this early?

Ruby: GOOD MORNING MY BEAUTIFUL FRIEND!!

Ruby: Are you SO excited about tonight?

Me: Beyond!!!!

I bite my lip, thinking.

Me: I hope Andy likes my dress…

Ruby: Emma. Stop it.

Ruby: Of course he will. I've seen you in that dress, and you are a stunner!

I smile. Ruby always knows how to make me feel better. She can boost my confidence in a way no one else can. Like, if Mom told me I was a stunner, I'd roll my eyes, but I *almost* believe Ruby when she says it.

Sometimes I feel so much more confident than I've ever been before. My boobs are getting bigger, I'm starting to master the art of the messy bun, and honestly, I kind of like myself. But then, other times, I look in the mirror and think, *Who are you kidding?*

Today, I'm channeling my inner Ruby and believing it.

Me: Thanks, Rubs.

Me: I CANNOT wait to see you in your jumpsuit!!! Did you get the sparkly heels?

Ruby: Ugh, it was so hard. I also found these like, iridescent, mermaid-y strappy ones. But Mom would only let me get one.

Ruby: So obv I went with the sparkles.

Ruby: *Ten fire emojis.*

Me: Obv.

Cher finally chimes in.

Cher: I will never understand why the two of you are always up so early.

Cher: BUT if you don't send me pics tonight, we are not friends anymore. I need to see everythingggg!!!!

> **Me:** Duhhhh.

Ruby sends a selfie of herself in bed, eyes closed, still wearing her satin bonnet, lips puckered and fingers in a peace sign.

> **Cher:** Not sure I need the before, Rubs…

> **Ruby:** *Winky face emoji*

Albus stretches at the bottom of my bed, and I lean forward to give him a couple pets. He immediately starts purring. He turns to face me, and I scratch him under his chin, which is his favorite.

My phone buzzes, and I assume it's another text from Ruby or Cher, but my heart flips when I see the name on the screen. I can't open the message fast enough.

> **Andy:** Hey. Can't wait to see you tonight. I bet you're gonna look beautiful.

Heat spreads across my chest. I'm about to screenshot and send it to the girls when he sends another one almost immediately.

> **Andy:** Not that you don't look beautiful every day. You do. But tonight is, like, special. *Monkey covering eyes emoji.*

He's so sweet. I ignore the second part because I knew what he meant.

Me: Thanks! Can't wait to see you, too.

I've been feeling pretty bold around Andy lately, and, in the spirit of believing I'm a stunner, I add one more thing.

Me: Save me a dance tonight?

He responds within seconds.

Andy: They're all for you.

Swoon!

4:30 P.M.
KITCHEN

"Mom. Not too heavy with the green, okay? I want it to be subtle, but like... *bam!*" Ruby punches an arm out to the side.

"I'm trying, but if you keep flinging your body around, you're going to have a green mustache," Georgia says, pointing the eyeliner at her.

Ruby frowns but then shrugs her shoulders. I giggle, and Ruby turns to smile at me.

"Ruby!" Georgia snaps. "Stop moving." Ruby stiffens, following her mom's instructions. "Thank you," she says more gently.

After a couple quiet seconds, Georgia lifts her concentration from Ruby's eyelids. "What are you thinking, Emma? The usual?" She drops the eyeliner in her makeup bag and digs around for a second before pulling out two different mascaras.

The usual is my sea glass eye makeup we discovered last year. It's a natural look, but it makes my eyes totally pop. I'd never realized I had pretty eyes until I saw another girl on social media with this makeup, whose eyes were exactly like mine. It was a big moment for me.

Georgia leans in close to Ruby, expertly applying the mascara, her mouth slightly open.

"Actually..." I glance at Mom, who's flipping through a magazine at the other end of the table. She gives me a small smile. "I was thinking maybe we could try something a little bit bolder?"

"Ooh, Emma, yes!" Georgia cheers. She turns to me as she puts the brush back in the mascara. "Let's see, maybe some Old Hollywood Glam?"

I nod excitedly.

Georgia claps her hands and rubs them together before turning to Mom. "Joanna, we're going to need a glass of wine after these beautiful teenage daughters of ours go off on their dates."

"More than one," Mom replies.

"And probably some ice cream," Georgia adds.

"Save us some ice cream!" Ruby says, standing up from her chair.

"Oh, Ruby," Mom says in quiet awe. "You are always beautiful, you know that." Ruby nods knowingly. "But wow," Mom continues. "You are growing into a stunning young woman."

Ruby's smile spreads across her face. "Aw, Mrs. Bishop, you're making me blush."

"I mean it," Mom says, giving Ruby one of her lingering mom-looks.

Ruby turns to me, putting her chin on her shoulder and raising both her eyebrows. I raise mine right back at her.

"Wait until you see the outfit, Jo," Georgia says, smiling at her mini-me.

5:50 P.M.
BEDROOM

Ruby and I stand next to each other, admiring ourselves in the mirror on the back of my bedroom door.

"Wow," I say, turning to admire myself from the side and then from the back.

"Girl," Ruby says, doing the same.

"We look…"

"Incredible," Ruby finishes.

Georgia killed it with my makeup. The sparkly eyeshadow and winged eyeliner make me feel like a movie star. My dress fits perfectly. For the first time ever, I'm happy with the size of my chest. Okay, maybe if they were a smidge bigger, I'd be even happier, but I fill out my dress enough that it's clear I have boobs, and that alone makes me so happy.

My silver shoes with the bowties on the toe go perfectly with the dress, making me feel like I'm about to walk a red carpet, and I feel confident that I could, too. I practiced walking in them for twenty minutes every day. Marie said I looked like a weirdo, walking around in regular clothes and fancy shoes in the kitchen, but it was totally worth it. I feel one hundred percent confident walking in them.

I shared Mom's shoe tip with Ruby, so we're both ready to walk the runway like models.

Speaking of, Ruby looks like a literal model. She had her braids taken out last week, so her natural hair is shorter and curly. She has three small braids on one side of her head, and the rest is curly and free.

No matter how many times I see the jumpsuit, I can't get over how fabulous Ruby is in it. The ruched, criss-cross top keeps her busty chest in control, the cinched waist highlights her incredible curves, and the wide-leg pants give the impression that her legs go on for days.

And she was right. The sparkly shoes are *so* her. Sparkly is almost an understatement.

After we send a picture to Cher, Ruby pulls me close, hooking her arm around my shoulder and squeezing me tightly.

"I'm so happy we get to go together," I say, giving her an equally tight squeeze around the waist

Ruby releases her hold on me and gives me a small hip-bump. "Me too." A second later, the doorbell rings. We turn to each other, frozen. The boys are here. "Let's do this," she announces, putting her arm out for me.

My heart thumps in my chest, and heat creeps up my neck and onto my face. I swallow the lump in my throat and nod, looping my arm through hers.

Ruby opens the door, and we make our way downstairs arm in arm.

CHAPTER 13

Like an angel.

SATURDAY, OCTOBER 9TH

6:01 P.M.

LIVING ROOM

The moms clap as Ruby and I enter the living room, Georgia the loudest of them all, my mom's eyes shining brightly.

My heart continues to thump inside my chest. It's so loud, Ruby must be able to hear it. Confident as ever, Ruby lets go of my arm and walks up to Jeremiah, offering her hand for a high five.

"What's up, Jer?" she asks.

"Ruby, wow," Jeremiah stutters.

"I know," she replies with a grin. They both laugh.

I'm still standing by the stairs, my heart trying to escape my chest. Andy walks over, his cheeks pink and his steps a little shaky.

"Hey," he says quietly. "You look..." He pauses, and I wait anxiously for him to finish his sentence. Beautiful? Stunning? Smart?

"Like an angel," he breathes out.

My cheeks warm, but also my stomach clenches. That's an *interesting* description. I'm not even wearing white. I know he's trying to tell me I look good, so I'll take it, but I wish he would have said something more... normal for a teenage boy. Luckily, there's so much going on in the room, I don't think anyone else heard him.

"Thanks." I glance down at the silver bows on my shoes, then smile up at him, telling myself it's actually romantic, being told I look like an angel.

One of Jeremiah's moms claps her hands to get everyone's attention. "Okay, teenagers. Time to take some pictures."

Andy places his hand gently on the small of my back, and I feel a jolt of energy and excitement.

This is going to be the best night ever.

7:15 P.M.
HOMECOMING DANCE

After about a thousand pictures, we all piled into Andy's mom's minivan so she could drop us off at the dance.

The gym lights are low, and the music is loud. There are streamers and balloons and strobe lights flashing along the floor.

We put our stuff down at a table, and the boys immediately pull us onto the dance floor. I'm not sure exactly what to do at first, but Andy is smiling and Ruby is laughing. The energy is so high, I stop overthinking it and start dancing. Andy reaches his hands out for mine, and I grab them. He twirls me around as the song crescendos.

7:40 P.M.
DANCE FLOOR

Ruby grabs my arm and shouts over the music, "I need some air. Come sit with me?"

I nod and motion to Andy that we're going to the tables. He gives me a thumbs up, but he and Jeremiah keep dancing. Jeremiah waves to someone.

It's the cute boy from Andy's story the other night. Matt. He's wearing a black dress shirt and black tie. His curly brown hair is a little wild, but in a cool, unbothered way. He's taller than I expected. Taller than Andy but shorter than Jeremiah.

My heart picks up its pace as he comes bounding over but drops when I see the girl following behind him holding his hand.

She's gorgeous. She has long, blonde, wavy hair. And boobs. Big boobs. She's also wearing a strapless dress, but she has some cleavage peeking out over the top. She actually reminds me of my middle school nemesis, Audrey. (Who, thank God, does not go to our school. I don't think I could handle watching Audrey whisper behind her hand for another four years.) This girl pulls her dress up as she and Matt approach the boys. She smiles brightly and waves.

I look down at myself, disappointed once again in what I have going on.

Ruby tugs my arm, and I shake my head. Why do I care about Matt and his beautiful girlfriend anyway? I'm here with Andy, who thinks I look like an angel.

7:48 P.M.
TABLES

Ruby and I are drinking punch, eating cookies, and people-watching. It's incredible. There's a couple fighting at the table to our left, another couple making out next to the bleachers to our right, and the dance floor is full of glances—stolen, lustful, and annoyed.

"That girl is so pissed at her date," Ruby says before popping another cookie into her mouth. She points to a girl, who I actually recognize from my art class. If looks could kill, this guy would be dead. He's dancing with another girl, and his hands are dangerously close to her butt.

"Whatever, Ben!" a different girl at the table next to us shouts. She stands up and starts walking toward the hallway. She turns back around to add, "Why don't you come find me when you actually want to be with me." Then she stomps off.

The boy, Ben apparently, watches her walk away, but he doesn't seem very upset about it. He runs his hand through his hair, stands up, and heads back to the dance floor.

"Ouch," Ruby grimaces. We both shake our heads.

"Are you ready to go back out there?" I ask. This is fun, but I want to hang out with Andy. And I wonder if Matt is still over there.

I swat that last thought away quickly.

Ruby ignores me. "Hey, there's Alejandra," she says, standing up. She waves both arms above her head and shouts, "Alejandra! Over here!"

Alejandra's dark head of hair turns, and her eyes dart around the tables. When she finally spots Ruby, who is now standing on a chair, her face lights up. She grabs her date's hand and trots over.

"Girl, you look incredible!" Ruby says as Alejandra approaches. Ruby wraps her arms around Alejandra for a hug and then spins her in a circle. Alejandra giggles before giving me a quick hug.

As she steps back, I take in Alejandra's full appearance. She *does* look incredible. Her long, straight, almost-black hair is smooth and shiny, pinned on one side with a sparkly flower barrette so that it all drapes over her other shoulder. Her dress is a soft pink with spaghetti straps and a heart-shaped neckline. The skirt is flared mesh, and the dress is adorned with stitched white flowers with pearls as the buds. She's wearing Converse sneakers the same color as her dress. She looks like a fairy.

Alejandra's date, Jimmy Sherwood, is standing off to the side with his hands in his pockets. His eyes scan the gym before turning back to us. He offers me a small smile, and I wave in return. I don't really know him, except that he's a sophomore in Alejandra's math class.

Alejandra is super smart. She tested out of Algebra I, which is what Ruby and I—and most freshmen—take. Instead, she's in Honors Geometry with mostly sophomores.

Ruby pulls Alejandra by the hand over to the table, and they sit down. Jimmy offers to get some more punch and cookies, and they both nod and wave him off.

"Rubs?" I call, still standing next to the table.

"Yeah?" she says, turning her face toward me. She's bouncing up and down in her seat, clearly excited that Alejandra is here. My gut twists.

"Don't you want to come dance?"

Ruby's eyes flit to the dance floor, to Alejandra, then quickly back to me. She shrugs.

"I'll meet you out there in a bit."

Not sure what else to do, I nod and head back to the dance floor. By myself.

8:35 P.M.
DANCE FLOOR

The music suddenly changes pace, and a slow song comes on. My heart is pumping, and the back of my neck is damp with sweat. We've been dancing nonstop.

Andy's been dancing behind me with his hands on my hips(!) but comes around to face me now.

"Can I have this dance?" He puts one hand behind his back and the other out like a prince. I giggle and glance around to see if anyone else sees this happening. I can't decide if it's romantic or cringey.

"Of course," I say, grabbing his hand.

I put my arms over his shoulders, and he wraps his around my waist. I take a step closer so there's basically no space between us. Andy adjusts his hands so they rest approximately one centimeter above my butt. My heart skips a beat at his touch. He leans back and opens his mouth to say something, but he must change his mind because, instead, he clears his throat and smiles.

I sigh happily at this perfect moment I'm having, slow-dancing in a boy's arms. I feel like I'm the star of the movie.

Off to the side, Jeremiah rubs the back of his neck and scans the crowd. We make eye contact, and he comes over to Andy and me.

"Have you seen Ruby?" he asks over the music.

I shake my head. She never came back onto the dance floor. I crane my neck to check the table we were at, but it's empty now.

"No, not in a while," I tell him. "She was sitting at one of the tables with our friend a little bit ago."

"Okay, I'll go check," he says, walking off with a wave.

It bugs me that Ruby is kind of ghosting Jeremiah. And me, too. She was supposed to come dance with me—with all of us. What is she doing?

I push my shoulders back and my annoyance with Ruby away, for now. I don't want to ruin my perfect movie moment with Andy. I lean into him a little bit more, and his hand dips down to rest even closer to my butt. A shiver runs down my body, and I smile into his shoulder.

When I lift my head back up, I lock eyes with Matt across the dance floor. His dark brown eyes dart away quickly, and I do the same. I can't help the uptick in my heart rate. Why was he looking at me?

I try to avoid looking at him again, but he and his girlfriend are directly in my eyeline, so after another few seconds, I can't help myself.

His girlfriend is up on her toes, whispering something into his ear. He gives her a slightly lopsided smile.

Then it happens again. He looks up over her head, and we lock eyes. This time, neither of us looks away immediately. It's like I can't. The air in the room suddenly feels heavier.

What is happening?

Andy rubs his hand up and down the small of my back, and I tear my eyes away from Matt's—a boy I've never even spoken to.

Andy leans in to talk over the music. "Are you having fun?"

"Yeah!" I nod enthusiastically, internally shoving my guilt into a box in my brain. I smile at Andy. My date. The boy I like. The boy I'm hoping to kiss tonight.

8:47 P.M.
TABLES

I finally find Ruby sitting at a different table at the back of the gym with Alejandra and a bored-looking Jimmy Sherwood.

"Ruby! Where have you been?" I throw my hands up in the air and sit down on the edge of the chair next to her. I pull up the top of my dress. My strapless bra keeps slipping. "Jeremiah's been looking for you. I set you up with this cute guy so we could double date and have fun together, but you've been totally ignoring him all night."

Ruby sighs dramatically. "Ugh, yes, I'm avoiding him. I'm not interested, okay? Have you seen his dance moves?" She shakes her head as she fluffs her hair a bit.

"What? But he's so cute!" I point to where Andy and Jeremiah are dancing with a group of guys. Ruby's not wrong. Jeremiah's dancing is like a fish flopping out of water. My cheeks flush with second-hand embarrassment.

"Okay, but he's still cute," I add feebly.

"Emma," Ruby says seriously. "Just because he's Black doesn't mean I'm going to like him. I appreciate it and all, but..." She pauses, looking over at Jeremiah's fish-dancing. She turns back to me with a wince. "No."

Alejandra snorts. She's also watching Jeremiah dance. I ignore her.

"I didn't set you up with him because he's Black. I set you up with him because he's Andy's friend, and he's nice and cute, and I thought it would be fun for us to go to the dance together."

"Okay," she says slowly. Waving her hand in the air she adds, "That doesn't change the fact that I don't like him."

I'm trying not to be hurt by all of this. All I wanted was to have a fun night with my best friend.

"Okay," I answer. I stand up, adjusting my dress again. This stupid bra is so annoying. I should have not worn one, like Mom suggested. "I'm going to dance with my date. I guess I'll see you later."

"Sounds good," Ruby says with a tiny shrug of her shoulders. She turns back to Alejandra and Jimmy, resting her chin on her hand. I watch them for a second. Jimmy pushes a plate of cookies in Ruby's direction, and she grabs one, munching happily.

I feel a pang of sadness in my chest but push it aside. If Ruby doesn't want to dance with us, then fine, whatever. I can still have fun without her. I take a deep breath and then run back over to Andy and Jeremiah.

8:58 P.M.
DANCE FLOOR

The music is loud and fast, and I can feel the bass in my chest. I spin, throwing my hands up in the air. Andy laughs and pulls me closer to his side. A big group of us—Andy, me, Jeremiah, Matt, his girlfriend, a girl from my Spanish class, and her date—are all dancing in a circle. Jeremiah dances into the middle and does the worm. Everyone whoops and cheers for him. Matt's girlfriend drags him out, and they dance together for a second. She pulls on his arms as he laughs reluctantly.

Suddenly, I feel a tug on my arm. Andy is pulling me into the center of the circle. Oh, God. Oh no. This is too embarrassing. What am I going to do? I barely know how to dance. I've just been watching the other girls tonight and trying to do what they do. I blush, hard, thinking about everyone's eyes on me.

But when we get to the center of the circle, he twirls me around. His smile is so big, and the music is so loud, and the lights are dancing across our faces, that somehow, it's okay. I'm not scared anymore. I laugh, throwing my head back. Andy twirls me one last time, then pulls his loosened tie off and drops it over my head. He puts his arm around my shoulder as our group cheers loudly, and we walk back to our spot on the perimeter.

My heart is thumping so hard in my chest that I can barely catch my breath. Next to me, Andy is panting slightly, but his smile is wide. I touch his tie around my neck. Is this even my life? What just happened? Is this what it feels like to be cool? I smile to myself before cheering for a boy I don't know dancing in the center of the circle now, his face red and his hair wet and matted on his forehead.

10:01 P.M.
END OF THE DANCE

The lights switch back on in the gym, and I feel as though I've been blinded. The magic of the dance fades away pretty quickly with the bright, fluorescent lights shining on our sweaty faces and balloons floating sadly across the floor. Groups of people are shuffling around or leaving. I can't believe it's over already.

Andy, Jeremiah, and I are sitting at a table in the middle of the gym. I'm still wearing Andy's tie. I make a mental note to take a selfie with him while I'm wearing it.

I reach down to put my shoes back on and notice Ruby meandering over to us. Jeremiah stands up.

"Ruby! We missed you out there. We were dancing up a storm," Jeremiah says with a smile.

Ruby shrugs casually. "Wasn't feeling it, Jer. I ate my weight in cookies instead."

"In good conscience, I can't hate on that choice," Jeremiah says, offering her a hand for a high five. She obliges with a smile, then pulls something out of her pocket and hands it to Jeremiah.

"For real? Sick, Ruby, thanks!" he says as he pulls a cookie out of the napkin Ruby handed him. He immediately shovels it in his mouth before he says, "You still coming for pizza?"

I continue doing the straps of my shoes, not wanting Ruby to see the desperation in my eyes. What if she made new plans with Alejandra and Jimmy, and she only came over to tell me that? I like Andy a lot, but I also really want to hang out with Ruby. Plus, Jeremiah hanging onto us like a third wheel all night has been kind of a buzzkill.

Andy appears in front of me, his hand out. I grab it, and he pulls me up to stand. His hand is warm in mine, and in turn, my chest warms on the inside, and my cheeks warm on the outside. He smiles at me with his mouth closed. I smile back and squeeze his hand.

Ruby's voice cuts in, and I tear my eyes away from Andy's pretty face.

"Yeah, I'm spending the night at Emma's. Of course I'm going to go. I can't leave my girl hanging, can I?" She smiles and skips over to grab my other hand. My worry and annoyance from earlier completely melt away, and I don't try to hide the happiness I'm feeling right now. My boy and my bestie on either side.

CHAPTER 14

This is it.

SATURDAY, OCTOBER 9TH

11:48 P.M.

WAITING FOR ANDY'S MOM TO PICK US UP

We're all standing in the parking lot waiting for Andy's mom to pick us up—Ruby, me, Andy, Jeremiah, Matt, and his girlfriend, Lily. My belly is full of pizza and pop, and my heart is full from all the laughter and fun we had.

Jeremiah didn't seem bothered by the fact that Ruby avoided him all night. They even made up a dance to the song that played three times while we were in the restaurant. While it makes me a little sad we won't be able to double date, maybe they're better as friends.

I watch the two of them now, sitting on the ground, watching a video on Jeremiah's phone. They're both laughing at whatever is happening on the screen.

Matt and Lily stand together next to Ruby and Jeremiah. Matt has his arm around Lily, and they're talking quietly. Lily is *so* nice. It's kind of unfair that she's pretty and also, like, a cool person. Matt was kind of quiet, but I think that's just how he always is. I didn't really talk to him, but that's probably because I was too busy laughing with Andy or Ruby the whole time. There was no weird eye contact either, which was a relief.

An arm slips around my waist, and I turn to find Andy smiling next to me.

"Hey," he says.

"Hi."

"Can I talk to you for a sec? Over there?" He nods his head in the direction of some trees to the side of the parking lot.

I nod with a cool smile as my heart tumbles in my chest.

Andy and I start across the walkway, holding hands. I give Ruby wide eyes as we step over her and Jeremiah. She wiggles her eyebrows back at me. Jeremiah sees this and makes a loud whooping sound. Matt and Lily turn, too, and Lily adds her own, "Woo!" to the noise. Andy ignores them, but a flush creeps up his neck the same way it's spreading across my cheeks.

Andy turns around the side of the building so we can no longer see our obnoxious friends.

"They're stupid," he says as he turns to face me.

"Totally," I breathe. I think I know what's coming. My legs feel like jelly. I don't know what to do with my hands. I've only kissed one boy, and it's been a long time since that happened. What if I don't know how to do it anymore?

"So..." Andy looks over my shoulder.

"Yeah..."

We don't say anything, and the next five seconds feel like an eternity. What's he waiting for?

Andy takes a deep breath and turns to face me. When I have my heels on, we're almost the same height.

"I like you, Emma," he says quickly, like he's afraid if he doesn't shove the sentence out of his mouth, he'll chicken out.

Everything inside me warms. I feel it from the top of my forehead down to my toes.

"I like you, too," I tell him. Andy's face breaks into a wide smile. I do, too.

"Do you think…" Andy starts but loses his courage. His gaze goes over my shoulder again. He lets go of my hand and fiddles with the sleeves of his dress shirt, which are rolled up to his elbows.

"Do you think…" he starts again and takes another deep breath. "Do you want to be my girlfriend?" He glances up at me and then immediately down at his shoes. "It's okay if—"

I cut him off before he can finish whatever he's about to say.

"Yes!" I fling myself into his arms for a hug. My boyfriend. I HAVE A BOYFRIEND.

"Awesome," he says into my shoulder. He takes a small step back so we can see each other's faces. He smiles nervously and tilts his head as he leans forward.

This is it.

His mouth presses to mine, gently at first, unsure.

I lean in.

CHAPTER 15

It was sweet.

SUNDAY, OCTOBER 10TH

12:12 A.M.

BEDROOM

"Did you have fun tonight?" I ask as I turn to face Ruby in my bed.

"I did, actually." She yawns and then pauses for a second, fiddling with the blanket. "I'm sorry about the whole Jeremiah thing. I didn't want to mess up your fun Homecoming plans because I know how excited you were, but being Jeremiah's date made me feel…" Ruby shifts and stares up at the ceiling for a second. "I don't know, icky."

I nod, not saying anything.

"I know it wasn't cool of me to avoid him all night, but it felt easier to hang out with Alejandra and Jimmy." She pauses again and throws her arm over me. "Emma. My best friend in the whole wide, beautiful world, can you forgive me?" She gives me her best puppy dog eyes.

"Yeah, yeah, I forgive you. Honestly, I get it. I saw him dancing," I say. Ruby snorts. "And I'm sorry if you thought I was setting you up with him because he's Black. I mean, I guess it did seem like a happy coincidence, but I didn't even know he was Black when I first talked to Andy about it."

Ruby smiles softly. "It's okay." She yawns again.

"But, I am bitter that you only danced with me for one song." I poke her on the arm. "One!"

Ruby rubs the spot on her arm but laughs. "I know, I'm sorry. Again, you saw Jeremiah's dancing! It was like..." She pauses, trying to think of the right description.

"A fish out of water," I reply helpfully.

Ruby's big brown eyes get even bigger, and she nods slowly. We both burst into a fit of giggles.

Once we calm down, Ruby says, "Okay, okay. Now that that's out of the way, please, finally, tell me what happened with Andy!" She wiggles her eyebrows the same way she did earlier.

I obviously couldn't tell her what happened when we were all in the car together. She grabbed my hand and squeezed it when we sat down in the very back of Andy's mom's minivan, her eyes wide, and tilted her head at Andy. My eyes darted to the front seat where Andy was buckling his seat belt and saying something to his mom. I shook my head and pointed to my phone, then sent her a quick text.

> **Me:** BIG NEWS!!!

> **Me:** We kissed!!! Tell you everything at home.

Ruby sent back like twenty heart eyes emojis.

Now, in my bed with Ruby, my cheeks flush, and I smile softly, thinking about Andy's lips on mine.

"It was nice. It was sweet."

"That doesn't sound like it was fireworks though," Ruby says skeptically.

I hesitate, sitting up and reaching to grab my stuffed pig, Piggy, from the foot of the bed.

"Yeah," I admit. Sweet was the best way to describe the kiss. It wasn't earth-shattering or anything. Does that even happen in real life? "There weren't any fireworks. But I didn't *not* like it."

"Better than Connor?" Ruby asks.

"Oh my God. Way better! Speaking of flopping fish!" We both burst into giggles again.

"He's my boyfriend now," I inform Ruby.

"Saw that coming," she says, wriggling down into the blankets. "I'm happy for you, Em."

"I'm happy, too." I squeeze Piggy tight to my chest.

Ruby's breathing slows, and I know she's asleep already. That girl falls asleep faster than anyone.

I roll over, facing away from her. Out my window, the night sky is sparkling—maybe more beautiful than I've ever seen it before. I have a boyfriend. We kissed. It was sweet. I smile as I stare at the stars and relive this perfect night in my head.

SUNDAY, OCTOBER 10TH

11:33 A.M.

KITCHEN

My phone buzzes nonstop with texts from Cher and Ruby (even though Ruby left my house literally only ten minutes ago). Obviously, I had to fill Cher in on what happened last night. I take a bite of my peanut butter toast as I walk over to the table. I sit down, then check the messages.

Cher: He's your BOYFRIEND???!!!

Ruby: Believe it. It happened. I was there. Sort of.

Cher: This is HUGE!

Ruby: Our little girl is growing up. *Sobbing emoji*

Cher: Okay. Wow. I can't hang out today, but let's talk later. I need to hear every. single. detail.

I lean back against the chair to reply, a dopey smile surely plastered over my face.

Me: Yesss!!!!

Marie comes strutting into the kitchen. I take a deep breath, trying to act normal and not look like I have a boyfriend. She eyes me quietly, walks over to the fridge, and grabs a string cheese. She shuts the door and comes to stand in front of me. She doesn't say anything.

"Hi?" I say, taking a drink of my water.

"Your hair is weird," she tells me before taking a bite off the top of her string cheese. (Weirdo. Who eats it like that?)

My hair is still curled from the dance. I didn't feel like brushing it out when we got home last night. It didn't look terrible this morning, so I thought I'd leave it for a little while longer, to savor the magic from last night.

But Marie is ruining it.

"You're so irksome," I say, using a vocabulary word from last year.

Marie shrugs. "I don't know what that means." She walks out of the kitchen and plops herself onto the couch next to Dad in the living room.

Mom walks in a second after Marie leaves, and I brace myself. It was late when we got back last night, so she didn't get to interrogate us about the dance. She waited up for us, but I think she fell asleep on the couch because she shot up onto her feet as we walked in and then shuffled us off to bed right away.

Mom walks past me now to refill her coffee cup. She adds some milk and stirs it, clinking the spoon against the cup like always. She turns and leans back against the counter. She smiles at me. I cautiously return the gesture.

"So...?" Mom starts.

There it is.

"How was the dance?" she finishes. She casually takes a sip of coffee. As if she isn't dying to hear everything. I roll my eyes internally.

"Good," I say.

"Did you have fun?"

"Yep."

She places her mug on the counter and crosses her arms across her chest. She's the one who rolls her eyes this time.

"Seriously? One-word answers are all you're going to give me?"

What does she want from me? It would take all day for me to tell her everything that happened. Plus, I am *not* telling her about the kiss.

"I guess."

"Two words. Impressive." Mom picks her mug back up and takes another sip. She stands up straight and walks toward the doorway. "I'm glad you had—"

I suddenly blurt out, "Andy is my boyfriend."

I didn't know that was going to happen.

Mom stops mid-step. On the other side of the wall in the living room, Marie coughs, and Dad turns the volume down on the TV.

Oh boy. What have I done?

Mom stays frozen for a second and then turns around slowly.

"Oh?" is all she says, but she comes over to join me at the table. We're both quiet for a few seconds. I think she's waiting to see what else I'll give up.

"Yeah. I, um... I like him." I focus on picking up some crumbs off the table with my finger and dropping them onto my plate.

"That's great, honey." Mom's eyes are bright and a little shiny. "He seems like a very nice boy."

Marie and Dad are conspicuously quiet in the next room, so I'm wary to share anything else. It's one thing to tell Mom stuff. It's a whole other thing for Marie and Dad to know. I'll never hear the end of it.

I nod, unable to stop myself from smiling. Mom clears her throat. Here comes the spiel.

"Emma," she starts.

"Mom, I know. Be smart. Be safe. Don't do anything I don't want to do. I'm in charge of my body." I list off the tidbits she's been hammering into my brain the past couple years.

Mom sits up a little straighter. "That's right." She puts her hand over mine. "I know it seems like I'm saying the same things over and over, but it's important."

My mind immediately flashes back to shouting "No!" at Connor last year when he kept trying to touch my (nonexistent) boobs.

I nod. Mom smiles and gently squeezes my hand.

"I'm glad you're listening, though. Can't always be so sure," she says, tilting her head and raising her eyebrows at me.

I roll my eyes but nod again.

"No kissing," Dad chimes in gruffly from the other room.

Too late for that.

"Sure, Dad," I say to appease him.

"Gross," Marie says quietly.

I can see a sliver of Dad through the doorway, and he nods, satisfied by Marie's response. I'm over this conversation.

"Okay, I'm going up to my room now." I bring my plate over to the sink and rinse it. Mom is watching me, so I put it right into the dishwasher.

Mom smiles softly as I make my way past her and up the stairs. I glance back down, and she's still watching me. I don't know what to do, so I wave. Mom chuckles and puts her head in her hand. I race the rest of the way up to my room.

CHAPTER 16

Having a boyfriend is so cool.

THURSDAY, OCTOBER 21ST

7:55 A.M.

MY LOCKER

Having a boyfriend is *so* cool. I close my locker as Andy walks up, a smile on his face.

"Hey, beautiful," he says, kissing me on the cheek.

"Hi," I say shyly, even though I don't actually feel shy.

Andy's been walking me to most of my classes since we started dating. We make our way toward the English hallway, and Andy grabs my hand. Ruby says we're disgustingly adorable.

"How'd your essay go last night?" Andy asks.

"Ugh," I groan. "I finished it, but it's not great. Why do we need to read super old books and write essays on them? What's the point?" I roll my eyes.

Andy's quiet for a second. Then he says, "I think it's for the messages they can teach us about life. And I guess old books show us that some of those lessons don't change throughout the years."

I look over at him, eyes wide. A pink blush creeps up his neck. He shrugs.

"I like English."

"You're lucky you're cute," I tease him. He smiles and adjusts his books under his right arm.

I've learned that Andy is way more into school than I am. Not that I'm a bad student, but school is definitely not my favorite thing. I'm generally a B student. Andy is an A+ student. Always. He's actually helped me with my math homework a few times, which has been nice. Another reason having a boyfriend is awesome: he can help you with homework.

I let go of Andy's hand as we reach my English classroom. The warning bell rings, and he glances down the hall, assessing how long it will take him to get upstairs.

"You better go. You don't want to be late," I tell him.

His blue eyes turn back to me. They crinkle at the sides when he smiles. "It's worth it if I'm with you." He leans in and pecks me on the lips.

As he steps back, my eyes dart around the hallway. Did anyone see us? Kissing in the hallway always gives me such a thrill.

Andy starts walking backward, and I give a small wave as I turn to go into class, a smile still playing on my lips.

3:18 P.M.
MY LOCKER

Ruby and Alejandra meander over to my locker from the band room at the end of the day. Andy and I are already there, discussing our plans for the weekend.

"Ruby, thank God," Andy says, reaching his arm out.

Ruby raises an eyebrow. "I know I'm wonderful, but why are you so happy to see me, Bio Boy?"

"When are you going to stop calling him that?" I demand, grabbing my backpack and shutting my locker. I lean one hip against it.

Ruby shrugs and smiles coyly at Alejandra, who giggles.

"It doesn't bother me," Andy says. "Back to my point, though: Ruby. Can you please tell your best friend that she should come to the football game tomorrow? It's the last one, and everyone is going. It would be so lame if my girlfriend didn't come."

Ruby turns to me, eyebrows raised.

"Ruby," I start. "Can you please explain to Andy that my mom is so not cool and will probably not let me go to the game with a bunch of people she doesn't know?"

Ruby shifts her books on her hip. "Sorry, Em. I'm going to have to side with Bio Boy on this one." My jaw drops. "Give your mom some credit. She's cooler than you think."

I roll my eyes. Andy turns to me and smiles smugly. I flick him on the arm.

"Plus," Alejandra adds, "doesn't she know Andy? Hasn't he been to your house?"

Heat quickly pulses through my veins. *Who asked you?* I want to say. I like Alejandra, but she's always around now. And sometimes, I'm not asking for her opinion.

Unfortunately, she's right.

"Yeah, for Homecoming pictures," I concede. "But she also knows Andy is my boyfriend. She's going to think we'll spend the whole night making out under the bleachers."

"We can totally do that," Andy says with a small shrug.

My cheeks burst into flame, and with a scoff, I lean forward and push him.

"What?" he says sheepishly. "Is that a crime?"

"Not. At. All," Ruby emphasizes. She turns back to me, pointing a long finger. "Do it. Go to the game. Make out with Andy. Alejandra and I will be watching you have fun from the band section, like the true losers we are."

"Speak for yourself," Alejandra says, poking Ruby playfully on the arm.

"Doesn't bother me," Ruby says, standing a little bit taller. "The weirdos always turn out to be the coolest adults."

I nod in encouragement, thinking of the story Georgia told us about her days in high school. She said she was always kind of lonely, like she never really fit in, until she found her group of weirdos. She said that once she found her people and could be who she truly was, and for her, that was a musical theater nerd (her words, not mine), she was finally happy and could grow into the person she was meant to become. And Georgia is the coolest adult I know.

"I like losers," I add to the conversation now.

"Duh," Ruby says, tossing me a smile.

"Wait, does that make me a loser?" Andy says, putting his hand to his chest.

"Yes," Ruby, Alejandra, and I say in unison.

We all burst into laughter.

CHAPTER 17

Can't have my sister looking like a freak at school.

THURSDAY, OCTOBER 21ST

5:12 P.M.

BEDROOM

I'm lying on my bed, pretending to study for my biology test, but I'm actually watching Celsius music videos. There's a quiet knock on my door.

"Come in."

Marie pokes her head around the door, not opening it fully.

"Emma?" she says tentatively.

"What?" I snap. Why can't she get to it? Marie's face falls. I rephrase and say more gently, "What is it, Marie?"

She pushes the door and steps fully into the room. Her hand is at the base of her neck, and her shoulders are pulled up almost to her ears. She looks down at the floor, and then at the posters on my wall, and then at my open closet—anywhere but at me.

Quietly, she says, "Can you help me?"

Normally, this encounter would annoy me. Marie is being shifty and not telling me what she wants. But I can tell by her demeanor that something is wrong, and my heart softens at that. She's annoying, but she's also my sister, and I guess deep down I care about her.

I sit up, closing my laptop. "With what?"

Marie lets go of whatever she's holding behind her neck—her hair, I realize now—and turns to show me. It's a tangled mess at the base of her neck, with a hair tie knotted up in it.

She turns over her shoulder and says with watery eyes, "I can't get it out, and it really hurts when I try." Her voice cracks at the end, and my heart breaks a tiny bit.

This is a moment for me to be the cool big sister. I can feel it. I bounce to the end of the bed on my butt and smile at my little sister.

"Come here. Grab that comb from my desk."

Marie picks up the comb and walks over, avoiding eye contact again. She hands it to me as I lean against the bed.

"It's okay," I tell her. She turns to stand in front of me. "I'll get it out." Marie's shoulders relax slightly. "What were you trying to do?"

"A messy bun," Marie says quietly. She rubs the side of her arm.

I nod but then remember she can't see me. "Mmm," I say. "I still haven't mastered that."

"Really?" she says, turning.

"Hold still," I remind her, working at the tangles surrounding the hair tie.

"Sorry." She's quiet for a second. "But your hair is always so cool."

"Thanks." I know it's Marie, but for some reason it actually means more coming from her. My hair isn't golden and luscious like Cher's or cool and stylish like Ruby's. It's just boring brown hair, usually in a bun on top of my head, which takes far longer than it should because it never looks the right amount of messy and cute at the same time.

But Marie's not the kind of kid who's going to butter you up just to do it, and she's not trying to get anything from me right now—except my help—so I think she means it. I smile at the rat's nest in front of me.

After a minute, I haven't made much progress.

"Maybe we should sit down," I tell Marie.

"Are you going to have to cut my hair off?" she asks quietly.

"Probably," I tease. She freezes. I pull lightly on her hair. "I'm kidding. Here come sit on the bed. I'll put some music on."

5:24 P.M.

"Girls?" Mom pushes my bedroom door all the way open. "What are you—" She stops short when she sees Marie and me sitting on the bed together. I finally got the hair tie out, and now I'm brushing her auburn hair smooth.

"Emma's going to teach me how to do a messy bun," Marie says brightly, bouncing slightly on the bed.

Mom doesn't say anything at first. She watches us for a second, a half smile on her face, then winks at me. I focus on the task at hand, but I smile to myself.

Mom heads down the hallway before calling back to us, "Dinner in about fifteen minutes."

"Let's go stand in front of the mirror so you can see what I'm doing," I tell Marie once her hair is smooth and tangle-free.

Maire hops off the bed and places herself in front of the full-length mirror standing next to my closet. She flips her hair behind her shoulders and smiles over at me.

"Thanks, Emma," she says.

I shrug. "Can't have my sister looking like a freak at school."

Marie giggles as I start pulling her hair up into a high ponytail.

8:40 P.M.

I open my bedroom door and step out into the hallway. "Mom?"

"Yeah?"

"Where are you?"

"Our house is not that big. Walk down the stairs."

I find Mom sitting on the couch, reading a book.

"Mom?"

"Yes?" She puts her book down on her lap and turns her attention to me.

My heart is racing. I'm not sure how to start. I stand there, silent, for a few seconds. I even open my mouth once but end up closing it without actually saying anything.

"Emma? What is it?" Her forehead crinkles. "Is everything okay? Did something happen?"

"No, everything is fine," I assure her.

"Okay," She places her book on the arm of the couch and leans forward.

"So, um, tomorrow is the last football game."

Mom nods slowly.

"And, um… I was wondering if… maybe I could go?"

Mom's face clears, and she sinks back into the couch.

"Sure, honey," she says. With a relieved smile, I clasp my hands in front of my chest and turn to head back up to my bedroom, but Mom stops me. "Oh, wait a second, it's not going to be *that* easy." She laughs softly.

I groan and turn. She laughs again and pats the spot next to her on the couch. The questions start as soon as I sit.

"Who's going? How are you getting there? How are you getting home? What time will you be home?" She ticks each one off on her fingers.

I swallow, prepared for the interrogation.

"Ruby and Alejandra will be there with band." Mom nods, pursing her lips slightly. "And also Andy and some of his friends."

"There it is," Mom says, pointing a finger at me. "That's why you're so fidgety."

I roll my eyes, even though she's right.

"Rides?" Mom prods.

"Um, I'd need a ride there, but Andy's mom can drop me off after. Or I'll get a ride with Ruby and Alejandra." I grab a pillow from behind me and put it on my lap, fiddling with a loose thread.

"No Cher?" Mom asks.

I shake my head. "She's going to the game at Woodlands."

"Home by?"

"Ten thirty?" I try. Mom raises an eyebrow in response. "Ten," I say with a sigh.

Mom is quiet for a few seconds. I continue pulling on the loose string of the pillow in my lap, definitely making it worse. *Please say yes. Please say yes.*

"All right," Mom says. Without thinking, I immediately wrap her in a hug. "Oh!" she says before putting her arm around me.

"Thanks, Mom," I say into her shoulder.

"But," she starts, pushing me off of her gently. I breathe in, ready for the spiel. "Be smart. Make good choices. Don't do anything you don't want to do." She pauses before giving me a mischievous smile. "People used to make out behind the bleachers when I was in high school. Do they still do that?"

"Ew, Mom!"

"What? Don't look so disgusted. I was cool." Mom gives me a sly smile, and I shake my head.

CHAPTER 18

Behind the bleachers.

FRIDAY, OCTOBER 22ND

6:57 P.M.

IN THE CAR

"I can get out here," I tell Mom. I reach to unbuckle my seat belt, but Mom throws her arm across me.

"Emma. We are in the middle of the street."

"But we're stopped."

"No," Mom insists.

I roll my eyes but lean back in the seat. There's so much traffic getting to the school, and I'm antsy. Up ahead, the lights are shining on the football field, and people are filing in at the gates. My phone vibrates with a text from Andy, and my heart tumbles.

> **Andy:** We're here. Want me to wait for you at the gate?

Ugh. How did I get so lucky?

Andy sends back a heart emoji. He's so sweet. But sometimes he does stuff like that—sending a heart—that makes me feel, I don't know, kind of embarrassed? I don't respond and shove my phone into my bag before looping it over my head and right shoulder.

Finally, Mom turns into the parking lot. There's a ton of cars in front of us, and I'll have to walk all the way across it, but as soon as she's stopped, I unlock the doors.

"Okay, thanks, Mom. Bye!" I pull on the door handle. Mom sighs but doesn't stop me.

"Have fun, be safe, be smart."

"I know, I know," I say, hopping out into the parking lot. I know I won't be able to see him yet, but my eyes still try to scan the entry for Andy.

"I know you do," Mom says. I turn back for a quick smile. "I love you, sweetie."

"Love you, too. Bye!" I shut the door and cut in front of Mom's car to head across the lot.

Mom rolls her window down to shout, "Be careful walking through this parking lot, Emma!"

My cheeks burn. Ugggghhhh. I hope no one heard her. I'm not six years old. I wave back in acknowledgment and trudge forward with my head down.

7:03 P.M.
ENTRANCE

I show the teacher at the gate my school ID, and she gestures for me to go in. I shuffle through behind a loud group of juniors, who are all talking about where they're going after the game.

"But can we stop at Taco Bell first?" a tall boy with broad shoulders shouts over his friends.

I scoot past them and scan the crowd for a boy with blond hair. My boy. I feel silly, standing here turning in circles by myself. I pull the zipper on my bag to grab my phone when I feel arms wrap around my waist. I turn and find Andy's face next to mine.

"Hi," he says, planting a kiss right on my lips.

"Hi." I smile, happy to have found him and be wrapped in his arms. He lets go too quickly and instead grabs my hand.

"Come on." He pulls me toward the bleachers. "Everyone's up here."

7:35 P.M.
BLEACHERS

There's a decent group of us hanging out together: Andy, me, Jeremiah, Matt, and Lily (who's mostly been sulking, a pinched expression on her face and her arms crossed across her stomach; I haven't heard her speak at all since I've been up here), plus Steve, Robby, and Paxton, who I'm meeting for the first time.

We can also see Ruby sitting with the band. She spotted us first, and in true Ruby fashion, stood up, waving both her hands above her head, shouting, "Emma! Bio Boy! Hey!" until we found her. I love that weirdo. I glance over at her now, and she's deep in conversation with the girl next to her, comparing their clarinets.

I lean back into Andy's legs. I saw a group of sophomore girls sitting like this with boys—leaning back in between their legs, like they're armrests—and thought it was so cool. And now I'm doing it with Andy. What even is my life?

I smile down at the football field, even though I have no idea what's happening there. The scoreboard says we're down by three, but then the crowd cheers and the band starts playing. They must have scored.

Andy leans forward. "Are you cold? You don't have a hat or anything." Truthfully, yes, I am a little chilly. But I wasn't going to ruin my hair by putting a hat on after it took me forty minutes to get it perfectly straight everywhere. Plus, I have a small head and usually look kind of stupid in hats.

I shake my head. "I'm okay."

"Darn," Andy says in my ear. "I was going to try to use that as an excuse to warm you up."

My cheeks flush, and I definitely don't feel cold anymore. I turn to face Andy, and his cheeks are pink, too.

"Actually, I am pretty cold." I rub my arms over my fleece jacket for emphasis.

"Cool," Andy says. He stands and nudges Jeremiah. "Emma and I are going to get something to eat. We'll be back."

"Surrrreeee," Jeremiah says. I pretend to be very interested in the game, but I can't even tell who has the ball.

Andy grabs my hand, and we climb down the bleachers, around groups of kids sitting between each other's legs and parents sitting on little square pillow pads.

My heart beats in time with the drum line. It feels like the drum roll they're doing is for me, rather than the guy kicking the ball on the field. I take a deep breath to try to calm it, but it only thumps harder as Andy helps me down the last step.

7:50 P.M.
BEHIND THE BLEACHERS

Andy and I walk hand in hand along the brick wall behind the bleachers. I feel jittery, and not because of the cold. It *is* cold, but back here behind the bleachers, the wind isn't blowing as much, so it's not too bad. Plus, Andy's hand is warm in mine.

I feel jittery because I know what's coming. Andy and I have been going out for two weeks now, but we've only kissed, *really* kissed, the one time after Homecoming. Hanging out in the hallway doesn't present a lot of opportunity for tongue-action.

We pass a group of kids standing around in a circle talking. One of the girls, who I recognize from my math class, waves to me. I wave back, pleased that someone is seeing me with my boyfriend. Andy and I continue walking all the way to the end of the wall, past the groups of people, past the bathrooms. We stop far enough away that we're alone and also can't smell the bathrooms. (Gross.)

Andy leans up against the wall and pulls gently on my hand. I step closer to him, breathing deeply, still trying to calm my racing heart. He smells like the cologne samples that come in magazines. I like it.

"You smell good," I tell him shyly.

"Thanks. It's called Fierce. It was a birthday present." He moves closer to me, and I think he's jumping right in, but instead, he leans back a second later. "You smell good, too."

Oh my God. He smelled me. My entire face bursts into flame, or at least it feels like it. Thank God I sprayed something before I left. I don't have any fancy perfume like Cher. Everything I have is from Bath & Body. I think I sprayed Enchanted Candy, which I picked because I liked the rose gold bottle with stars on it. I make a mental note to add something nice to my Christmas list this year. And to ask Cher what she buys.

"Thanks," is all I say, glancing behind me.

"I'm glad you came tonight," Andy says. He's holding both my hands now and sways them slightly.

"Me too."

He's making some serious eye contact. I feel like I should keep it, but it's making me feel weird, like I'm under a magnifying glass. Instead, I look up at the bleachers, wondering what everyone else is doing right now.

He squeezes my hands, and a warm sensation floats through my chest as he takes a step closer and our mouths press together. Thoughts of anyone else are gone. Andy wraps his arms around my waist, and I wrap mine around his neck.

He leans back from the kiss, his deep-blue eyes examining mine. I smile, still warm all the way through. My heart is racing, and I can feel his beating up against my own. It's fast.

He smiles before moving his face back toward mine, and this time, we really go for it. Open mouths, tongue—we are full-on making out behind the bleachers at a football game. This is so fun. I wonder if anyone is walking by.

The warmth in my chest spreads all the way down through the rest of my body. Andy tries to pull me closer, although I'm not sure it's possible.

Someone clears their throat, and Andy and I both whip our heads around to find our biology teacher, Mr. Milo, standing near the entrance to the boys' bathroom.

"Probably time to head back up, my friends," he says. Andy's neck is as red as my face feels. We scurry off before Mr. Milo can say anything else.

8:03 P.M.
CONCESSIONS

"Oh my God. I can't believe that happened." I burst into giggles and cover my face as Andy and I reach the crowded concessions area. "How are we going to face Mr. Milo on Monday?"

Andy shrugs, a small smile playing on his lips, even though his neck is still pink. His lips are a little red. Probably from the kissing. Instead of feeling embarrassed, it makes me want to kiss him some more.

Seemingly out of nowhere, Jeremiah's head pops up over Andy's shoulder.

"Hey, buddy!" Jeremiah grabs Andy's shoulders and shakes him.

Andy jumps a little but smiles when his friend comes around to stand next to us. Matt follows not far behind.

My heart skips. *Stop that,* I scold it. I barely even know him. I've never spoken one word to him directly. We were all together after Homecoming, but we didn't have a conversation or anything.

"Hey," Matt says, eyes flitting from Andy to me. I swear they linger on me for an extra second.

"Hey," I say back. *That's one word,* my heart taunts me as it skips again.

I grab Andy's hand and ignore whatever is happening inside my body. Matt averts his eyes and turns to the concession stand.

"What have you two been up to?" Jeremiah says, pointing at Andy and me. He wiggles his eyebrows. He and Ruby are so much alike. Maybe that's why they didn't work out. I wouldn't want to date the boy-version of myself either.

"About to get some food," Andy says casually.

Jeremiah purses his lips and nods theatrically. "Totally." He nudges Matt with his elbow.

"Leave them alone, Jer," Matt says cooly.

I like Andy. I really do. But I can't deny that Matt is... hot. And cool. He's standing half a step behind Jeremiah, with his hands deep in his pockets. He's probably cold because he's not wearing a jacket, just a hoodie and a beanie hat.

Whereas Andy is cute and kind of dorky. But so am I. That's why we're a good fit. Not that it even matters, but Matt would never be interested in a girl like me. His girlfriend, Lily, is tall and blonde and beautiful and confident. And I am... none of those things. Which is okay because I. Am. With. Andy.

I squeeze Andy's hand as we all walk over to the concessions line. He smiles and squeezes back. I'm happy.

"Where's Lily?" Andy asks Matt.

Matt's mouth straightens into a flat line. He shrugs and turns to the football field. I guess that's the end of the conversation. Jeremiah leans over and does a "cut it out" gesture, flicking his hand across his throat a couple times.

I wonder what happened.

9:12 P.M.
BLEACHERS

The game ended. I think we won. I was too busy talking and cuddling with Andy to even pretend to pay attention.

One thing I did notice, though, was that when we came back up to the bleachers after getting snacks earlier, Lily was gone and didn't come back.

Did she and Matt get in a fight? Did they break up?

Whatever. It's not my business.

Andy wraps his arm around my waist. "So now what?"

I check the time on my phone. "I have to be home by ten," I say, rolling my eyes.

"No worries," Andy replies. "Want to walk?" He raises his eyebrows and smiles at me.

"Yeah, that sounds perfect."

How romantic. My boyfriend is going to walk me home! I told Mom I'd get a ride, but as long as I'm home on time, it'll be fine. It's not that far of a walk anyway, and I won't be alone.

Andy stands up and says to the boys, "Hey, we're going to walk to Emma's house. Her curfew is ten." My cheeks warm. He didn't have to tell everyone about my curfew.

"Oh man, you know what? That's perfect," Jeremiah says. "I have to be home by ten, too. Did you know I only live a few blocks over from you?"

"Really? Where?"

"On Mansfield." Jeremiah turns to the group. "You guys want to hang at my house after?"

The group murmurs and nods in agreement. Okay, so my boyfriend and his friends are going to walk me home. Not quite so romantic, but I'll take it.

"Helloooo!" Ruby throws her arm around my shoulder. "What's happening, people?"

I smile and grab Ruby's hand near my neck. She's still in her black-and-gold band uniform with her clarinet in her other hand.

"Ruby!" Andy says loudly. He opens his arms in welcome. "Excellent playing tonight." He gives her an a-okay sign.

Ruby and I exchange a quick glance, and Ruby tries to stifle a giggle. That was so dorky.

"Thanks, Bio Boy," she says.

"Rubs, we're all going to walk home together. Want to come?" What's one more person on my romantic walk home?

"Duh," she says. "Can you wait for me? I have to change out of my uniform."

"We'll meet you by the big rock on the other side of the parking lot," I tell her.

"Perf." She runs off toward the school.

We make our way down the bleachers, clunkily and noisily.

"Sorry our walk home totally got hijacked," Andy says quietly. He wraps his arm around my waist again. It makes it kind of hard to walk, but I like it.

"It's okay. It'll be fun."

"As long as you're there, I'm happy." Andy pulls me in and kisses me on the cheek. He stops walking. The rest of the group keeps moving ahead of us, laughing at something Jeremiah said.

"Hey," he says expectantly, his face still very close to mine. "A real one please." He leans in to kiss me on the lips. I glance behind us, and there's a bunch of people waiting. We're blocking the exit. My cheeks burn, and I nudge him away quickly.

"Come on. There's people behind us." I unwrap myself from his grasp and pull him by the hand to catch up with everyone else.

CHAPTER 19

I can totally do a cartwheel.

FRIDAY, OCTOBER 22ND

9:31 P.M.

WALKING HOME

I'm sort of glad our walk home got hijacked. Sometimes Andy tries a little too hard to make the moment romantic. It's embarrassing. Like that kiss on the bleachers. I heard a girl behind us sigh loudly while they were waiting for us to move. Just thinking about it makes me want to crawl under a rock and hide.

I mean, obviously I'm glad he likes me, and I like him a lot, too. But I wish he'd take it down a notch.

All I've ever wanted was for someone to like me, really like me. And now that I do, it's kind of embarrassing.

Weird.

I shake these thoughts out of my head and focus on what's happening in front of me. We're walking down the middle of a quiet side street, lit only by street lamps. Ruby and I trail slightly behind the boys, who are half jumping, half walking, and being very loud.

Andy turns around and walks backward. "I bet Ruby can do one," he says.

"Of course I can," Ruby says. After a beat, she adds, "Do what?"

I giggle, and she nudges me lightly in the ribs.

"A cartwheel," Jeremiah says, also walking backward.

"Oh. Duh. Easy." Ruby hands me her backpack and jogs to catch up with the boys, hopping into a beautiful cartwheel as she approaches them, her legs gliding perfectly up and over their heads.

"Incredible. Teach us," Jeremiah says, flipping his baseball hat backward and rubbing his hands together. The group continues walking more slowly while Ruby explains the logistics of a cartwheel.

A few seconds later, Jeremiah announces, "I think I'm ready." He turns to Andy. "You with me, man?"

"Of course," Andy says, smiling over at me. He points and says, "This one's for you."

I blush but also smile back and give him a thumbs-up.

"Wait!" Andy calls out. He jogs to me, where I'm now standing with Matt and Robby. He gives me a quick kiss on the lips, and I blush even harder. I'm very aware of Matt and Robby next to me.

(Okay, fine, mostly Matt.)

"On my count," Ruby announces. "Three, two, one!"

Jeremiah, Andy, Paxton, and Steve all attempt a cartwheel. And they're all pretty pathetic.

Ruby shakes her head and rubs her fingers over her eyebrows. "No, no, no..."

Robby, Matt, and I all laugh at the pitiful attempt. Robby bends over and puts his hands on his knees, and Matt laughs into his fist. I let my head drop as the giggles subside.

"Hey, I'd like to see you try this," Jeremiah calls back to us.

"I can do a cartwheel," I retort. Feeling brave, I drop Ruby's backpack on the ground and take a couple steps forward. My hands touch the rough asphalt beneath me as I put my weight onto them, and I kick my legs up and over my head, even remembering to point my toes. For a fraction of a second, I'm very aware of the skin exposed on my stomach, but rather than be embarrassed like I normally would, a shiver of exhilaration shoots through my veins. I finish the cartwheel gracefully, landing softly right in front of Andy.

"Incredible!" he says and pulls me in for a kiss. Everyone claps, but I'm not sure if it's for the cartwheel or the kiss.

I push my hair behind my ears and smile as I walk back to pick up Ruby's backpack, where Matt and Robby are still standing.

"Impressive," Matt says, turning his head toward me.

Robby nods and walks over to the rest of the group. "I gotta try this," he says.

This is the second time tonight Matt has spoken to me directly, and it's making my heart whir and my cheeks hot. Matt and I continue walking behind the group, alone, now that Robby has joined them.

"Thanks," I mumble. I shake it off. Andy is my boyfriend. He is the one who makes my heart do funny things, I remind myself. More confidently, I say, "I was in gymnastics from, like, three to ten, so I'm basically a pro."

A lopsided smile breaks onto Matt's face, and my heart starts whirring again. *Stop it!* I clear my throat in another attempt to control my body.

"Don't tell those guys," he says, nodding his head at the group a few feet in front of us. I hear Ruby telling them to point their toes and let out a small giggle. Matt continues. "But I can totally do a cartwheel. I did gymnastics, too."

My mouth opens in surprise. "Really? You strike me as more of a football, baseball, soccer kind of dude."

He nods. "I am now. Mostly soccer and baseball. But when I was little, my older sister was in gymnastics, and I wanted to do it, too." He shrugs, his smile back for a second, and I notice his front teeth overlap slightly. It's cute.

"I bet my cartwheel is better than yours," I say.

Wait. Was that me? It sounded way more confident than I ever sound in my head, and even a little… flirty. I push his arm lightly when he doesn't say anything. Definitely flirty. *What am I doing?*

Matt seems to notice it, too. He glances in front of us at Andy and the others, who are giving another poor attempt at a cartwheel, and pushes some of his brown curls out of his eyes.

"Okay, better," Ruby says. "Jeremiah, you actually lifted both of your legs that time." She gives him a small clap.

"Oh, come on," I say in an attempt to salvage the situation. I don't want Matt to think I'm being weird or inappropriate or anything. I bite the edge of my lip and push my own hair behind my ear. "I'm messing with you."

Matt nods, his eyes still on the group ahead of us, sliding over to me for half a second. Rather than drop it, something comes out of my mouth unexpectedly.

"Unless you're a chicken."

"What?" Matt says, turning his head.

What am I doing?

"I said, 'Unless you're a chicken.'" I raise my eyebrows and put my hands on my hips.

Matt chuckles and tilts his head back, his face up to the sky.

"Okay," he says. He pushes up the sleeves of his burgundy hoodie. "Let's do this."

My heart starts thumping. "You're on," I say when a hilarious idea strikes me. Once again, I drop Ruby's backpack on the ground. I quickly grab my phone and hold it in my right hand while Matt is on my left.

Matt jogs a little in place, and I giggle to myself. I pretend to stretch my legs, leaning one out in front of me and then the other.

"Ready?" he says.

"Yup."

"I think I need a running start," he says, his voice a little softer than before.

"Sure, sure. Whatever you need," I say kindly.

He narrows his eyes at me, and I smile back innocently.

"Three..."

"Two..." Matt joins in.

"One!" we both say.

Matt runs a couple steps forward, and I point my phone at him. He lifts his arms in the air and hops forward into a pretty decent cartwheel. And I capture it all on video. I'm laughing, hard, and I can't stop. It's really more like a cackle.

Matt turns around, clearly impressed with himself, but it fades when he sees me in the same spot, pointing my phone at him.

Ruby and the boys behind him are all clapping and cheering. "Now *that* is what you want to look like," Ruby says, gesturing at Matt.

Matt pays them no mind, though, and instead, starts running toward me, that lopsided smile back on his face with a mischievous twist.

A loud squeak escapes my mouth, and I try to run, but Matt is already right in front of me. Before I realize what's happening, he scoops me up and over his shoulder. Barely slowing down, he continues running in the opposite direction of our friends.

"What are you doing?" I shout, but I'm also still laughing.

"This is payback!" he says.

All I can see is the street bouncing by as he runs. Then I hear a bang. I try to peek around Matt's side and see green plastic.

I scream and instinctively wrap my arms around his waist. "Are you putting me in the garbage?"

"Yup." Matt laughs.

"No!" I start kicking my legs trying to get down, but Matt must be strong because he holds on, until...

"Yo!" Andy's voice breaks through our laughter.

Matt immediately flips me over and places me back on the ground. I straighten my fleece jacket, which had ridden up my middle while Matt was carrying me.

Everyone is quiet.

"Dude," Andy says, throwing his hands up. "My girlfriend's butt was totally in your face. What the hell?"

Matt pushes his hair back, and I cross my arms over my chest, rubbing them like I'm cold, even though my cheeks are on fire.

Matt still hasn't said anything.

"We were just messing around," I tell Andy. I walk over and stand awkwardly in front of him. He doesn't look at me, glaring at Matt instead.

"Not cool, man," Andy says coldly.

Matt's eyes flick from the ground, to Andy, to me. "Dude. You heard her. We were messing around." He pulls the hood of his sweatshirt over his head and a shadow covers the top of his face.

Andy nods curtly. He grabs my hand, and without another word, he turns and starts walking. His arm is stretched out behind him as I kind of hop-walk to catch up. I glance over my shoulder once I'm next to him, but everyone is cast into shadow behind us.

CHAPTER 20

It was no big deal.

We're almost at my street, and Andy hasn't said anything. He and I have been walking silently ahead of the rest of the group, who are trailing behind us, talking in whispers or not at all.

It's weird.

I swallow and stop walking at the corner. He's being kind of a baby about this whole thing, but I'm tired of his silence, so I want to fix it.

"Hey," I say quietly. The rest of the group keeps walking.

"Emma, I'm gonna head home. Text me later," Ruby says as she passes us, blowing me a kiss. I nod and wave.

Andy's eyes are on the ground. I squeeze his hand.

"Want to sit?" I ask.

"Sure," he says quietly.

We sit next to each other on the curb. I stretch my legs out in front of me. Andy has his knees up with his arms crossed on top of them. He's still silent.

"So..." I fold my hands in my lap.

Andy finally looks at me. His usually bright, blue eyes are dim. I don't know if it's because it's dark or because he's mad. Maybe both.

"Are you mad at me?" I ask, wringing my hands.

Andy shrugs. He faces the street again, resting his chin on his folded arms.

"I'm sorry. It wasn't—"

"It's fine," Andy interrupts.

I freeze, unsure what to do or say next. Andy is still looking out at the street.

"Okay," is all I say. I check my phone. I need to be in my house in five minutes.

"I think I was jealous," Andy says, unfolding himself and stretching his legs out, too. I don't know how to respond, so I wait for him to continue. "I like you so much." He grabs my hand and rubs his thumb up and down the side.

"I like you, too," I tell him. *And I do,* I remind myself. He's cute and nice and funny and smart. What's not to like?

"Good," he says. He scooches closer to me, and I can see his blue eyes shining under the streetlight now. He smiles and licks his lips, moving in.

We kiss for a minute or two. Andy's lips smile on top of mine. I think I'm getting good at this. I smile back, pleased.

"What?" Andy says, scanning my face.

"Nothing." I give a small shrug. "I like kissing you." My cheeks flush slightly, but I'm impressed with myself. A year ago I never would have been bold enough to say something like that.

"I *love* kissing you," Andy says, but at that exact moment, the alarm blares on my phone.

"That's my two-minute warning," I explain, showing Andy the screen. "My parents are super strict about curfew." I roll my eyes for effect.

We both stand up, wiping gravel remnants off our butts.

"Thanks for walking me home," I say, glancing down the block toward my house. I better hurry.

"Thanks for being my girlfriend," Andy says, pulling me in for a hug.

"I gotta go," I say after a second. "Bye." I give him a quick peck on the lips, like kissing a boy is the most normal thing in the world for me to do. Which, I guess it kind of is now.

I run down the street. Over my shoulder, Andy is still standing there, watching me. I wave as I hop up onto the porch step. He waves back and starts walking.

10:00 P.M.
HOME

Mom is waiting for me on the couch in the living room. "Right on time," she says as I open the door. The time on my phone changes from 10:00 to 10:01. *Phew.*

"Mmhm," I reply, locking the door behind me.

"Did you have fun?" Mom asks.

"Yep."

"Is that all you're going to give me?"

"Yep." I walk up the stairs.

Mom sighs dramatically. I smile to myself but don't say anything else.

10:38 P.M.
IN BED

I crawl into bed, and my phone vibrates. It's a text from Ruby. I also have one waiting from Andy. I open Ruby's first.

Ruby: DISH.

I laugh out loud to myself.

Me: We're fine. I said I was sorry, and before I could say anything else or explain, he said it was fine and that he was jealous.

Ruby: Wow.

Ruby: Well, that's good.

Me: Yeah. Then we kissed on the corner.

Ruby: Oooooh how romantic!!!

I smile. It was pretty romantic.

Ruby: But like, for real, what WERE you doing with Matt?

Me: What do you mean? We were messing around.

Me: I recorded him doing a cartwheel, and when he saw me, he ran over and picked me up. He was acting like he was going to put me in the garbage can as revenge. It was no big deal.

Ruby: IDK girl. If I was Andy, I probably would've been pissed, too. You were giggling and shouting.

Ruby: It sounded like some hard-core flirting to me.

My cheeks flush, heat rising from my chest all the way up.

Ruby: What's the deal? Are you into him?

Ruby: Matt, that is.

Me: What? No.

Me: I like Andy. My boyfriend, remember?

Ruby: Ok, just checking.

I lie back on my pillow and stare up at the ceiling.

Ruby: It WAS pretty impressive that he could carry you over his shoulder like that.

I can't stop the grin that sneaks onto my face.

Me: I know, right?

I feel slightly giddy, and I'm about to dive into this more deeply when my phone buzzes with a new text. Andy.

Oops. I forgot I had a text waiting from him. I tap over to that conversation.

Andy: Hey. Thanks for being a great girlfriend. And a great kisser.

I smile, thrilled to be known as a great kisser.

Andy: Maybe you're asleep already. Good night, beautiful.

I reply quickly.

Me: Sorry, not asleep. Was talking to my mom and then Ruby texted, too. Thanks for always making me feel special.

Andy: You deserve it. Night, Emma.

Me: Night, boyfriend.

Andy sends back a gif of two penguins hugging. Cute. But I don't know why, I can't look at it for more than a second. I turn the screen off.

10:50 P.M.

I should be more grateful that my boyfriend is so sweet. Lots of boys are not like that at all.

I meant it when I said he always makes me feel special. Our kiss on the corner was pretty great. I like kissing Andy. His lips are soft, and his kissing is gentle—almost... sensual? Ew. That word makes me feel slimy.

I force my brain to focus on the romantic (not sensual) kiss with Andy.

Very rudely, my brain shoves Matt into the forefront. His lopsided smile as he ran at me. Throwing me so easily over his shoulder. His laugh as he ran to the garbage can. My arms around his waist, trying to escape.

We were definitely flirting. Or at least I was.

Was he?

10:52 P.M.

It doesn't matter if he was flirting. I have a boyfriend. Andy. Sweet, cute, slightly cringey Andy.

10:59 P.M.

I like Andy a lot.

11:02 P.M.

But why do I have to keep reminding myself that?

CHAPTER 21

I'm allowed to have other friends, you know.

THURSDAY, OCTOBER 28TH

1:25 P.M.

BIOLOGY

The bell rings, and Andy and I pack up our books. How cute is it that I sit next to my boyfriend in class?

"What are you doing tomorrow night?" Andy asks as we walk together out the door.

I shrug. "Probably hanging out with Ruby?"

The girls and I were texting about our weekend plans last night. Cher's going to a movie with Jacob on Friday, and then she's at her dad's all weekend. Ruby has to help her mom organize their kitchen at some point. I have to go to my sister's basketball game on Sunday.

"Want to come over to my house? I'm going to do a big movie night." He holds the door open for me, and I smile at him. Always so sweet.

"Yeah, that sounds fun. What movie?"

"I'm thinking a scary one," he says. I make a face. I don't really like scary movies. Andy adjusts his books and grabs my hand. "Don't worry, I'll keep you safe. We can snuggle under a blanket together."

I bite my lip, still unsure. He leans forward, squeezing my hand, and his eyes bore into mine. His eyebrows are raised, and his smile is so eager, I reluctantly give in.

"Okay, but you have to protect me," I say, eyeing him seriously.

"Of course. That's my job." He squeezes my hand again and stares into my eyes meaningfully. I blush, but I'm not sure if it's because it's sweet, or too much.

"Heyyyy, Bio Boyyyy!" Ruby calls as we approach. She closes her locker and leans up against it. She grins like the Cheshire Cat and tosses her braids over her shoulder. My best friend is so effortlessly cool.

"Hey, what about me?" I tease.

"I'm always happy to see you. You're my favorite."

I smile and lightly bump my shoulder against hers.

"Movie night at my house tomorrow," Andy says. He points at Ruby with a finger gun motion. "You in?"

Ruby's brown eyes turn to me. I nod.

Pointing her own finger gun back at Andy, she clicks her tongue and says, "You bet, BB."

Andy's forehead crinkles. "BB?"

Ruby sighs. "BB—Bio Boy. Keep up."

I giggle, and Andy nods, a tiny smirk on his face.

"Are you ever going to call me 'Andy'?" he asks.

"We'll see," Ruby says, standing up straight.

Andy laughs and steps closer to give me a kiss goodbye.

"Oh, BB, wait, before you go—can Alejandra come tomorrow, too?"

I whip my head around. Why is she inviting Alejandra? If she feels my eyes on her, she doesn't show it.

"Of course," Andy says. With a wave, he leaves for his next class. Ruby and I start the walk to PE without Alejandra today.

I hesitate before saying anything. It's not that I don't like Alejandra, I do. Ruby's been hanging out with her so much, though, it's starting to feel like she'd rather spend time with Alejandra than with me. Something stirs in my chest, and I decide I can't hold it in.

"So..." My heart thumps. I don't want Ruby to get mad at me. Ruby raises her eyebrows, waiting for me to finish my thought.

"You're hanging out with Alejandra a lot lately."

Ruby shrugs. "Yeah. I like hanging out with her."

"It's just, like..." Again I hesitate. I don't know how to explain what I'm feeling. "A lot," I finish feebly.

"What's that supposed to mean?" Ruby's tone changes, deeper and quicker.

"Nothing... I don't know." We pause in front of the locker room doors, and I stare at the floor.

"Emma. Don't lie." Ruby's lips are pursed, and her eyes are dark.

"I'm not. It's—"

Ruby cuts me off. "I'm allowed to have other friends, you know." She sucks in a quick breath. "Plus, I'm surprised you noticed since you've been spending so much time focused on Bio Boy."

I blush, heat spreading up my neck and onto my cheeks like wildfire. I don't say anything.

Ruby rolls her eyes with a sigh and opens the locker room door. She doesn't wait for me.

3:10 P.M.
ALGEBRA

Ruby didn't speak to me in PE. We're playing soccer this month, so we didn't have much time to sit around anyway. At least Ruby didn't. I tried to sit on the sideline as much as possible.

I think Ruby may have been imagining my head as the soccer ball. She was out there running and kicking that ball like it had offended her.

Alejandra came in late with a pass, so we didn't even see her in the locker room. I was worried it was going to be weird at the end, but I quietly changed while she and Ruby talked about something that happened in their English class this morning.

Now, I'm watching the minutes drag by, waiting for the bell to ring so I can sprint to my locker and try to catch Ruby before she leaves the band room.

3:14 P.M.

Come on. Only one minute left.

My algebra teacher, Mrs. Anderson, is talking about the homework, but I'm only half listening as I scribble the assignment in my planner.

The bell rings, and I fly out of my seat. Apparently, everyone in my class has somewhere to be because there's a traffic jam leading into the hallway.

I push myself through the crowd and move as quickly as I can amongst the throngs of people on the stairs. There's a group of girls stopped in the middle, gasping at something on someone's phone. I roll my eyes and snake myself around them.

Finally, I make it to a clearing in the hall and speed walk past the cafeteria, the art room, and the vending machines, and turn right.

Not that I expected her to be, but Ruby is not waiting for me at my locker. I didn't see her in the hallway, though, so I must not have missed her. I slow down to catch my breath and casually peek into the band room as I walk past it. Ruby's braids trail down her back as she bends over to pick up some papers.

My heart leaps, and I scuffle over to my locker, opening it while glancing back over my shoulder every other second to watch for Ruby.

She and Alejandra (of course) walk out of the room together. Neither of them even glance my way. I wonder if Ruby told Alejandra what I said. My stomach clenches as a flicker of shame creeps in. I hope not. I *do* like Alejandra. But I want my best friend to be *my* best friend.

"Ruby," I call out. I'm nervous, though, so it comes out too quiet. "Ruby!" I try again. She stops.

"What?" she says. She looks over her shoulder but doesn't turn her body. Her eyes are slightly narrowed.

"Can I talk to you?" I squeak out.

Ruby says something to Alejandra, who adjusts her black frame glasses on her nose before waving to me with her usual closed-mouth smile. She must not know why Ruby is mad at me.

Ruby watches Alejandra continue down the hallway for a second before making her way slowly to me. She walks like she has all the time in the world. When she stops in front of me, she adjusts her books on her hip. She doesn't say anything.

"Hi," I say. My mouth is suddenly very dry, and I swallow quickly.

"Hi," Ruby mutters dully. She stares at me expectantly.

"Look, I'm sorry." I decide not to filter myself and let all the word vomit out, even if it's embarrassing. "I didn't mean to make you mad earlier. I like Alejandra. I guess I was feeling jealous. You're my best friend. And, yeah, I prob- ably have been focused too much on Andy lately, but I don't want Alejandra to replace me."

Ruby's body relaxes. Her shoulders lower slightly, and the crinkle between her eyebrows smooths itself out. A smirk plays on her lips.

"Jealous, huh?"

I shrug but smile softly because her tone has lightened, too.

"Give me a hug, you big nerd." Ruby puts her books on the ground and opens her arms. I happily step into them. She squeezes me tightly, then pushes me back to hold me at arm's length.

"Emma Bishop. You are my best friend." She shakes me a little. "Always. Okay?" I nod earnestly. She lets go of my shoulders and reaches down for her books. "But I *am* allowed to have other friends. Just like you're allowed to have a boyfriend."

My eyes go to my feet, and I nod again. Ruby is so wise.

"Plus, Alejandra can't even come tomorrow. She has family coming into town."

"Oh, bummer," I say automatically.

"Uh-huh, sure," Ruby scoffs, but she's smiling, too.

"Okay, but I meant it when I said I like Alejandra," I defend myself. I grab my backpack and close my locker. Ruby and I walk down the hallway.

"I know, I know," Ruby says with a laugh. She throws her arm around my shoulder and leans her head against mine. I lean mine back.

CHAPTER 22

It feels like too much.

FRIDAY, OCTOBER 29TH

5:12 P.M.

MY BEDROOM

"What should I wear tonight?" I ask Ruby.

She's lying on my bed with her top half hanging over the edge. Her braids are coiled into a big bun today, which is resting on the floor. Ruby turns her phone off and tries to toss it on the bed, but her center of gravity is off-kilter, and it ends up on the floor. She sits up, shaking her head slightly, before reaching down to grab it.

"Something cute," she says simply.

"Duh." I stand in front of my closet, scanning the options. "Okay, what about this?" I pull out a pink cropped hoodie and show it to Ruby.

She immediately shakes her head and comes over to stand next to me. She stares into the closet for a second before diving into the back. She pulls out a baby-blue spaghetti-strap dress I wore to my cousin's wedding over the summer.

"This," she says. "Your boobies will look so good in it now that they're bigger."

Exasperated, I say, "We're watching a movie in his basement, not going to a dance. Also, it's October."

Ruby shrugs. "You asked for my opinion. This is it."

I roll my eyes and laugh. Ruby hops back over to my bed, now snuggling under the light-pink comforter. I glance at her over my shoulder.

"Don't get too cozy," I warn. "We have to get ready."

"I *am* ready," Ruby says, closing her eyes.

5:50 P.M.

After about twenty nos from Ruby, we finally decided on an outfit: leggings, a white tank top with a gray zip-up sweater over it (zipped to just under my boobs), and gym shoes. For jewelry, I'm wearing gold hoops and my favorite necklace with the pink quartz gem. We were going for cute-but-casual-base-ment-hang.

"Love it," Ruby says, still in my bed. "Pull up your boobs to give yourself a little cleavage."

My face must say exactly what is in my head: *Huh?* She sighs and comes to stand next to me. She shakes her chest slightly and bounces up and down.

"Okay, so you stick your hand in your bra and sort of pull your boob up and over a little bit." She demonstrates on herself. "Then, same thing on the other side. See? Perkier cleavage." She nods at me in the mirror. "Your turn."

Hesitating, I reach my hand into my bra and fiddle with my left boob, attempting to pull it up and over. I do the same on the right. When I'm done, I sort of have cleavage!

"Wow! Look at me!"

Ruby tilts her head to the side and nods, pleased with herself. "You're wel-come."

I study myself from the side, running my hands down my chest. This is a game-changer. I smile at my reflection.

6:54 P.M.
IN THE CAR

"And who is this boy?" Dad asks. He's dropping us off at Andy's.

I roll my eyes. "Andy. You met him on Homecoming, Dad. He was my date."

"He's Emma's boyfriend," Marie chimes in from the back seat. I give her the evil eye. Marie smirks at me and checks for Ruby's reaction. Ruby's texting, though, and not paying attention.

"Boyfriend?" Dad rubs his forehead. "Did anyone approve this?"

"Don't worry, Mr. Bishop," Ruby says. "He's a nice boy. I wouldn't let Emma date a jerk."

"What would we do without you, Ruby?" Dad asks, glancing in the rearview mirror.

"Honestly, who knows?" Ruby says seriously.

Dad turns onto Andy's street and slows, scanning the address numbers.

"It's okay. We can get out here." I unbuckle my seat belt, and Ruby does the same. Dad slows to a stop.

"Are you so embarrassed of me that you want me to drop you off down the block?" He puts his hand to his chest as though he's offended.

He's joking, but I know there's some truth to it, too. I bite my lip as I reach for the door, feeling a little guilty. It's not that I'm embarrassed of him exactly, but it would be way cooler if Ruby and I walked up on our own instead of my dad dropping us off.

"No, I—" I start to explain as I hop out of the car.

"So rude," Marie interrupts as she climbs into the front seat.

"Who even invited you?" I spit back at her.

"Dad did," she says, nodding in his direction. "We're getting ice cream."

I ignore her. "Bye, Dad. Love you," I offer as consolation.

"Love you, too, Peanut," he says, using my childhood nickname.

"Love you!" Ruby adds with a wave.

"Just so you know, I'm waiting here until you go in the house," Dad says, leaning over Marie and shouting out the window.

"Daaaaad," I groan. He shrugs and gives Marie a conspiratorial smile. She giggles.

"Come on," Ruby says, grabbing my hand.

We start walking, and the door to Andy's house opens. Andy steps out, grinning at us.

"Hey, BB!" Ruby shouts, dropping my hand and waving.

How did he know we were coming? I hadn't even texted him that we were here yet. Was he watching for us? Something stirs in the pit of my stomach. I shake it off, though, instead focusing on having fun tonight. A jolt of excitement goes through me as Ruby bumps her shoulder against mine, and Andy, my boyfriend, beams at me from the doorway.

7:01 P.M.
ANDY'S HOUSE

Andy's house is gigantic. Like, the front door is actually two doors. He opens one of them for us, offering me a kiss as I step in. The entryway is wide, and off to the left is a living room with cream walls, cream carpet, and white furniture.

Ruby whistles. "Wow, BB. Impressive. Does anyone ever go into the white room?" she asks, pointing over her shoulder.

Andy laughs as he leads us down the hallway. "Nope. Never."

7:06 P.M.
ANDY'S BASEMENT

The usual crew of boys is here: Andy (duh), Jeremiah, Matt, Steve, Robby, and Paxton. Ruby and I are the only girls. I'm not going to lie, it makes me feel very cool.

Jeremiah raises his hand for Ruby, who gives him a high five and a, "What's up." I wave at the group.

"Scooch, man," Andy says to Jeremiah so the three of us can sit down on the giant sectional couch. Matt and Paxton are sitting on the floor, playing a video game.

While the rest of Andy's house seems very formal and fancy, I'm a bit more at ease in the basement, which feels like an average, everyday basement—with the exception of the massive TV. The walls are beige, the carpet is blue, and the couch is a dark gray, situated right in front of a huge TV. Seriously, it's the biggest TV I've ever seen in my entire life.

So maybe it's not an average basement, but at least I'm not afraid to sit on the couch. Ruby elbows me and mouths, "Wow!"

"I know," I whisper back.

There's a bunch of snacks on the coffee table in front of us—three bowls of popcorn, two bowls of chips, an assortment of candy, and a bucket with water, pop, and Gatorade in it. Ruby leans forward and grabs a Twizzler. She takes a bite, then twirls it between her fingers.

"Is anyone else coming?" Ruby asks. "What about Lily?"

Andy whips his head around, then leans in close. "No," he says quietly. His eyes dart to Matt, who's still focused on the video game. Even quieter, he says, "They broke up. Last weekend. He broke up with her."

Oh.

"Dang. I liked her," Ruby says. I keep my face neutral and nod in agreement. None of us say anything for a few seconds.

"So, what are we watching?" Ruby asks, finally dispersing the awkward air around us.

"It's a surprise," he says ominously. Then he jerks his head at the boys on the floor. "If these two ever finish this game."

"Bro!" Paxton shouts over his shoulder. "I'm up by three. Two minutes left. I haven't beat Matt in like a year. This is a huge moment for me!" He pushes Matt, who barely moves or acknowledges Paxton. "What's breaking your concentration, Matteo? Am I finally in your head?" Paxton laughs, but it quickly turns into a groan. "Noooooo! How?"

Matt throws the controller down and pushes Paxton over. Paxton lies on his back, staring up at the ceiling. "I was so close," he whispers.

Matt stands up with a self-satisfied grin on his face. His eyes scan the room, quickly landing on Ruby and me before he flops onto the opposite end of the couch.

I try really hard not to notice how cute he looks with his new haircut. With a little less hair in his face, you can see his big, brown eyes better.

Not that I care.

Andy puts his arm around me, and I snuggle closer to him. He always smells so good. I smile, reminding myself how lucky I am to have a boy this cute who likes me.

8:10 P.M.

I was nervous about watching a scary movie, but I really didn't need to be. First, Andy has kept his arm around me the entire time, so I can easily hide in his shoulder if something scary is happening on screen. And more importantly, we're not actually watching a lot of the movie. The boys are goofing around, throwing popcorn, pushing each other off the couch, and making jokes.

Ruby and I lean together and giggle as Jeremiah comes up from behind the couch and sticks a Twizzler in Andy's nose.

"What the hell, Jer?" he says, pulling it out. Clearly, he did not find it as funny as we did.

"You just got Twizzled!" Jeremiah taunts, pointing and jogging backward. Andy hops up and chases after him. Ruby and I giggle some more before Ruby picks up the Twizzler.

"Ruby. Don't."

"What? It's perfectly fine." She examines each end, unsure which side was in Andy's nose.

"Do ittttttt!" Jeremiah calls from the floor where Andy has him pinned down. I'm impressed. Andy's kind of lanky. I wouldn't expect him to be able to take down Jeremiah.

Ruby takes a confident bite of the Twizzler, and the boys cheer.

"Ruby!" I gasp, covering my mouth in disgust.

"Delicious," is all she says in return, chomping the whole thing down and into her mouth. The boys cheer again. I shudder but can't help laughing, too.

8:17 P.M.

The lights are off and everyone is quiet. After the Twizzler debacle, we started actually watching the movie. I think something scary is about to happen because the main girl is creeping around the hallways of the house, and there's quiet, ominous music playing. My heart is thumping in my chest, waiting for it.

"Hey," Andy whispers in my ear. I jump about a foot in the air.

Ruby lightly pushes me from the other side before tossing some popcorn into her mouth.

"Sorry," I hiss back at her.

"I didn't mean to scare you," Andy says.

"It's okay. I get a little spooked during scary movies. They're not my favorite."

"Want to hang back there for a bit?" He points his thumb over his shoulder and pauses for a second. "Alone?"

I hesitate. I sort of don't. I'm having fun hanging out with the group and realize that I'd rather stay here than go make out with Andy. That can't be good.

I can't say that, though, so I nod and follow him when he stands up. I glance over my shoulder as we head to the back of the basement, and Matt's eyes dart away. He was watching us. My heart skips. I ignore it.

8:20 P.M.

Andy leads me behind the stairs where it's mostly storage. He walks backward, bringing me over to a concrete post. He leans against it and pulls me close. My heart skips (again).

Andy and I kiss for a few minutes. He's really a good kisser. Not too much pressure, but also his tongue isn't flopping around. I've only kissed one other person, but this is pretty good.

Andy pulls back and locks his eyes on mine. The eye contact feels very intense, so I look down at our feet.

"I really like you, Emma." Andy's voice is soft and earnest. I force myself to raise my head. His eyebrows are knit together as his eyes bore into mine. It feels like too much. Something twists in my stomach. But I have to say something.

"I like you, too," I tell him. And I do. Really.

I think.

"No." His arms are still around my waist, and he pulls me closer to him. "I really, *really* like you."

I smile, but it's forced. Andy's staring at me with puppy dog eyes, but rather than making me internally swoon, it's making me squirm. I don't know what to say, and I don't want to keep this conversation going. Who knows what he'll say next? So, I kiss him. That seems to shut him up.

8:27 P.M.

I wonder what everyone else is doing.

8:32 P.M.

When we finally stop kissing, Andy smiles at me in a dazed way, and I smile back, staring into his pretty blue eyes. He has really long eyelashes. I *do* like him.

So why did the "I like you" profession make me feel so... twisty? Shouldn't I love something like that?

"I guess we should go back out there, huh?" Andy says. His arms are still around my waist, and he's rubbing his fingers in small circles against my back.

"Yeah," I say, trying not to sound too eager. "Ruby's probably wondering what happened to me."

Andy nods, not letting go of my waist. He's giving me those puppy dog eyes again, and I don't think I can stand it another second, so I break away from his grasp and walk back to the group.

"About time," Ruby teases. I plop down next to her on the couch, and she bumps her shoulder against mine. "Did you have fun?"

"Mmhhm," I reply, grabbing some popcorn from the bowl in her lap. Andy sits down next to me, casually putting his arm around my shoulder. The boys make a bunch of noise to mess with him, and Jeremiah comes over and rubs the top of his head.

"Our little boy," he says. Andy swats Jeremiah's arm away.

I scan the room and stop on Matt, who's focused on the movie. I quickly avert my eyes and turn back to the TV. I have no idea what's going on.

In the movie, or my head.

CHAPTER 23

But I don't NOT like him.

FRIDAY, OCTOBER 29TH

10:12 P.M.

IN BED

Rudely, Mom wouldn't let Ruby spend the night. So instead of talking everything out with her after the movie night at Andy's, we're texting. I explained the puppy dog eyes and the twisty feeling in my stomach.

> **Me:** What do I do?

> **Ruby:** You break up with him, obv.

Ugh. I had a feeling she was going to say that.

> **Me:** But I don't NOT like him.

Ruby: But you are clearly not as into him as he is into you.

I stare straight ahead. She's right. It's very clear that Andy *really* likes me. Like, a lot. And I don't feel the same way. And I keep thinking about his friend.

Me: I guess you're right. But I've never dumped anyone before. How do I do it?

Ruby: Dumped is such a mean word.

Ruby: Poor Andy. You're going to break his little heart.

Me: NOT HELPING!

My heart sinks into the pit of my stomach. To make it even worse, another text comes in.

Andy: Thanks for coming over tonight. You're the best girlfriend. I'm so lucky you're mine.

I groan. I never imagined that a boy liking me so much would make me feel so squirmy. I screenshot the text and send it to Ruby.

Ruby: He's a goner.

I close my eyes, contemplating. Do I end it right here, right now? It could be a quick and easy text: *Listen, Andy, I think we're better off as friends.*

No. You don't break up with someone in a text. That's so uncool. Instead, I decide to keep up the facade a little longer. I'm not going to break up with him yet, but I am going to pull back a little—ease him into the breakup.

I respond to Andy's text with the blushing smiley face emoji. Then I turn off the light and hug my stuffed Piggy tightly to my chest.

What am I going to do?

10:49 P.M.

I bolt upright in bed when I have a sudden realization. I text Ruby. I hope she's not asleep.

> **Me:** WE SIT NEXT TO EACH OTHER IN BIO.

She doesn't respond. I send another text.

> **Me:** If we break up, that's going to be SO awkward!!!

No response. I sigh.

11:01 P.M.

What do I say? And how am I going to be able to get the words out if he's looking at me with those big, blue, puppy dog eyes?

My stomach clenches. I'm not even doing anything yet, and I already feel nauseous.

11:40 P.M.

I wonder what Matt is doing right now.

Stop it, Emma!

SUNDAY, OCTOBER 31ST

3:32 P.M.

RUBY'S LIVING ROOM

Ruby, Cher, and I are passing out candy for the trick-or-treaters at Ruby's house. We've got Halloween movies (not scary ones) playing in the background. The lights are dim, and the three of us are squished together on the two-seater couch in the living room.

"I can't believe we're not doing *anything* for Halloween this year," Ruby complains.

"We're in high school now," Cher says as if this explains everything. It was her idea to stay in and watch movies. Part of me suspects it's only because Jacob is out of town for a hockey tournament.

"So?" Ruby counters. "We could still dress up and go out."

"You *are* dressed up, Ruby," Cher says.

Ruby has on a calf-length black dress, a black shawl, and a witch's hat. She's wearing a lot of heavy, black eyeliner and purple lipstick.

"And no one is seeing it," Ruby sighs.

"I'll take a pic for you to post," I offer.

"Maybe later," Ruby says glumly. She gazes out the window longingly.

Suddenly, Ruby takes her hat off and stands up. Her demeanor changes instantly.

"We have other important matters to deal with right now, friends," Ruby says. She points a finger at me. "Emma. What is the breakup plan?"

"You're breaking up with Andy?" Cher asks, surprised. "Since when? Why? Ugh, you never tell me anything anymore." Cher rolls her eyes.

"We only decided on Friday night," Ruby says. She comes over and puts her hand on Cher's shoulder. "You were sucking face with Jacob, remember?"

Cher's mouth twists into a satisfied smile. "Yeah," she concedes.

"We will definitely come back to *that*," Ruby says, pointing at Cher before standing in front of me again. "But for now—breakup plan."

I sigh, quickly unwrapping a fun-size Reese's and popping it into my mouth. I shrug.

"I don't have a plan," I say through my chewing.

"Wait. Can we back up, please?" Cher says. "What happened?"

I put a finger up while I finish chewing my candy. Ruby steps in and explains what happened on Friday. I don't add the part about Matt, and the fact that I keep thinking about him. I've never mentioned it to either of them. I'm too embarrassed, and I don't want them to think I'm a horrible person.

"So, it's time. Emma has to end it. Soon." Ruby punctuates "soon" with another point in my direction.

I nod solemnly.

Outside, there's a group of teenage boys walking down the sidewalk. They turn up Ruby's pathway, and my heart plummets into my stomach when I notice a familiar blond head. Ruby gasps.

The doorbell rings.

3:45 P.M.

"What do we do?" I hiss.

"Does he know this is my house?" Ruby tries to whisper. She is not a good whisperer.

"Is that him? Is that Andy?" Cher hops off the couch and peeks out the window.

"Cher!" Ruby and I whisper-shout in unison.

"They'll see you!" I add.

"We can't ignore them," Cher says reasonably. "I'm sure they noticed people sitting on the couch as they walked up, and there's literally a sign on the walkway that says, *Ghosts and Ghouls Welcome*, so it's not like this is a house that doesn't do trick-or-treating."

I take a deep breath. "You're right. Just act natural."

Ruby nods and grabs the candy bowl. The three of us approach the front door, and Ruby swings it open.

"Well, well, well. Look who it is!" Ruby says. "Hey, BB. Hey, boys."

Cher throws me a quizzical look at Ruby's nickname for Andy. I wave her off and push my way next to Ruby.

"Hey!" I say, a little over-eagerly.

Andy's face lights up when he sees me, but it hurts my heart, so I glance away quickly, and my eyes accidentally find Matt's. He's standing at the back of the group. As soon as our eyes lock, he turns away. I do the same.

I grab the bowl from Ruby and open the door, stepping out onto the front porch. I hold it open for Ruby and Cher to follow me.

"Are you going to do it now?" Ruby loudly whispers into my ear as she steps out. I shoot daggers at her with my eyes, which she hopefully understands as, *No, I'm not going to break up with him now in front of all these people.*

Andy walks over and wraps his arm around my neck, pulling me in for a kiss on the cheek. My face warms, and not because of the sweet moment, but because I know what's coming, and he doesn't.

"What are you up to?" Andy asks. He notices Cher. "Is this the famous Cher? I feel like I'm meeting a celebrity." Andy walks over and opens his arms for a hug.

Cher's not a big hugger, but she sucks it up, and with a grimace, gives Andy a quick hug.

The boys aren't in costumes, but they're all very dirty and covered in shaving cream.

"You guys smell," Ruby says, wrinkling her nose.

The boys chuckle and push each other around in response.

"Shaving cream and eggs," Matt says with a smirk.

"Gross," Ruby and I both say. She makes eyes at me, and we giggle.

"Why?" Cher asks.

"Why not?" Andy replies. He pulls a can of shaving cream out of the pillowcase he's carrying and points it at Cher. "Want to join?"

Cher stiffens but doesn't move. "No," she says icily.

Andy chuckles, but his smile doesn't reach his eyes. He shrugs and puts the shaving cream back in the pillowcase.

"For real, though, you should come out with us," Andy insists, walking back over to me. His eyes search mine. They're so pretty. Maybe I don't need to break up with him.

3:59 P.M.

We sent the boys off on their way down the block. As soon as we close the door, we hear Jeremiah bellow, "Every man for himself!"

I peek out the window. Matt grabs hold of Andy and covers the top of his head in shaving cream.

Cher sits back down on the couch, crossing her legs. "You need to break up with him," she announces.

My cheeks warm. "What—why?" I stammer as I join her. I pull a knitted blanket down from the back of the couch and spread it across Cher and me.

"Because he is *so* into you," Ruby says, coming through the doorway with a big bowl of popcorn.

"And, he's…" Cher pauses, thinking. "Cringey."

I can't deny that. When the boys were getting ready to leave, Andy pulled me behind a tree so we could have a "proper goodbye," but everyone saw us. Then a big group of little kids and their parents were coming up the block. The whole thing was mortifying. I let him kiss me for half a second before I pulled away, blaming the approaching group.

I sigh now, leaning my head back against the couch cushion.

"What do I say?"

Ruby shrugs, pulling half the blanket onto her own lap and away from Cher and me. Cher pulls some of it back, narrowing her eyes at Ruby.

"Maybe practice it," Cher suggests. She sits up straighter. "Oh! Try writing it all out on paper first, and then practice saying it out loud. Like when you have to do a presentation at school."

I nod slowly. That's not a bad idea.

"It's settled then," Ruby announces. She turns the volume up on the movie, and we each grab a handful of popcorn.

"Who was that boy with the curly brown hair?" Cher asks. My heart jolts.

Before I can say anything about Matt, though, the doorbell rings, and all three of us scream. Ruby spills popcorn all over the floor. Cher grabs the candy for the trick-or-treaters. I stay on the couch, my eyes glued to the TV, but not paying attention to the movie at all.

You weren't supposed to see that.

TUESDAY, NOVEMBER 9TH

12:32 P.M.

RUBY'S LOCKER

Ruby closes her locker as I walk up. She's smiling brightly at Alejandra, but her face turns serious when she sees me.

"Emma Bishop." Ruby adjusts her books and puts her hand on her right hip. She raises her eyebrows and tilts her head expectantly. Alejandra's eyes slide over to me, and she smirks. We filled her in on the Andy situation earlier in the week.

I shake my head solemnly. Alejandra rolls her eyes. This annoys me.

"You can't keep dragging it out like this," Ruby says, exasperated. "It's been over a week."

"I know," I say quietly. I examine my white gym shoes on the dirty hallway carpet. The carpet is so worn and discolored, I think it might have been red at some point, but now it's a muddy brown.

"He *has* to know something is up by now," Alejandra says, adjusting her black frame glasses on her nose. She's not wrong. At my locker this morning, I was putting all my stuff away, avoiding eye contact with Andy. He asked me three times if I was okay.

"Emma," Ruby warns.

"I'll work on it tonight," I promise.

7:18 P.M.
MY BEDROOM

I'm all set up at my desk, with a notebook and a selection of colorful pens in front of me, ready to write my breakup speech. Except, I don't even know where to start.

Ruby's right, though. I can't keep putting this off. It's been a long week. And every night, Cher sends the text, "Did you do it today?"

Finally, I write in my notebook, *Dear Boyfriend...* Okay, I guess this is a letter.

I stare at the notebook in front of me, my brain as blank as the page.

Let's not overthink this. I'm not giving him this letter. It's just practice.

So, I start writing, and I don't hold back.

7:28 P.M.

I'm finished. And I feel lighter. I really do need to do this. It's like a heavy weight has been sitting on my chest all week. I'm avoiding it because I know I'll feel bad, but I also feel bad because I'm avoiding it.

I reread the letter.

Dear Boyfriend,

It's been really fun being your girlfriend this last month. You always make me feel pretty and special. And I've always dreamed of someone making me feel that way. Plus, you're sweet and funny and cute and smart. You always have gum, you smell really good, and you're a great kisser.

But I think we need to break up. All of those things I said before are true. And I really liked you. But sometimes, it's all too much. Like, when you wanted to have a "proper goodbye" on Halloween? That was so cringey and embarrassing. Everyone was watching us and knew what we were trying to do. And you do stuff like that kind of a lot.

Plus, it's really clear to, like, everyone, that you like me A LOT. And I like you, too. But you like me a lot more than I like you, and that doesn't seem fair. Your feelings keep growing, and mine are the same. I like you, but not enough.

I hope you can forgive me, and maybe we can still be friends. We do sit next to each other in bio, so there's that.

This was really hard for me to do. I don't want to hurt you, but I can't keep pretending I feel the same way you do. Because I don't anymore.

So yeah… not sure how you end something like this.

xoxo,
Emma

Is it cruel to put *xoxo* since I'm not going to be kissing and hugging him anymore? I shake my head. It doesn't matter. This was practice. I'm not actually giving him this letter.

I read the letter a third time. I need to be a little nicer in person. I can't tell him he's cringey and embarrasses me. That feels too mean.

I'll show it to Ruby tomorrow and see what she thinks.

By tomorrow—or maybe the next day—I'm going to break up with Andy.

WEDNESDAY, NOVEMBER 10TH

12:10 P.M.
LUNCH

Ruby reads over the letter as she munches on some chips. She folds it in half and puts it on the table. She nods encouragingly.

"I think that about covers it," she says.

"Is it too mean, though?" I ask. "Like, I call him cringey and embarrassing."

"He *is* cringey and embarrassing," Ruby says. She shrugs. "When are you giving this to him?"

"I'm not!"

Ruby wrinkles her forehead and leans forward. "Then what was the point of the letter?"

"For practice! Aren't you supposed to break up with someone in person?"

"Yeah, I guess," Ruby says, leaning back on the bench. "Sounds unpleasant though," she adds as an afterthought.

"Yeah. I'm not looking forward to it." I put my head in my hands.

"Okay, so if you're not giving him the letter, let's hear the speech."

My mouth dries up, and my heart starts racing. This isn't even the real deal, and I can't choke out one word. I shake my head.

"I don't know what to say," I manage, picking apart my sandwich.

"Emma," Ruby warns. "You have to do this. He's a dork, but BB's a nice guy. You can't keep leading him on. That's not fair. Plus, you're torturing yourself!"

I nod, feeling miserable.

"Ok," I concede. "Today. After school."

Ruby claps her hands together once. "You've got this, Em. You're a strong, badass lady, who deserves a boy who doesn't embarrass her."

I smile at Ruby, and my chest warms slightly. Matt flits into my brain, but I shove him to the side.

"You're right. Thanks, Rubs."

"I'm always right," she says, flipping her braids over her shoulder.

12:34 P.M.
BIOLOGY

Andy totally knows something is up. He smiles at me as I sit down next to him, but it's a little forced.

"Hey, cutie," he says. "Where were you this morning? I missed you at your locker."

I don't tell him that I didn't even go to my locker this morning. All my stuff is in Ruby's because I knew Andy would be waiting for me at mine.

Yeah, it's definitely time.

"Hey. Sorry, Ruby and I were running late today," I lie.

The bell rings for the start of class, and Mr. Milo immediately starts talking about our new unit on cellular reproduction. I pretend to be very interested in the schedule for the next three weeks of class. I feel Andy's eyes on me. I ignore them.

1:23 P.M.

I pull out my planner to write down our homework. Andy leans down to pick something up. I focus on the assignment and then sigh. This is going to take forever to do.

I glance at Andy, who's bent over his textbook. His eyes dart across the page as he reads. His eyebrows are furrowed, and his neck is growing redder by the second.

What is he reading? I lean over.

When I see what it is, I freeze. My stomach drops. My mouth goes dry, and everything is suddenly silent around me. And then my heart starts racing, beating faster than it ever has in my entire life.

Andy's not reading the textbook. He's reading my letter.

The breakup letter.

1:25 P.M.

The bell rings. I panic. I start packing up my stuff as quickly as I can. Maybe I can escape and not have to deal with this.

"Emma," Andy says quietly. He holds up the letter. "What is this? Do you want to break up?"

The answer seems obvious, but I can't manage to say anything. All I can do is stare at the floor.

Andy stands in front of me, unmoving. I have to say something.

"You weren't supposed to see that."

"It fell out of your planner. I picked it up for you and saw that it said *Dear Boyfriend* at the top, so I assumed it was a note for me..." He trails off as he scans the paper in his hand again.

"Everything okay, you two?" Mr. Milo calls from the front of the room.

We both nod and leave the classroom. Once we're in the hallway, Andy stops and leans against the wall next to Mr. Milo's room, his shoulders slumped forward and the letter held loosely in his hand.

"So, are we broken up?" Andy asks. His voice cracks at the end, and his eyes are red. Oh my God. Is he going to cry? I can't bear to look at him anymore. Instead, I focus on the crowds of people moving past us, the white noise of everyone's conversations muddling together. I wish I was one of them, walking to class like it's a totally normal day.

Andy clears his throat. "Emma?"

"Yeah," I finally give in. "I'm sorry."

"K," Andy says. He walks off in the opposite direction, dropping the letter as he goes. I scramble to grab the paper off the ground without getting stepped on. The last thing I need is for someone else to pick it up and read it.

Once I have it secured, I take a deep, shaky breath and head to Ruby's locker.

1:27 P.M.
RUBY'S LOCKER

"It's done," I announce to Ruby and Alejandra.

"What—" Ruby starts to say, but then her eyes go wide. "You broke up with him? When? What happened? Oh my God!"

"How do you feel?" Alejandra adds.

"Horrible," I say. "He was so quiet and sad."

"You broke his poor little heart," Ruby says dramatically. Alejandra pushes her on the arm.

"Not helpful," Alejandra says. For once, I'm grateful she's here. Alejandra is calm, cool, and collected. It always seems like she has a handle on what's going on. It's comforting, actually.

Ruby nods and steps over to give me a big hug, rubbing my back sympathetically. I feel a prickle behind my eyes. I swallow and step back, forcing a small smile.

"Come on. We're going to be late. I'll tell you everything on the way."

CHAPTER 25

Breakups suck.

WEDNESDAY, NOVEMBER 10TH

8:15 P.M.

BEDROOM

Mom knocks on my door, peeking her head around it before I can say, "Come in." I roll my eyes, but I don't have the energy to complain about it.

"You were quiet at dinner tonight. Everything okay?"

I nod but don't trust myself to speak. The well of tears builds behind my eyes. It's been there since this afternoon, and I keep ignoring it, hoping it'll go away.

Mom must notice. She comes fully into my room and sits on the edge of my bed.

"Do you want to talk about it?" she asks. She reaches out and runs her hand down my hair. I can't hold it in anymore. The tears start to fall. I wrap my arms around my knees, hiding my face. Mom comes to sit right in front of me, reaching around to rub my back without a word.

I lift my head, and with a shuddering breath, whisper, "I broke up with Andy," My voice is small and weak.

"Oh, Em. I'm sorry, honey. A breakup is never easy." She pulls me into a tight hug, and I let myself cry for the first time today. For the first time in a while, actually.

"I thought being the dumper was supposed to be easier than being the dumpee," I say into Mom's shoulder. I lean back with a sniff, grabbing a tissue from my nightstand. The whole box tumbles onto the ground. I leave it there. I don't care.

"Yeah, you'd think so, but breaking up with someone you care about isn't easy. It hurts to hurt someone, even if it's the right thing to do."

I nod. "That sucks."

"It really does," Mom says. She smiles at me, her eyes crinkling at the corner. "Want me to make you something? Some toast? Tea? A hot chocolate?"

I sniff. "I could go for some hot chocolate."

8:27 P.M.
KITCHEN

Mom places a steaming cup of hot chocolate and a bag of small marshmallows on the table. She sits down across from me with her own mug.

We're quiet for a minute. The steam warms my face as I blow into the mug. I drop in a few mini marshmallows and watch the chocolate swirl and dance around them.

"Do you want to talk about it?" Mom asks again.

I think for a second. It might feel good to get everything off my chest. But it also sounds exhausting. I don't think I can go through the details again.

I shake my head, taking a sip of my drink. I burn my tongue. It makes me want to cry again.

"Okay. The offer always stands. Let me know if you change your mind," Mom says. She takes a sip from her own mug and then swears quietly.

"Burn your tongue?"

Mom nods. "Every time." We're quiet again for another minute. "You know what I used to do after a breakup?"

I don't say anything, my face blank.

"I'd put on some loud music and just let myself feel my feelings. Sometimes it was a super sad song; sometimes it was a celebratory song. But either way, I drowned out the sounds of the rest of the world and let myself… feel. Sometimes we don't let ourselves do that, and it's actually so important."

I nod. It's not a horrible idea, I guess.

"What was your worst breakup?" I ask her, taking a sip of my now-drinkable hot chocolate.

She looks up at the ceiling for a few seconds, then smiles to herself.

"David. David Nichols. I was a junior, and he was a senior. He broke up with me at the beginning of the summer before he went away to college. I was devastated. I thought we'd be together forever—that we'd get married and have kids. But he wanted the freedom to go to college without a girlfriend still in high school." Mom smiles softly, her eyebrows pushed together. "Looking back, it was the right choice for him to make, but to me, it felt like the end of the world. My boyfriend broke up with me so he could go to college parties and kiss other girls who weren't me. And I was stuck at home, another year of high school to go, with a broken heart."

"Sounds rough," I say.

"It was hard," Mom agrees. "But I survived. And I survived a few other breakups, too. And so will you." Mom reaches out and grabs my hand. She squeezes it before standing up. "I love you, Em."

"Love you too, Mom."

She puts her mug in the sink and walks out of the kitchen. Alone with my thoughts, I slurp up a couple marshmallows from my cup and decide her breakup with David Nichols sounds way worse than mine. It makes me feel a tiny bit better.

9:10 P.M.
BEDROOM

My phone vibrates as I work on the bio homework. My heart drops when I see the name: Andy.

Andy: Hey, can we talk?

I don't know what to do. I don't want to talk to him. What's there to say? I imagine his face in the hallway earlier today, his shoulders drooping, his blue eyes watery. I can't. Maybe it's selfish, but I can't talk to him right now.

I put my headphones on, pick a Celsius album at random, click shuffle, and close my eyes. The song "Breathing" starts to play. I haven't heard this song in ages, but it's one of Ruby's favorites.

I lie back on my bed, leaning against the wall, feeling sorry for myself. The beat picks up, and I nod along.

It's like I can't breathe

My lungs are constricted

It's too much

Yes, ugh, I feel that so hard. I nod more emphatically and bounce on the bed.

But you know what?

It's time.

It's time, yeah,

And now,

Then the chorus kicks in, *I can finally breathe, yeah, yeah, yeah,* and my heart is pumping, my head is clear, my shoulders feel light, and I can't stop myself—I hop up on the bed and start dancing. Dancing away the guilt. Dancing away the fear. Dancing away the embarrassment.

I take a video of myself dancing on my bed and belting out the lyrics and send it to Ruby and Cher. The caption says, *I did it.*

I'm free.

10:22 P.M.
IN BED

I'm still riding the high of my dance party as I lie in bed, thinking about today. What a whirlwind.

Ruby and Cher were both proud of me. Cher sent a bunch of clapping emojis, and Ruby sent back her own dancing video, banging her head to some classical music she's studying for band.

I still feel bad about breaking up with Andy. But like Mom said with her boyfriend, David, it was the right thing to do. While I feel guilty about making Andy sad, I'm also relieved because I don't have to go to school tomorrow and pretend that I still like him.

Albus hops up onto my bed, and I pull him close to give him some pets. He allows it, but when my phone buzzes, he goes flying out of the crook of my arm. He sits at the door with an expression that says, *Why did you have to ruin the moment?*

"It wasn't my fault," I tell him out loud. He licks his paw in response.

My stomach twists when I see the name on the screen.

It's Andy. Again.

Andy: Sorry to bug you. It's fine. I get it.

Even in a text, he sounds miserable. My mood droops again.

10:25 P.M.

I stare at the screen, not doing anything, for what feels like a long time. Should I respond?

I screenshot the texts from Andy and send it to Ruby and Cher. I'm sure Ruby's sleeping, but Cher might still be up.

> **Me:** Do I respond? What do I say?

Surprisingly, Ruby is the first to text back.

> **Ruby:** Poor guy. Idk. Tell him you're sorry? That you can still be friends? That he's a nice guy?

> **Cher:** No. Don't respond. Don't give him any false hope. It's over. Period.

I wish there was something in the middle I could do. I feel bad totally ghosting him.

Cher sends another message.

> **Cher:** Seriously. Don't respond.

With a sigh, I put my phone face down on my nightstand and roll over to face the wall.

10:47 P.M.

I can't stop thinking about Andy, lying in his own bed, heartbroken. Probably crying. Over me.

Wow. A boy is heartbroken over *me*. I feel horrible thinking it, but it's kind of... cool. Someone liked me enough to be upset when we broke up.

10:50 P.M.

Ugh, self-centered much, Emma?

11:12 P.M.

I wonder what Matt is doing...

11:14 P.M.

Am I a horrible person?

11:17 P.M.

Bio is going to be so awkward tomorrow. What do I say to Andy? Do we pretend like nothing happened? Should I ask Mr. Milo to change my seat? Would that make it worse?

Thinking about it makes my heart race, so I try to focus on something else.

Kitties. Kitties are cute. Maybe Mom will let us get another cat.

11:22 P.M.

Breakups suck.

166

CHAPTER 26

The seat next to mine is empty.

THURSDAY, NOVEMBER 11TH

7:55 A.M.

MY LOCKER

Andy doesn't come to my locker this morning. I mean, of course he doesn't, but it feels a little lonely. The girl whose locker is next to mine smiles as she closes hers and heads down the hallway. I stare blankly into my locker for a few seconds, thinking.

While it does feel weird having no one to talk to, I'm also glad Andy's not here. Part of me was worried he might try to talk to me about the breakup, and I don't think I can handle that right now. I swipe at a tear and continue to stare into my locker, trying to mentally prepare myself for the day.

I feel a tap on my shoulder, and my stomach drops. Oh no. He did come to talk to me.

When I turn around, though, relief floods over me. It's Alejandra.

"Hey," she says, pushing some of her dark hair behind her ears.

"Hey, what's up?" I close my locker and turn to face her. I want to say, "What are you doing here?" but I worry it'll sound rude. But what *is* she doing here?

Alejandra shifts foot to foot, adjusting her books in her arms.

"Ruby told me you were pretty upset last night," she says.

What the hell, Ruby? Yeah, of course I was upset, but why is Ruby immediately telling Alejandra about it?

"Oh," is all I say. I press my lips together and glance down the hallway.

"Yeah, so I wanted to check on you. See if you're okay." Her eyes search mine, and she offers a half smile.

"Oh," I say again, taken aback. "That's really nice of you." And it is. Alejandra and I started talking last year when she sat behind me in English, and it's really because of that that she and Ruby are close now.

Alejandra shrugs. "You're my friend. And I know Ruby was worried about you."

My cheeks warm thinking about some of the less-than-kind things I've thought about Alejandra lately. She really is a cool person.

"Thanks," I say. The warning bell rings. People in the hallway start moving more quickly to class. "I'm okay, I guess. Sort of." An exasperated chuckle escapes, and I roll my eyes. "I don't know. It sucks."

"It sounds like it. You're a nice person. I'm sure it wasn't easy telling someone you don't like them anymore."

I nod, grateful for her kind words.

"Thanks, Alejandra."

She nods, smiling with her mouth closed and shrugging one of her shoulders. We both suddenly notice the hallway is basically empty.

"Shoot!" Alejandra says.

We run down the hallway, but before we turn in opposite directions, I pull Alejandra in for a quick hug.

"Oh," she lets out quietly, surprised by my sudden affection.

I let go quickly and sprint down the hallway to English, feeling a peace I haven't felt in awhile, like everything is going to be okay.

12:33 P.M.
WALKING TO BIO

I've never walked slower than I have leaving the cafeteria today. People were pushing past me on the stairs. I drag one foot in front of the other, my heart pounding, dread pooling in the pit of my stomach as I approach Mr. Milo's classroom.

I haven't seen Andy all day. But now it's the moment of truth. I don't know what to expect. Will he ignore me? Will he be mad at me? Will he pretend nothing happened?

Outside the door, I take a deep breath, trying to calm the jitters throughout my body. I don't think I was even this nervous when Andy and I kissed the first time.

Mr. Milo steps into the hallway. "You coming in, Emma?" he asks, gesturing into the classroom.

I nod and take another deep breath like I'm about to step into battle. Mr. Milo raises an eyebrow and quirks his mouth downward slightly but doesn't say anything, and I enter the classroom.

The seat next to mine is empty. Andy's not here.

12:35 P.M.

For the second time today, relief washes over me, and I let out a long sigh as I sit down in my chair. The bell rings, and I check over my shoulder to be sure he's not coming in late. He's not. Mr. Milo closes the door and heads to the front of the room, already talking about today's assignment.

My relief lingers, but I also feel a pang of worry. I hope Andy's okay. Maybe I shouldn't have ignored him last night. The knot in my stomach twists and grows, and Andy's sad face appears in my brain.

7:12 P.M.
BEDROOM

I worried about Andy all afternoon. I could barely pay attention in my classes. Mrs. Anderson stopped me as I was leaving algebra to see if I was okay.

"You don't seem like yourself today," she said. It's weird how teachers notice stuff like that.

I nodded and told her I was fine before shuffling out of the classroom.

Now, I'm trying to distract myself by binge-watching my favorite TV show about teenage vampires for the ninth time. Cher thinks it's weird that I watch it over and over, but I find comfort in it. I love the show, and I always know exactly what's coming. Unlike my life.

My phone buzzes. I immediately tense, staring at it for a second before cautiously reaching an arm out to grab it.

I thought about texting Andy, but if he's really upset, I don't want to make it worse, or give him any false hope, like Cher said.

Cher: How'd today go?

I relax my shoulders. On my computer screen, my favorite couple is in the midst of an argument. The fangs come out, and they start fighting.

I turn my attention back to my phone and tell Cher about Andy's absence today.

> **Me:** I'm worried about him, I think. I feel bad.

> **Cher:** Sounds like he's being a little dramatic.

> **Ruby:** I told you he was going to be heartbroken.

> **Me:** Neither of you are helping me feel better.

> **Cher:** He can't stay home forever. He'll get over it.

> **Cher:** Jacob's friend Alec and his girlfriend broke up after they'd been dating for six months. He was sad for like a week, moping around the hallway, being super quiet, and then one day he came to school and was his normal self again. I'm sure the same will happen with Andy.

That makes me feel better. At least I know it's normal to react this way. I'm sure I'd want to stay home if I'd been dumped, too.

> **Ruby:** Or he'll pine after you forever because you're his one true love.

I send an eye roll gif in response, snuggle under the blankets, and keep watching my show.

CHAPTER 27

I miss you, Emma.

FRIDAY, NOVEMBER 12TH

12:34 P.M.

BIOLOGY

I stop in my tracks in the doorway of the bio classroom. The back of Andy's blond head is staring right at me. I feel like I'm moving through mud as I force myself to walk to our desk table. The bell rings, and Mr. Milo comes in behind me, so I shuffle quickly to my seat and slide into it without a word.

My heart pounds inside my chest. I glance at Andy. He's looking back at me. What do I do?

"Hey," he says quietly before turning his attention to Mr. Milo at the front of the room. In one word, I know that Andy is upset. His voice was low and somewhat gravelly, like he hasn't been using it much.

"Are you feeling better?" I whisper. I'm going to try the let's-act-normal route.

"No," he says, deadpan, not even looking in my direction. His neck is pink.

I swallow heavily, my cheeks on fire. I nod and take out my notebook, praying that we are not doing partner work today.

1:31 P.M.
LOCKER ROOM

"It was awful. Seriously. He wouldn't even look at me," I tell Ruby and Alejandra as we get changed for PE.

"Woof. That sounds rough," Ruby commiserates. Alejandra nods quietly in agreement. Her eyes linger for a second on Ruby.

"Oh, but it gets worse. We had to do a partner activity today—"

"Noooo," Ruby interrupts.

"Yes," I say seriously. "Even then, he wouldn't look at me. I was basically copying off him because he wasn't talking to me about the answers."

"At least the semester is almost over," Alejandra says. "Maybe his schedule will change?"

"Oh my God. Yes," I sigh with relief. Hope surges in my chest. I can't stand this for another semester.

"If nothing else, I'm sure you'll change seats," Ruby says. We push the doors of the gym open, and I groan when I see the racks of basketballs. Could today get any worse?

TUESDAY, NOVEMBER 30TH
1:03 P.M.

It's been over two weeks, and Andy is still not back to normal. His mood fluctuates each day, along with his attitude toward me.

One day he's quiet and cold, the next he's quiet and mopey, and the next he's quiet and seemingly unfeeling. But he's always quiet. He only speaks to me if he absolutely has to.

Well, when we're in person.

I gave up on ignoring the texts over Thanksgiving break. They would come every couple nights, usually something uninteresting, like "Hey," or "Can we talk?" or one night, "Are we ever going to talk again?"

That's when I responded. I don't even know why. Maybe because I hadn't seen him in a few days? Maybe because I was bored?

Me: Yeah, we can talk again.

Andy: Wow. Didn't expect you to actually respond.

I felt a flicker of annoyance at that. Then why did he keep texting me?

Andy: But I'm glad. I miss you, Emma.

Now we're texting most nights. We don't talk about *us* or anything like that. Mostly school and homework, the shows we're watching, our siblings—that kind of stuff. It's fine. Ruby and Cher don't approve, but honestly, it's nice. I got so used to having him around and talking to him all the time, I was feeling a little lonely after the breakup.

1:07 P.M.
BIOLOGY

Today, Andy is quiet and mopey. He's kept his eyes down on his desk the entire class, and I've heard him sigh three times. Luckily, we're taking a quiz, so we don't have to do any work together.

Andy's mood swings really bug me. He acts like this at school, and then tonight he's going to text me and act like everything is normal? I don't get it.

8:28 P.M.
BEDROOM

I stand in the middle of my room, contemplating the basket of laundry Mom left for me to put away, but I can't muster the energy to actually bend down and do it.

My phone buzzes on the desk at the foot of my bed. I pick it up, and a couple lip gloss tubes roll onto the floor. Right on time, it's Andy.

Andy: Whatcha up to?

I'm still annoyed from earlier, so I keep my response short and curt.

Me: Laundry.

Andy: Cool. Any fun plans for this weekend?

Me: Nope.

Andy: Oh…

Andy: You ok? You don't seem very talkative.

I let out an exasperated sigh and sit cross-legged on the floor, next to my still-full laundry basket. I run my hands through the fuzzy, soft pink rug underneath me while I think about how to respond.

No, Andy. I'm not okay. You act totally normal while we're texting but then act like a sad puppy at school. Pick one and stick with it. Either we're friends, or we're not.

I don't say any of that, though.

Me: Yeah I guess… just kind of confused by how you've been acting at school.

8:49 P.M.

Andy still hasn't responded to my last text. Whatever. I'm not wrong.

8:52 P.M.

Marie is trying to teach herself to braid, and it's not going well. I had to go into her room to brush out a giant knot she'd made in her hair, while she complained the whole time.

That girl in her class is still being mean. Marie has embraced her low-pony, but she's working on other hairstyles, too. And, apparently, I'm the one who has to help her.

It's annoying. But not as annoying as the girl that's bullying her.

When I come back into my bedroom, I have five messages from Andy.

My face gets hotter and hotter as I read.

> **Andy:** Yeah… I'm sorry, Emma. It's just so hard when I see you.

> **Andy:** I really miss you.

> **Andy:** It makes me so happy to be able to talk to you again every night, but then when I see you in school, it's a reminder that you're not my girlfriend anymore. Which makes me sad, or mad, or whatever.

> **Andy:** If there was anything I could do to fix this, to get us back together, I would do it.

> **Andy:** I miss hugging you and kissing you and walking you to class and hanging out on the weekend.

I can't respond. Not right now. I can't even look at it. I put the phone face down on my nightstand, crawl onto my bed, and stare up at the ceiling.

9:10 P.M.

Part of me is embarrassed for him, but another, smaller, part of me admires it. It had to take a lot of courage to send that, knowing I would probably reject him. Again.

I think back on our time dating. He *was* a good boyfriend. He's so sweet and a really good kisser. I wouldn't mind kissing him some more. Warmth spreads down my body as I flash back to Homecoming, behind the bleachers, and under the streetlight.

Maybe I should give him another chance…

CHAPTER 28

What? How? Why?

WEDNESDAY, DECEMBER 1ST

7:51 A.M.

OUTSIDE SCHOOL

"You're *what*??" Ruby exclaims as we approach the school doors. I examine the dead grass in front of the school, avoiding eye contact.

"Emma. Look at me," Ruby demands. She stops walking.

I force my gaze to meet Ruby's, her brown eyes glaring at me. She waits for me to say it again.

"I'm back together with Andy," I mumble.

"What? How? Why?" She can't seem to decide on a question. "Em, what happened?"

"I don't know. He was so sad. And you know, we've been texting—"

Ruby interrupts me. "I told you that wasn't a good idea. So did Cher. You were giving him false hope. And now you're back together with him? Do you even like him?"

"Yes, Ruby," I say defensively. "Of course I do."

"Then why did you break up with him in the first place?" Ruby says.

I bite the inside of my cheek. She has a point. People shuffle around us, a crowd forming near the doors to get inside and into the warmth of the building. Ruby sighs and puts a hand to her forehead.

"Ugh. This is not a good idea."

I adjust my backpack and stare at my feet, not saying anything. A bitter wind whips my hair into my face.

Ruby sighs. "Come on. It's cold. Let's go in."

My eyes prickle, and I rub my palms over them, hoping Ruby doesn't see as she trails off ahead of me. I tell myself it's because of the wind, even though I know it's not true.

7:56 A.M.
MY LOCKER

Andy bounds down the hallway, a grin plastered across his face. My heart jumps into my throat, but I'm not sure if it's because I'm happy to see him.

"Hi," he says excitedly, pulling me into a hug. He sighs happily. "I missed this. I missed you."

This is why I broke up with him in the first place. So. Cringey. Like, it's sweet but feels over the top for the moment. Why can't he give me a hug and say hi, and leave it at that?

I ignore the thought and instead smile at him as I remind myself of all the things I like about him: he's sweet, funny, smart, cute, a great kisser, fun to be around. Of course I like him. I focus on his ocean-blue eyes and widen my smile.

"I missed you, too."

Andy leans in and gives me a soft kiss on the lips. My cheeks warm pleasantly. It's nice.

5:03 P.M.
RUBY'S BEDROOM

Ruby, Alejandra, and I are sitting on the floor in Ruby's bedroom, doing homework, or at least, pretending to.

"So," Ruby says, reaching up and grabbing one of the many, many stuffed animals on her bed. She tucks a little bear in a hoodie into her lap. "Spill." She tilts her head and purses her lips slightly.

Next to Ruby, Alejandra uncrosses her legs and gently places her open laptop on the floor. Why is Alejandra even here? She seems to be part of a lot of my life moments lately.

I roll my eyes. "Spill what?"

"Everything," Ruby says, spreading her arms wide. "How did you end up back together with Andy? How did it go today? How are you feeling?"

I don't know where to start. I shrug, staring at the Celsius poster on Ruby's wall, admiring each of their beautiful faces.

"How are you feeling about being back together with him?" Alejandra asks gently.

While I am slightly annoyed she's here, I appreciate that Alejandra asks the question without any judgment in her voice. Her warm, brown eyes give me their full attention, and she smiles softly.

Ruby, on the other hand, is making a face like she bit into a lemon. Her lips are puckered, and her eyes are slightly narrowed. She nods.

I sigh. "Fine, I guess."

Ruby rolls her eyes and flops onto the bean bag chair behind her with an *oof.*

I blush. I don't know if Ruby's ever reacted like this to something I've done before.

"Are you happy?" Alejandra asks.

"Um, yeah." I mean, I am. Today was definitely much less stressful, not worrying about what kind of mood Andy was going to be in.

"Then I guess that's what matters, right?" Alejandra says. She picks up her laptop and raises her eyebrows at Ruby. The two of them have a moment I'm totally not part of, communicating without actually saying anything.

A flame of jealousy lights in my chest. When did they get so close? What have I missed?

Ruby sighs loudly, sitting up and adjusting herself in the bean bag chair.

"Yes," she says solemnly. "If you're happy, that's all that matters." She gives me a small smile. "How was BB today? Was he over-the-moon happy?"

"Yeah, he was like a golden retriever puppy." I giggle. "It was like he wanted to be touching me all the time. If he wasn't holding my hand, he was giving me a hug. He even put his hand on my thigh in bio today," I tell them conspiratorially.

Ruby gasps. "Scandalous!"

I wave her off. "But yeah, it was nice not worrying about him being all mopey today."

Ruby nods and then gets serious again. "Have you told Cher?"

I shake my head. Ruby makes a "tsk" sound.

7:12 P.M.
MY BEDROOM

My heart thumps. My whole face is warm. I'm even sweating a little bit. I'm going to text Cher about Andy. It's not a big deal. I don't know why my body is acting this way. I take a deep breath and hit send.

> **Me:** So I have some news… Andy and I are back to-gether.

I lean my head over the back of my desk chair while I wait for a response. It takes only a couple seconds.

Cher: Seriously?

Me: Yeah…

Cher: That is so dumb.

Cher: You clearly don't like him. I met him once and could tell immediately.

I swallow the lump in my throat. I really did not expect my two best friends to be so unsupportive about all of this. I wallow in self-pity for a few seconds, allowing my annoyance at their reactions to build up until I feel like it's sitting on my chest. I furiously type out a response.

Me: You know, it's really lame that both of you are making me feel so crappy about this. I'm back together with Andy. It's already done. I'm happy with my decision. You can either like it or not, but it's not going to change anything.

I send it with a flourish and then toss my phone onto the bed. On my desk, there's an arched mirror with a white frame propped against the wall. I stare at my reflection, and my sea glass eyes stare back at me. They feel tight, which I know means they want to cry. But my brain doesn't want to.

My eyes don't care. A tear slides down my face. I swipe it away quickly and decide to go downstairs and distract myself with a snack.

8:23 P.M.

I come back to a bunch of messages from both Cher and Ruby.

> **Cher:** Wow, Emma. Sorry. I was just trying to be honest. Chill.

> **Ruby:** We're not trying to make you feel crappy. Like Cher said, we're trying to be honest about what we think.

> **Ruby:** But I want you to know that I support you. You're my best friend, and whatever makes you happy, makes me happy. And if that's Bio Boy, then great.

I'm guessing Ruby texted Cher on the side because Cher really changes her tune at the end.

> **Cher:** If you like him, then that's great. He's cute and seems like he's a really
> great boyfriend.

> **Cher:** I'm sorry if I made you feel bad. I didn't mean to.

SATURDAY, DECEMBER 11TH
6:17 P.M.
ANDY'S BASEMENT

"Pizza's here," Andy's mom calls down to the basement. The boys cheer and run up the stairs like a stampede of buffalo. I linger on the couch, not wanting to get bowled over by the group.

Andy and I have been back together for a little over a week now. And everything is… fine. Andy is his usual, sweet, kind of cringey self.

Earlier, before the rest of the boys came over, we were making out in his basement, and he kept stopping to, like, gaze into my eyes. I think he thought it was romantic, but it just made me uncomfortable.

At one point, we were kissing, and he leaned back to stare into my eyes again. I shifted my weight on the couch, distracted by the fact that I kind of had a wedgie, but obviously, couldn't get it out.

"Can I?" he whispered. At first, I wasn't sure what he was talking about. Then I noticed his hand, hovering over my chest and shaking slightly. Heat immediately spread all over my face, but a shiver of excitement also ran down my body.

I nodded, and Andy leaned in to kiss me again while he gently cupped my boob from underneath. His touch was tentative, but once it was there, he left it for a while, readjusting his hand to sort of rest on top of it. It wasn't unpleasant, but I still don't really get the appeal.

So, now I've officially been to second base. The whole thing didn't feel like a big deal, but shouldn't it? Shouldn't I care more?

Someone clears their throat, and the sound jolts me out of my thoughts and back to the present moment. I thought I was the only one still down here.

Matt stands at the edge of the couch, and we make eye contact. He doesn't say anything. I don't say anything. My heart beats a mile a minute, though. Why?

Literally nothing is happening. Matt quickly averts his eyes and heads for the stairs. I follow suit. Neither of us speaks.

But why do I feel like we had a moment?

And why is it making my heart thump so loudly?

9:35 P.M.
BEDROOM

The rest of the evening was uneventful. It was kind of fun being the only girl, though. I mostly sat on the couch and watched them do whatever they were doing—playing video games, wrestling, arguing about soccer. It sounds boring, but I actually had a good time. A better time than when Andy and I were alone, if I'm being honest.

9:38 P.M.

I can't stop thinking about that moment with Matt in the basement. And later, we were arguing about the superior ice cream toppings (caramel vs. strawberry syrup—obviously, caramel is the winner). It's silly, but it was one of the highlights of the night. It was so fun to go back and forth with Matt. It was like there was an electricity flowing between us as we argued. It made me tingle all over.

He came over to shake my hand after conceding to my victory, once the rest of the group got on my side. He gave me a small smile that made my heart tumble to the bottom of my chest.

Why?

9:40 P.M.

I think I know why.

But it makes me feel horrible. I *just* got back together with Andy.

9:44 P.M.

I like Matt.

9:45 P.M.

And I think he might like me, too.

9:49 P.M.

Crap. What am I going to do?

Ignore it. I'm going to ignore it for now. I think that's the smartest option.

CHAPTER 29

Is this really what you want?

MONDAY, DECEMBER 20TH

3:17 P.M.

MY LOCKER

Andy calls my name as he walks to my locker at the end of the day. He waves, his arm up high above his head, a big smile on his face. I blush but give a small wave back. I reach into my locker to put my algebra book away.

"Emma!" Andy calls again. He's only a couple feet away at this point. In my head, I think, *Yeah, dude. I see you.*

Then it happens. Andy trips. But he doesn't just trip and catch his balance. No. He falls to the floor.

I gasp and cover my mouth with my hand. "Oh my God! Are you okay?"

Andy stands up, a sheepish grin on his face. "Yeah, I'm okay. I guess I'm *falling* for you." He dips his chin and raises his eyebrows. "Falling? Get it?"

My body tenses. He did that on purpose? Oh my God. This is so embarrassing. There are two girls standing at the locker next to mine. They stifle giggles. A tingling sensation travels up the back of my neck, and I cross my arms over my stomach. I want to shove myself into this locker and hide. Andy is still smiling at me, waiting for me to react.

I decide right then and there. I have to break up with Andy. Again.

8:22 P.M.
BEDROOM

I text Ruby and Cher.

> **Me:** I'm breaking up with Andy tomorrow.

> **Cher:** That didn't take long.

I send an eye roll back.

> **Ruby:** How come?

> **Me:** You were right. I got back together with him out of pity. And he's so cringey. I can't take it anymore.

I fill Cher in on what happened in the hallway today.

> **Cher:** OMG. No. That is… just no.

> **Cher:** When are you going to do it?

> **Me:** Tomorrow morning. First thing.

> **Ruby:** You've got this, Em!

That's it. I've committed. There's no going back.

TUESDAY, DECEMBER 21ST
7:56 A.M.
MY LOCKER

I stand at my locker, organizing my books for the morning. I'm trying to act normal, but my heart is racing, and my hands are shaky. I know this is the right thing to do, to break up with Andy, but I'm so nervous.

I didn't really plan out what to say either. It didn't work out great last time, so I decided to wing it this time. I realize now it might have been a bad idea. I put my hand on the door of my locker and lean my head against it, staring at the floor.

"Hey, beautiful," I hear behind me. Ugh. Why does he have to be so sweet *and* so cringey? If it was one or the other, this would be so much easier.

"Hey." I try to smile, but it feels weird on my face. My eyes immediately go to the ground. I can't look at him while I do this. I don't want to see the hurt on his face.

Okay, no dilly-dallying this time. You can do this. I take a deep breath, trying to calm the pounding of my heart.

"Is something wrong?" Andy asks. He says it quickly and quietly. Does he know what's coming?

"Um, sort of..." What do I say? How do I do this? I should have prepared. Maybe the letter was better.

Andy grabs my hand and squeezes it. "What's going on?" he asks.

God, this is awful. My eyes are still on the ground, examining Andy's sneakers. There's a scuff on the toe of his left shoe. Probably from when he *fell* yesterday.

"Emma, look at me." I pull my gaze up to his. His eyebrows are knit together, and his eyes dart across my face. "You can talk to me."

Just do it, Emma. Dragging it out is only making it worse. I clear my throat.

"I... um..."

Do it!

"I think we should break up," I force out, but it's barely above a whisper.

Andy immediately drops my hand. The warning bell rings, and there's a cacophony of closing lockers around us. Andy stares at me, his eyebrows still knit together, but his eyes narrowed now.

"What? Did you say we should break up?"

I nod solemnly. People rush past us to get to class.

Andy runs his hand through his hair aggressively. His neck is suddenly red and blotchy. He sighs loudly.

"Why?" His tone changes. It's sad and confused. "I like you so much."

Tears prickle the back of my eyes. I cannot cry. I will not cry. I stare at the ground again.

Andy leans down, trying to make eye contact with me. "Emma. Please." His voice cracks, and now I'm afraid *he's* going to cry.

I shake my head. "I'm sorry," I squeak out.

He stands up and lets out another heavy sigh.

"We should go to class," I say meekly, still not daring to look at Andy's face.

"Okay," he says dully, turning on his heel and heading down the hallway with his shoulders slumped.

I trail behind him awkwardly until we turn in our opposite directions. When we finally do, I take a huge breath in and let it out through my mouth.

That was horrible.

And yet, I feel better. I take another deep breath and roll my shoulders back before sprinting the rest of the way to English.

12:33 P.M.
HALLWAY

Andy finds me in the hallway before biology.

"Can we talk for a second?" he asks, putting his hand on my arm. I stop walking and move to the side, so we're not blocking everyone's path. We're only a few steps from Mr. Milo's classroom. He's standing in the hallway, and I see him see us.

"Why won't you look at me?" Andy asks, his voice pleading.

I turn away from the goings-on of the hallway to face him. He's pale, and his eyes are a little bloodshot. Oh God, has he been crying? I swallow, heat creeping onto my cheeks. I hate this so much.

I don't say anything. I can't handle his sad face. The hallway is starting to clear out. We probably only have a minute until the bell rings.

"Is this really what you want?" Andy asks quietly. Now his eyes are on the ground. He shifts his weight slightly and rubs the back of his neck with his free hand.

I clear my throat. I have to stand by this. I'm not doing him any favors by pity-dating him.

"Yeah." I try to say it kindly but also so he knows I mean it. I muster up some courage and add, "It's not working. For me." I pause. "But we can still be fr—"

Andy raises his face to the ceiling and groans, cutting me off.

"Christmas is in four days, Emma. What the hell?" His neck is red, and now we're two of the only people left in the hallway.

"The bell is going to—"

"Yeah," Andy mutters, storming off to the classroom.

We walk past Mr. Milo as the bell rings. He doesn't say anything, nodding toward our seats.

12:35 P.M.

At the end of class, Andy hops out of his seat so fast, I don't even have my stuff gathered before he's out of the room.

He ignored me the entire period. Luckily, we only have one more day until winter break. And tomorrow is our semester final, so we won't have to talk then either.

I walk quickly to Ruby's locker, and I'm relieved to see Alejandra isn't there yet.

"I did it," I say immediately, leaning against the locker next to Ruby's.

Ruby's face is confused at first, but then she registers what I'm talking about. Her eyes widen.

"How'd it go?" she asks eagerly. She closes her locker and turns to me. She quickly glances over my shoulder, probably checking for Alejandra.

"Horrible," I moan. "He was so sad."

Ruby nods sympathetically. "I bet. That boy is like a puppy. But you did the right thing." Ruby reaches her arm out to give me a hug, and I put my head on her shoulder, soaking in the comfort of my best friend.

"Then he was mad because it's almost Christmas," I add, standing up straight.

Ruby pulls her face back and wrinkles her eyebrows. "So?"

Alejandra walks up quietly, tapping Ruby's shoulder with a finger but not interrupting the conversation.

"My thoughts exactly," I say. "I broke up with Andy... again," I inform Alejandra.

She nods, adjusting her glasses on her nose. "Mmm, I'm sorry," she says, reaching out to squeeze my arm gently.

I give her a half-hearted smile back, and the three of us walk down the hall.

9:30 P.M.
BEDROOM

No text from Andy tonight, which I think is a good thing. What more is there to say?

I still feel bad that he's so upset. My heart twinges with guilt every time I think about his bloodshot eyes.

9:34 P.M.

And I don't understand the whole Christmas comment. It's the last thing he said to me, and I can't get it out of my brain.

But, really, would he rather I pretend to like him so he can give me a Christmas present? Also, phew, because I did not get him one. It didn't even cross my mind.

9:41 P.M.

I hope he's okay, though. I never wanted to hurt him.

9:47 P.M.

What do you even buy a teenage boy for Christmas?

9:53 P.M.

I wonder what Matt is doing over break.
Shut up, Emma. Not cool.

CHAPTER 30

I think maybe I'm in love, too.

WEDNESDAY, DECEMBER 22ND

11:36 A.M.

HALLWAY

I haven't seen Andy all morning, which has been a relief. I know I'll have to face him in biology later, but the less I have to see him, the better.

I stop at my locker before lunch. As I shut it, a familiar head of brown, curly hair approaches. My heart jolts. It's Matt. What's he doing over here? I almost never see him in the hallways.

His eyes are laser-focused on me, and my heart rate ticks up a notch.

"Uh, hi," I say as he stops in front of me. The corners of his mouth are turned down, and his eyes are stony. I swallow. I don't think this is a friendly visit.

"What are you doing over here?" I ask. I fidget with my books. I'm nervous. Being around Matt makes me feel jittery in general, but the grim look on his face and his stiff body language are making it worse.

"You have to stop messing with Andy," he says. His voice is quiet, but forceful.

My eyes go to the ground guiltily. But then I look back up at Matt. No. I don't need to feel guilty, I decide.

"I wasn't messing with him," I say defiantly.

"You never should have gone back out with him in the first place. And now he's all upset. Again."

I bite my lip and nod because he's not wrong.

"I didn't mean to hurt him," I say more gently.

"Yeah," Matt says with a sigh. "But you did."

My heart lurches.

"Just stop. Okay?" Matt says. I nod. He turns and leaves without another word.

As he reaches the end of the hall, he looks back over his shoulder, and we make eye contact. He gives me the tiniest smile, lifting just one corner of his mouth, as if to say, *Maybe you're not so horrible*, before disappearing into the crowded hallway.

What does it mean?

11:42 A.M.
LUNCH

Ruby is telling me all about how she aced her Spanish final this morning, but I'm barely listening.

After my conversation with Matt, Andy should be at the top of my mind. Or at the very least, the fact that Matt basically scolded me. But instead, I can't stop thinking about that tiny smile playing on his lips.

This is not good.

Ruby waves her hand in front of my face. "Emma? You okay? What's going on in there?"

"Yeah," I answer immediately. "Yeah, I'm fine. Let's have a sleepover tonight," I suggest. I think I need to talk about this with the girls. Tell them everything.

"Oh, great idea," Ruby agrees, taking a bite of her pizza. "We have a lot to discuss."

I nod, my head a jumbled mess.

7:20 P.M.
RUBY'S BEDROOM

Despite the weird day I had, I can't help but enjoy the buzz of excitement in Ruby's room. It's winter break—no school for two weeks, Christmas is coming up, I'm free of a cringey boyfriend, and I'm spending the night with my two best friends. My heart is light, and there's a sense of hope fluttering in my chest.

We're sitting in a circle on the floor, munching on a tub of Twizzlers. Cher leans against Ruby's bed, giving us all the updates on her and Jacob.

"So, yeah, I'm going to go to his family's dinner on Christmas Eve, and he's going to come to my dad's on Christmas day," she explains.

"Wow, that all sounds so grown up," Ruby says, taking a bite of her Twizzler.

I nod, impressed.

"Have you said, 'I love you'?" I ask coyly.

"Oh yeah," Cher says nonchalantly. "Like, a month ago."

"You didn't tell us that!" Ruby yelps. She sits up straighter, scooching closer to Cher.

"When was I supposed to?" Cher says somewhat icily. "You're both busy, like, all the time now. We haven't even hung out in weeks."

Ruby and I glance at each other, unsure what to say. My mind flits to all the times Cher said she couldn't hang out with us because she was doing something with Jacob, but this doesn't feel like the time to point it out.

Cher sighs. "It's fine. I know we go to different schools now. But sometimes it feels like I'm being forgotten while you two still get to do everything together."

We're all quiet for a few seconds, and the air is thick with the silence. Ruby stares at the ceiling. Cher picks a fuzz off her sweatshirt. I bite my lip.

Cher sighs again. "It's not like I don't have other friends at school. And I have Jacob, obviously. I'm not a total loser. It just—" She lets out a breath. "It sucks that I'm not with you guys every day anymore."

I nod solemnly. Ruby reaches out to grab Cher's hand, squeezing it.

"We'll be better," Ruby promises. "All of us."

"You're still our best friend," I tell Cher.

She nods. "I know." She runs her hands through her hair with a huff. "It'll be easier next year when I get my license and can drive myself places." Cher's taking Driver's Ed over the summer so she can get her license right when she turns sixteen in September. "My mom acts like driving twenty minutes on a Friday night is going to kill her." Cher rolls her eyes.

"Oh my God, that'll be so cool!" I squeal. "The three of us driving around together?" I imagine it now, rocking out to music, laughing, the windows rolled down, giddy with the freedom of driving ourselves somewhere. It feels like a far-off dream, but I guess it's not.

Cher smiles, her blue eyes sparkling with excitement. "I know," she says. "I think my dad is—"

"Wait," Ruby interrupts. She puts her arms up, her long, slender fingers splayed out. "Let's not forget where this whole conversation started." She folds her hands in her lap and faces Cher fully. "Soooo, what's it like, being in love?" she asks dreamily.

I almost forgot about this development. This is huge. I also face Cher directly. Ruby and I are like students in a classroom, looking to our teacher for all the answers.

Cher tries to play it cool, but she can't hide her happiness. Her eyes are bright, and a big smile spreads across her face. She pushes her blonde hair behind her ears, thinking.

"I don't know. It's... nice, I guess?"

"Nice?" I ask. "What about the fireworks? The magic?"

"Yeah, that was all there at the beginning," Cher explains. "But now, it's easy. Besides you two, he's my best friend. I feel like I can tell him anything. And, like, kissing him was such a big deal a few months ago, but now I can't imagine not being able to kiss him."

"Wow," I whisper. "I want that."

Ruby nods, leaning back onto her bean bag chair, her hand on her chin like she's deep in thought.

"I mean, don't get me wrong. There are still exciting things—like, we haven't done *it* or anything—"

Ruby interrupts her. "I would hope not! If you had done *it* and not told us, I don't know if I could ever forgive you."

I blush. I can't believe we're talking about sex. Not that we're doing it yet, but that it's an actual conversation. That it's on the table for one of us. It gives me kind of a funny feeling in my chest, kind of like a longing—maybe for the days where sleepovers were movies and makeovers? Now they're about more serious things like sex and breakups. I've always wanted to be older and wiser and cooler, and now that I'm (sort of) getting there, it's making me feel... weird.

Cher's laugh breaks me out of my thoughts. "Oh my God. Never. We'll have to plan every moment leading up to it. I'm not ready for that yet anyway," she says. "And I want it to be special."

Ruby and I nod in agreement.

"Because you're in love," Ruby suggests.

Cher nods with a smile. "Yep."

Ruby's round, brown eyes dart between Cher and me. She clears her throat, sitting up straighter in the bean bag chair.

"I think maybe I'm in love, too," Ruby bursts out. Her eyes continue to dart between us.

Cher's brow is furrowed, and her mouth is slightly agape. Ruby's hands are still folded in her lap, like she's waiting for us to answer a question.

I'm the first to speak. "With who?" Ruby has never even talked about any boys being cute, let alone being in love with them.

Ruby hesitates. She wrings her hands together but then takes a deep breath and puts them on her knees. "Alejandra," she announces firmly.

My jaw drops open. Cher is silent next to me. I don't know what to say.

Cher nods. "Okay... yeah. That makes sense," she says slowly.

I think back over the past few months. Alejandra always being around. Ruby ditching Jeremiah at Homecoming to hang out with Alejandra. Doing their homework together and hanging out all the time on their own. The way they exchange looks and communicate without saying anything.

Duh.

I jump up and barrel over to Ruby to give her a hug. She lets out a surprised, *Oh*, as I tumble on top of her.

"Rubs, wow," I say after a long hug. I lean back and put my hands on her shoulders. "Thank you for telling us. I love you so much."

Ruby's eyes are shining, and she's more relaxed than she has been all night. I didn't notice the tension buzzing around her until it was gone.

Cher comes over and pulls Ruby onto her feet to give her a hug, too.

Ruby swipes at her eyes. I can't remember the last time I saw Ruby cry. Maybe sixth grade when her hamster died?

The three of us sit back down on the floor, and Ruby reaches out to grab our hands.

"Thanks," is all she says.

"Why didn't you tell us sooner? When did this happen? Are you two dating? Does Alejandra know you love her?" I have so many questions.

Cher puts a hand out. "Slow down, Emma." She turns to Ruby and gives her hand a squeeze. "Tell. Us. Everything."

A huge grin spreads across Ruby's face. She lets go of our hands and puts hers over her cheeks.

"Yeah, I guess we're dating," she says. "I mean, we've kissed... a lot." Cher and I both squeal, and we all burst into giggles.

"But why didn't you tell us sooner?" I ask again.

Ruby thinks for a second. "I guess, before, I'd never really thought much about labeling myself. I mean, I knew I had no interest in boys. Like when you kissed Connor last year, Emma? The idea of him sticking his tongue in your mouth really grossed me out." She shivers dramatically.

We all laugh at the memory of my first, tongue-flopping kiss.

"It grosses me out, too," I say.

Ruby continues. "And then Alejandra and I started hanging out more, and I realized that I really liked hanging out with her. I liked the way she made me feel. And then it dawned on me that I was having those feelings you two always talked about—with Connor, with Jacob, with Andy. But for me, it was with Alejandra. You know, I'd get a little tingly when I was with her. And then one day, it happened. I kissed her. And she kissed me back, and I knew I wanted to keep kissing her."

Ruby pauses to take a breath. She's serious, but she's also smiling.

"I wasn't sure how to tell you. It's not that I was embarrassed or anything, but, I don't know, it felt... different. I've always known I was different. I mean, look at me." She motions to herself, to her hair coiled up inside of her satin bonnet. "I'm Black and have these two, cute little white girls for my besties. I'm the girl with the dead dad. This was just another way I was different."

Cher and I both nod.

"So, I don't know," Ruby continues. "We kept it to ourselves. I guess it felt easier." Ruby's eyes are wide as she searches mine and Cher's. "I didn't mean to lie to you."

"Oh, Ruby, it's okay," Cher says softly.

"I get it," I say.

Ruby smiles softly. "No, you don't. I appreciate it, Em, but you can't get it because you've never lived it."

My cheeks flush, and I suddenly want to hide under the pile of stuffed animals on Ruby's bed. I open my mouth to say something, but nothing comes out.

Ruby squeezes my knee. "It's okay."

I smile gratefully at my best friend. "You're so wise."

"I know," Ruby says.

Cher snorts, and Ruby reaches up to grab a giant stuffed frog to throw at her.

"Ah!" Cher gasps. A mischievous grin twists onto Cher's face. She stands up quickly and grabs an armful of stuffed animals, throwing each of them at Ruby and me.

Ruby drops to the ground, covering her head. I hop up and grab a few to retaliate. Briefly, I wonder how many stuffed animals Ruby has. It's got to be more than fifty.

I pelt one at Cher's chest, but she catches it expertly and throws it back at me.

"I surrender!" Ruby shouts from the floor. She waves one arm above her head. Cher and I nod at each other before both throwing our remaining stuffies at Ruby's long body.

"I said, *surrender*!"

Cher and I flop back onto the floor. We're all laughing and gasping for air. It feels like one of those precious moments. One I don't want to forget—ever.

CHAPTER 31

I'm not embarrassed.

WEDNESDAY, DECEMBER 22ND

RUBY'S BEDROOM

8:40 P.M.

Once we've all calmed our giggles—which takes a while because every time we think we're done, someone else lets one escape—we resume our lounging and chatting and Twizzler eating.

"Okay, Emma, your turn." Ruby takes an aggressive bite of a Twizzler and wiggles her eyebrows at me.

I sigh and lean my head back. This is my chance. It's not a huge revelation like Ruby's, but it still feels like a big moment.

"Obviously, Andy and I broke up. We all know this." I gesture toward both of them.

"Phew," Ruby says. "Just making sure you didn't get back together with him again without telling us."

I grab the stuffed owl next to me and pelt it at her face, but she raises her arms to block my attack.

"I'm sorry, I'm sorry! Last joke, I promise," Ruby says with a laugh.

"How'd it go this time?" Cher asks.

"Better, I guess?" I don't know, did it go better? I shrug. "He hasn't been texting me. So that's good. I feel bad, though." I fiddle with the sleeve of my sweatshirt.

"Don't," Cher says.

Ruby nods emphatically. "It's done," she says, swiping her hand across her neck.

"Definitely." I hesitate before casually adding, "Matt came to my locker today."

"Who's that?" Cher asks.

"Andy's friend," Ruby says, then asks, "For what?"

"He told me to stop messing with Andy." I explain the interaction with Matt.

"Sounds like he's looking out for his friend," Cher says with a shrug.

"Yeah," I agree. I want to say more, to tell them how I can't stop thinking about Matt's tiny smile, or the way his curly hair falls into his eyes, or the fact that my heart slams against my chest when he looks at me, but I can't seem to get any more words out.

"Your cheeks are pink," Ruby says. "Why are your cheeks pink?" She points an accusing finger at me.

"Um, because she's embarrassed?" Cher suggests, flicking her hand up as if to say, *Duh*.

This is my chance. I cross my legs beneath me and pull at a string at the end of my sock. I shrug.

"I'm not embarrassed," I say quietly.

Ruby gasps. "The cartwheels! Do you *like* Matt?"

I don't say anything. I stare at Ruby, and I know I must be blushing harder because I feel the warmth spreading across my face.

Cher looks quickly between Ruby and me. "Wait, wait. Which one is Matt? Is he the one with the curly hair?"

I nod, biting my lip, trying to stop a smile.

"Okay, yeah. I noticed him watching you on Halloween," Cher says.

I turn my head so quickly, I hurt my neck. "Wait, really?" I ask, rubbing the spot.

"Emma Bishop, you naughty girl." Ruby clicks her tongue and smirks.

I put my face in my hands. "I know," I wail. "I can't help it, though."

"How long has this been going on? Does he know you like him?" Ruby asks.

"Oh my God, no! Nothing is 'going on.'" I put air quotes around "going on." Ruby raises her eyebrows at me. "I mean, we've had a few, like, moments, I guess."

"Like the cartwheel night," Ruby says. I nod.

Cher sighs loudly. "What's the cartwheel night?" Then she mumbles, "This is exactly what I was talking about before."

Ruby and I tell Cher about the night walking home after the football game, everyone doing cartwheels, and Matt throwing me over his shoulder.

"I thought we told you about this," I say when we're finished.

Cher shakes her head. "Nope." She pauses. "But he totally likes you."

"You think?"

Cher nods.

"Does he make you feel tingly in all the places?" Ruby asks with a smirk.

I flush again but smile. "I think about him all the time. And I've felt *so* guilty about it because, like, Andy, you know? That's his friend. And Andy's like a sad, lost puppy."

Ruby taps her chin with a Twizzler. "It's definitely tricky," she says slowly.

"What do I do?" I moan.

"Give it time," Cher advises. "If it's meant to be, something will happen."

"When did you become such a sap?" Ruby asks, pushing on Cher's shoulder.

We all say the same thing at the same time, "Jacob," and burst into another fit of giggles.

1:11 A.M.

Ruby and Cher are asleep in Ruby's bed. I'm on the air mattress on the floor. I can't sleep.

What a night. Cher's in love, Ruby's (maybe) in love, and I'm in… *like*, I guess.

Matt's face pops into my brain, and for the first time, I don't try to shake him off right away. It's a relief to have finally said it out loud: I like Matt. I mean, how could I not? I think about his lopsided smile and the way his front teeth kind of overlap, and warmth spreads not only across my cheeks but also down into my chest.

But what am I going to do?

Cher seemed pretty convinced that Matt likes me, too, but I don't know. Andy is one of his best friends. He's not going to turn around and start dating his ex-girlfriend.

Plus, how would he even know I like him? I'm not going to go up to him and announce, "Hey. I like you. Let's date." That's not how it works. Not for me, at least. I could see Ruby doing something like that.

1:29 A.M.

I can't believe Ruby has been dating Alejandra for so long, and I had no idea. I mean, I guess I had an idea that something was happening. We did get into that fight about her spending so much time with Alejandra, but I didn't see it for what it really was.

Georgia caught on way faster than us, though.

"My mom asked me about it a couple weeks ago," she said earlier. "I told her."

"And?" I asked.

Ruby shrugged but smiled softly. "She was cool."

1:40 A.M.

I wonder what it would be like to kiss Matt. Would it be gentle, like Andy? Or floppy, like Connor? Or something totally different?

I sigh and roll over. It doesn't matter. I can't do anything about it—not right now. Andy's too heartbroken.

1:43 A.M.

Cher bought Jacob a flat-brim hat for Christmas. Apparently, hats are expensive.

1:45 A.M.

I still can't sleep. I sigh and pull my phone out from under my pillow and start scrolling. Matt has a story posted. My heart skips when his face pops up on the screen. It's a video of him and his dog. He's laughing as the dog licks his face.

I watch it four times.

1:51 A.M.

Matt looks cute in a beanie hat. How much do beanies cost?

CHAPTER 32

A sophomore?

TUESDAY, JANUARY 4TH

7:54 A.M.

MY LOCKER

"You used to date Andy Williams, right?" The girl whose locker is next to mine—I think her name is Jenny—leans over toward me.

Taken aback, I glance over my shoulder to make sure there's not someone behind me that she's actually speaking to. Jenny and I don't really talk. She's a sophomore and has always been perfectly nice, but she's never seemed interested in chatting beyond a "Hi" when we see each other at our lockers.

I clear my throat. "Uh, yeah. Why?"

Jenny closes her locker and leans up against it conspiratorially. "He's dating my friend Angela now," she says matter-of-factly.

"A sophomore?" I say, disbelieving. I'm embarrassed as soon as it leaves my mouth. Jenny chuckles.

"Yeah," she says, shaking her head slightly.

"Oh." I don't know what else to say.

Jenny stands up straight. "I hope it's okay I told you. Personally, I'd want a heads up."

I nod. "Yeah, thanks."

Jenny gives me a small smile before walking away.

Andy has a girlfriend? Already? But he was so heartbroken over me! It hasn't even been a month!

8:54 A.M.
HALLWAY

I make my way down the crowded hallway, still thinking about Andy and his new girlfriend. And not just a new girlfriend, but a sophomore. How did this even happen? Do I care?

An older boy, maybe a junior or senior, runs down the hallway and almost mows me over. He barely pauses to touch my arm and stabilize me before continuing his sprint down the hall, shouting, "Sorry, wrong way!" over his shoulder.

I'm fine, but my cheeks flush as people turn to see what happened. I put my head down and pick up the pace to second period art, relieved I didn't have any schedule changes for the new semester and can stick to my usual routes.

I stop short as soon as I enter the art room. The girl who walked in behind me huffs, but I can't be bothered as my heart drops into the pit of my stomach, bounces back up, and starts thumping. There, in the middle of the classroom, is a familiar head of brown, curly hair.

It's Matt. In my art class.

I find my name on the new seating chart projected at the front of the room, and right behind *Emma Bishop*, it says *Matteo Martinez*. No way. I casually walk over to my seat and put my stuff down. Matt is already sitting at the table behind me, but I haven't looked directly at him yet. My heart is still thumping, and, based on the temperature of my face, I'm sure I'm red as a tomato.

Should I say something to him? Did he notice me come in? He must have, right? I walked right past him, and I'm sitting at the table directly in front of him. I can't ignore him. That would be weird.

I definitely wasn't this nervous around him before I admitted I liked him. Ugh. I'm both excited and mortified for some reason. I was not expecting this, especially after the bomb that Jenny dropped on me only an hour ago.

I take a deep breath and turn around in my seat.

"Hey."

Matt looks up from his phone. He stares at me for a beat before saying, "Hey, Emma."

My heart skips when he says my name.

"So, your schedule must have changed, huh?"

Matt nods, tight-lipped, and doesn't say anything else. He glances around the room, not making eye contact with me. If it's possible, my cheeks burn even hotter. Is he not going to talk to me?

"Okay, then…" I say, turning back around as the bell rings.

That was weird. And disappointing.

9:43 A.M.
ART

I have not been able to concentrate for the entire period. Is Matt watching me? It's all I can think about. Oh God, what does my hair look like from behind? I can't remember if I checked it this morning.

Why was he being so cold to me? Is it about Andy? He has a new girlfriend now, apparently, so why is Matt still mad?

The bell rings and everyone gathers their stuff. I try to calm my racing heart as I stand up, but it jolts to a stop when I realize that Matt is already gone.

Cher was wrong. Matt clearly does not like me. I shove the disappointment deep into the back of my brain as I head out into the packed hallway and pretend like I'm not looking for Matt in the sea of people.

12:33 P.M.
BIOLOGY

Andy is still in my biology class, but like in all my other classes today, we changed seats. He's in the room before me, talking to one of the boys on the soccer team when I come in. He smiles when he notices me. I smile back.

Good, let's not make this weird. I sit down at my new seat, and Andy walks over to stand in front of me. So much for not making it weird.

"Hey," he says with a bright smile.

Okay, would it kill him to tone down the happiness a smidge? I've been in a crappy mood all day.

"Hey." I force a smile back up at him.

"How was your break?"

"Good," I reply simply. I don't want to seem rude, but are we really going to do this small talk? Who cares? Andy nods, glancing at the clock. The bell is going to ring any second.

"So listen," he starts, putting a hand on my desk and leaning closer.

I cut him off. "I already know about your new girlfriend," I say clearly, but I can't stop a slight blush from creeping across my cheeks.

I'm suddenly embarrassed. *I* broke up with *him*, but he's the one with a new girlfriend already. It makes me feel very small, especially as he hovers above me at my desk.

I clear my throat and sit up straighter, trying to exude more confidence than I feel.

"Oh," he says. "Um, look, yeah." Andy rubs the back of his neck, which is pink now. Good. I'm glad he's embarrassed.

I smile at him cooly.

He's stumbling for his words now. "I didn't, you know, plan it, or anything. It just kind of happened."

"I'm happy for you," I lie sweetly.

The bell rings. Andy nods and walks to his seat at the front of the room. He glances back over his shoulder once and gives me a small smile. I wave back.

I let out a sigh and slump in my chair as Mr. Milo starts talking about this semester's syllabus.

1:27 P.M.
RUBY'S LOCKER

"Rubs, what's wrong?" I ask as I approach her locker. She scans the hallway, her eyes wide and darting among the crowds of people.

"Nothing," she says too quickly. She closes her locker. I give her a pointed look to let her know I don't believe her.

Ruby sighs. "It's stupid." She pauses, again glancing over her shoulder down the hallway. She bounces her knee a little. "It's just that, you know, now you know about Alejandra and me." She bites her lip. I reach out and squeeze her arm.

"Ruby. Hey."

Ruby stops bouncing and locks her brown eyes on my green ones. Hers are still wide, and I can almost feel the buzz of her anxiety.

"Everything is fine. I'm not going to act any differently around Alejandra." I pause. "Honestly, I might be a little nicer now that I know she's not trying to steal you as my best friend."

Ruby smiles and drops her books to envelop me in a hug. "You're a good friend."

My spirits lift a little. Who cares about these boys? At least I have Ruby. What else do I need?

Alejandra walks up as Ruby and I gather her things from the floor. "Everything okay?" she asks, adjusting her glasses stiffly.

"Of course," I say, standing up. "Everything is great." Alejandra doesn't need more than that to know what I mean. She turns to Ruby, and as she does, her soft smile transforms into a wide grin. Ruby's eyes are shining, and she reaches out to squeeze Alejandra's hand.

They're totally in love.

I just wish I wasn't so jealous.

CHAPTER 33

Forget her.

TUESDAY, JANUARY 4TH

5:34 P.M.

DINNER

Marie is unusually quiet at dinner tonight. She stares down at her plate, pushing her food around. Mom keeps glancing at her but doesn't say anything.

Marie takes a drink of her milk, then stares at the glass for a couple seconds before saying quietly, "May I be excused? I'm not really hungry today."

Mom's forehead is creased with concern, but she nods. Marie scooches her chair back and makes her way around the table. Dad reaches out to tickle her, but she pushes him off with a grunt and goes upstairs.

"That was weird," I say.

"Maybe you could go talk to her," Mom says casually. She takes a sip of her water. "She might tell you what's going on."

I roll my eyes.

"Emma," Mom warns.

"Okay." I put my hands up in resignation. "I'll talk to her."

5:44 P.M.
MARIE'S BEDROOM

I knock on Marie's door, half-hoping she'll tell me to go away. I have my own stuff to be worried about. I don't really need to add a ten-year-old's drama to that.

Marie swings the door open, though. Her eyes are on the floor, and she stands straight, not even a hand on her hip, which is very unlike her. Marie always has some sort of flair about her presence. This must be serious.

"What?" she asks flatly.

"Are you okay? Do you want to talk?" I try to take a step forward.

"No." She doesn't move to let me in.

"You know I was in fourth grade once, too," I remind her. Oh God, I sound like Mom. I roll my eyes internally at myself. Marie rolls hers, too.

"Fine," she says with a sigh.

She takes a step back to allow me into her room, then closes the door behind me. I walk over to her bed and sit cross-legged at the end. I lean forward and pat the spot in front of me. She climbs up and pulls her hot pink comforter and lime green sheets over her knees.

"So what's going on?" I ask.

Marie sighs but doesn't say anything. Her big brown eyes turn to me briefly before focusing on the poster of a golden retriever puppy to her right.

"Come on," I say kindly. After another second of silence, I add, "You're freaking me out. You've never been this quiet in your entire life."

This gets a half smile from her, but she's still not talking.

"Is it that girl in your class? Addy?"

"Ally," Marie corrects. "And yeah."

I knew it. That little brat. I don't even know her, but I hate her. Are you allowed to hate a ten-year-old?

"What happened?"

Marie sighs again, which tests my patience. I'm trying to be the understanding big sister here, but the dramatics and the sighing are starting to irk me. I take a breath and wait, staring at my little sister, mentally telling her, *Spit it out.*

Finally, she does. The words tumble out of her mouth, and once she starts, she doesn't stop.

"Ally makes fun of my hair every day. Like, every single day, Emma. And it doesn't matter if I do it, or you do it, or Mom does it. Whatever it is, Ally thinks it's dumb and has to tell me that. And everyone thinks she's *so* cool. I'm the only one who sees her for what she is. But, like, why me? Why did she choose *me* to pick on? What did I do to her?" Marie's eyes brim with tears, and I feel like a mama bear who needs to protect her cub.

"Come here." Marie crawls over next to me, and I wrap my arms around her. "That girl is a bully." She nods against my shoulder. "What do your friends do when she says this stuff to you?"

Marie sniffs. "She does it when we're alone. Like today, we were in the bathroom. I came out of the stall, and she snorted at me. So I said, 'What?' and she said, 'Do you have a mirror at your house?' So obviously I said yeah, and she was like, 'Oh, I thought maybe you didn't because there's no way I would come to school if I saw my hair like that.'"

I want to scream. This Ally girl reminds me of my middle school bully, Audrey.

"Maybe you need to tell your teacher about what she says to you."

Marie groans. "No, that's even more embarrassing. Then everyone will know what she's saying." She pauses before whispering, "And what if they all start making fun of me?"

"Hey." I put my hands on her shoulders. "You are cool. Like, actually cool. Way cooler than I was when I was ten."

"Obviously," Marie says with an air of her usual bravado. I flick her on the arm.

"So, you can tell the teacher, or not. You can tell Mom and Dad, or not. It probably won't stop her anyway." Marie nods solemnly. "But, forget her." I have a flashback to jumping in the school bathroom with Ruby and Cher last year, chanting the same thing. "Seriously. Forget her. She is *not* cool. And you are."

"Thanks. You're cool, too. Sometimes."

We both giggle, and I pull her in for another quick hug before I get up. As I'm leaving, I pause in the doorway. Marie is already busying herself searching for something on the floor of her closet.

I hope she believes me. Because I mean it.

10:58 P.M.
BEDROOM

What a day. Andy's new girlfriend. Matt in art class. Ruby and Alejandra. Marie. My brain feels all jumbled. And so does my heart.

I put my headphones on and play some music. Loud.

I let the sound wash over me, not really paying attention to the words, just trying to drown out the seemingly never-ending barrage of thoughts barrelling through my brain.

How does Andy already have a new girlfriend? Why does it bother me so much? I should feel relieved, right? But instead, I'm mad, and, honestly, kind of embarrassed.

Why did Matt ignore me in art? How can he be mad if even Andy isn't upset over the breakup anymore?

Then, there's Ruby and Alejandra. I can't believe I didn't see it before. It's like they're looking at each other with cartoon heart eyes all the time.

And, Cher. She sent us a picture from the basketball game at Woodlands tonight. She's in the middle of a big group of people, Jacob's arm casually thrown over her shoulder, her head leaning on his chest, a genuine, laughing smile on her face.

I'm happy for both of my friends. I am. But I'm also jealous. Is it so horrible that I want someone to love me?

You had Andy, my brain reminds me. But I didn't feel that way about him. It's not the same.

I wonder if Matt thinks about me as much as I think about him. Based on our interaction today, I'm going to guess, no.

My heart hurts thinking about Marie. She's annoying, of course, but that's what little sisters are for, right? No one else is allowed to be mean to her.

The music in my ears changes to one of my favorite Celsius songs, "Don't Stop (Loving Me)." James, my favorite, really has his moment in this song, belting out,

Don't stop
loving me
It's all I can do
to think of you.
We were meant to be
baby
please don't stop
loving me.

I sigh and stare at the ceiling, my thoughts circling back to Matt. His brown curly hair. His lopsided smile. His overlapping front teeth. I feel tingly and warm. But there's also an ache in my chest. What am I going to do? Do I try to talk to him again tomorrow, or do I ignore him?

We *have* had a few moments. The cartwheel. Andy's basement. My locker. His eye contact always feels so intense. Like he's not just looking at my face, but really looking at *me*, like, who I really am.

Crap. I really like him. Like, a lot.

I'm screwed.

CHAPTER 34

Everything feels like a mess.

WEDNESDAY, JANUARY 5TH
7:02 A.M.

I wake up feeling grumpy.

About Andy. About Matt. About Ruby. About Cher. About Marie. About my life.

I snap at both Marie and Mom while we eat breakfast.

Mom gives me a warning look but simply says, "Why don't you go finish getting ready?"

9:43 A.M.
ART

I ignore Matt in class. I feel him see me as I come in and sit down in front of him, but I don't turn around.

I want to know if he's looking at me. But I want to show him I don't care if he's looking at me more.

When the bell rings, I grab my stuff and strut out the door, feeling somewhat vindicated.

12:35 P.M.
BIOLOGY

Andy smiles at me when I walk into bio. I ignore him and go to my seat without a response. His shoulders slump and a frown quickly replaces his smile. I drop into my seat, cross my arms, and stare straight ahead.

1:28 P.M.
WALKING TO PE

Alejandra, Ruby, and I make our way down the crowded hallway to the locker room. Alejandra says something about a viral video of a marching band performance.

"That's dumb," I grumble.

Ruby looks me dead in the eyes. "Chill. Out." She and Alejandra walk a little ahead of me, but I don't try to keep up.

7:13 P.M.
BEDROOM

It was a long day, and I'm still in a sour mood. I sit cross-legged on my bed, my laptop open, but I'm not actually working on anything. I stare off into space, sulking.

My phone vibrates. It's Cher.

> **Cher:** What's going on? How did it go this week? Any Matt updates?

> **Me:** No.

> **Ruby:** Don't bother with Emma today. She was a crab ALL DAY.

She sends a gif of a lady giving side-eye.

My cheeks burn. And even though I know it's true, I'm annoyed. Am I not allowed to have a bad day once in a while? Sorry I can't always be the person lifting everyone up and making them feel better.

I turn the screen off and toss the phone next to me. It vibrates a few more times, but I ignore it.

8:24 P.M.

There's a knock on my door.

"Come in," I say dully.

Marie pushes the door open tentatively. Her left hand is cupped around something small in front of her. She doesn't say anything as she walks over to me.

"Here." She reaches her hand out.

It's a mini Reese's cup. My favorite.

"Why are you bringing me this?" I ask as I grab the chocolate.

Marie shrugs. "I have a few pieces left in my Halloween stash. Seemed like you could use it." Without another word, she turns on her heel and leaves my room, closing the door behind her.

I stare at the little Reese's for a few seconds. My eyes prickle. Am I going to cry?

8:28 P.M.

Yes, yes I am. A tear slowly runs down my face. I swipe at it. This is stupid.

I unwrap the candy and pop it into my mouth.

The tears keep pouring out of my eyes, and I keep swiping at them. Why am I crying? It's a stupid Reese's.

But it was really nice of Marie to bring it to me, especially knowing how she hoards her candy.

And I had a really crappy day.

And everything feels like a mess.

I can't keep it bottled up anymore. The floodgates open, and I'm full-on crying, alone, in my bed. I couldn't even tell you exactly why. But it's a cry so deep, I'm not even making any noise. My mouth is open, tears are streaming down my face, but no sound is coming out.

I gasp for air, and it stops as suddenly as it started.

I feel better.

I mean, I'm still annoyed that Andy has a new girlfriend. I'm still feeling conflicted about Matt. I'm still jealous that my friends are in love and I'm all alone.

But, it's all less than before.

MONDAY, JANUARY 10TH

8:54 A.M.
ART

Matt gives me a small, tight-lipped smile as I come into class today. We don't talk, but it feels like progress.

12:35 P.M.
BIOLOGY

Andy's in his seat when I come into bio. I make a point to give him a wave and a friendly smile. He sits up and smiles brightly back at me.

That's better.

7:02 P.M.
HOME

I text the girls.

> **Me:** Matt smiled at me today.

> **Ruby:** Ooer!

> **Cher:** Did you talk?

> **Me:** No. But that's ok I guess.

> **Me:** Also, I'm happy for you both. That you're, like, in love or whatever.

> **Ruby:** Or whatever. LOL.

> **Me:** You know what I mean!

7:31 P.M.
MARIE'S BEDROOM

I knock on Marie's bedroom door. After a few seconds, it swings open, and my little sister stands in front of me.

She's getting taller. I don't think I've grown much, if at all this year. I read somewhere that you don't really grow after your period comes, so I guess I'll be kind of short forever. But Marie clearly has—her head comes up to about my nose now. I hadn't noticed before.

"Yes?" she says, one hand on the door and the other on her hip.

"What are you doing?" I ask her.

"Why?" She narrows her eyes at me, closing the door a hair.

"No need to get all twitchy. I was going to see if you wanted to practice doing your hair."

Her hand goes to the bun at the nape of her neck. She hasn't been rocking the colonial pony as much lately, but her bun is still pretty low and droopy.

Marie takes a step back and opens the door to let me in. "Okay," she says quietly.

8:02 P.M.

Marie prances down the stairs to Mom and Dad, who are in the living room. Mom is reading a book on the couch. Dad is "resting his eyes" in his recliner chair while the TV plays in the background.

"Hello!" Marie announces to the room, spinning around with her arms out.

Mom looks up, and Dad opens his eyes. Mom glances at me, standing quietly behind Marie, who is now in the center of the room with one hand on her hip.

"Sooooo, what do you think?" She puts her hands on either side of her face. Her auburn hair is in a ballerina bun on top of her head. I helped her do the bun part, but she did the ponytail part herself. It took a while for her to figure it out, and she kept complaining that her arms were getting tired, but we got there. And it turned out pretty cute.

Mom closes her book and claps her hands together.

"Very impressive," Dad says.

Marie nods, satisfied, and heads back upstairs. I turn to follow, but Mom stops me.

"Emma?"

"Yeah?"

"Thank you." Mom smiles at me with shiny eyes. I glance at Dad, who gives me a smile, too.

"For what?" I didn't really do anything.

"Being a good sister," Mom says softly.

Something pleasant swirls in my chest, and I nod.

9:38 P.M.
IN BED

Today was a good day.

CHAPTER 35

ALERT. ALERT.

TUESDAY, JANUARY 11TH

7:07 A.M.

KITCHEN

Marie comes bounding down the stairs and into the kitchen. She grabs a bowl and some cereal and sits down across from me at the table. She's humming quietly. Her hair is back in her colonial pony.

"Marie, what about your ballerina bun?" I ask tentatively. Maybe she was having a hard time getting the ponytail high enough.

Marie shrugs. "I like my low pony," she says matter-of-factly.

"Are you sure? I can help you—"

Marie cuts me off. "Yes, Emma. I like my hair like this."

I sigh but stop myself from rolling my eyes. "Okay, if you're sure."

"I am. Who cares what anyone else thinks? Forget them." She shrugs and goes back to her breakfast.

FRIDAY, FEBRUARY 4TH
7:55 A.M.
MY LOCKER

Ruby and I are chatting at my locker before first period. Ruby glances over my shoulder, and her eyes widen slightly.

"Be cool," she says out of the corner of her mouth.

I am not cool, so of course, I look over my shoulder and see Matt walking by. I turn swiftly back to Ruby, hoping he didn't see me checking him out. Ruby and I stare at each other, both grimacing.

Weird. He doesn't usually come this way. I lean slightly and watch him over Ruby's shoulder. He never turns back, but my heart still flutters in my chest.

"Is that new?" Ruby asks.

I nod, staring down the hallway, even though Matt has already turned the corner. Ruby closes my locker and comes around to stand next to me.

"I smell love brewing." She hip-bumps me.

"Shut up," I say, but I also let a little flame of hope light in my chest.

8:54 A.M.
ART

I feel jittery as I walk into second period but try to rationalize with myself. There's no proof Matt walked down that specific hallway this morning to see me. He didn't even say anything to us. He probably got dropped off at the door there or something.

Matt glances up and gives me a small, close-lipped smile. I blush but return the gesture, hoping he doesn't notice the pink of my cheeks.

That flame in my chest burns a tiny bit brighter.

FRIDAY, FEBRUARY 18TH

9:44 A.M.

ART

Matt gives me his usual smile, like he has every day for the past two weeks. Class goes on like usual. I half pay attention to whatever directions Ms. Lesh gives us while the rest of my brain thinks about Matt, wondering if he's looking at me. I pretend to check the clock behind me while, really, I'm casually sneaking glances at Matt.

Today, when I turn to "check the time," Matt is staring at me. His eyes dart back to his drawing, and my cheeks burn as I whip around in my seat.

That hasn't happened before. I stare, unmoving, at the paper in front of me. What does it mean? Was he watching me? Does he always watch me? What is he thinking?

The bell rings and startles me out of my thoughts. As everyone shuffles out, Ms. Lesh reminds us that our stills are due in a week. I sigh, my pitiful drawing of Albus staring up at me.

I close my sketchbook and stand up, instinctively glancing at the table behind me. Matt is already standing, but he's looking at me again.

"See ya," he says, and then he turns and walks out the door. I don't even have time to say anything.

It's tiny, but it's something. My heart soars.

WEDNESDAY, FEBRUARY 23RD

8:54 A.M.

ART

"Hey," Matt says when I walk into class. Another first.

"Hi," I say back.

These are the only words we speak to each other.

THURSDAY, FEBRUARY 24TH
8:01 P.M.

Today Matt said, "Hey," and "See ya."

I spend far too long thinking about these three words.

What does it mean? Does he want to talk more? Is he just being nice? And a very small voice in the back of my head dares to ask, *Does he like me?*

TUESDAY, MARCH 1ST
9:45 A.M.
ART

Matt said his usual "Hey" at the start of class today, but I swear his eyes lingered on me as I sat down. I could feel it. It made my whole body vibrate.

The bell rings, and I gather my stuff like usual. Behind me, Matt hesitates at his seat. He adjusts his books under his arm. I'm expecting the usual, "See ya," but something else happens instead.

We lock eyes. My heart feels like it's twirling in circles inside my chest.

"It's my birthday," he blurts out.

"Oh," I say, taken aback. I wasn't expecting a chat, much less a birthday announcement. "Happy birthday." I put my hand up for a high five. He looks at it for a second before hitting it.

I feel the flush rush up my neck and onto my face. What was that? Why did I give him a high five?

He's still standing there. I don't know what to do, so I start toward the door. Matt falls into step beside me. I swallow and try to mentally calm the alarms blaring in my brain.

ALERT. ALERT. BOY IS DOING SOMETHING. ALERT. ALERT.

I don't know what to do or what to say. I can feel the energy radiating off his body next to me. He lets me pass through the door ahead of him. Do I wait for him?

I keep walking, but slowly. Matt catches up. My heart pauses its twirling to do a flip-flop. What should I say? I don't want to ruin this.

PROCEED WITH CAUTION, my brain warns.

"Are you doing anything fun for your birthday?" I ask.

He shrugs. "Not really. Tuesday's kind of a boring day for a birthday." He pauses, looking right at me. His eyes are a soft, soothing brown. So different from Andy's deep blue ones, which were like diving into the ocean. Matt's are like being wrapped in a warm blanket.

"Anyways," Matt says. "I'm this way." He gestures to the right. "English."

I point up ahead. "Spanish."

"Ha," he lets out a chuckle, and I can see his full, lopsided smile. I bite my lip, trying not to let on how much of a thrill I'm getting out of this conversation.

"Well, see ya." He lifts a hand slightly as he crosses behind me to turn down the hallway.

I let out a heavy sigh.

WHAT DOES IT MEAN? my brain asks.

I'm not sure. I take a deep breath, trying to calm the buzzing throughout my body. My legs are shaky as I walk the rest of the way to Spanish.

11:51 A.M.
LUNCH

"Alejandra says I should get the sweater, but I don't know, it feels kind of impersonal. It's her *fortieth* birthday!" Ruby says.

I nod, waiting my turn to talk.

"Emma, are you listening to me? This is important. My mother is turning forty. I need her present to be perfect. You are not helping."

"I am, I promise. It's…" I bite my lip and lean in closer to her. "I have news," I say conspiratorially.

Ruby gasps and drops the sandwich in her hands onto her tray. Then she spews out a list of questions at me. "What is it? Is it good news or bad news? Is it Matt? Cher? Your dad? What's going on? Why didn't you tell me this morning?"

I put my hand on her arm to stop her from going into full freak-out mode.

"Good news. It happened this morning."

Ruby puts her hands flat on the table and levels her gaze on me. Her dark-brown eyes are eager.

"Dish," she demands. I smile and stifle a giggle.

"Okay, so in art this morning—"

"Oooooooh so it *is* about Matt!" Ruby shouts.

"Ruby! Shh!" I slap her arm and glance around. She mimes zipping her lips and gestures for me to continue.

I tell her all about my interaction with Matt today—the way he blurted out his birthday, walking down the hallway together, and the butterflies fluttering nonstop in my stomach.

When I finish, Ruby is smirking and shaking her head lightly.

"He totally likes you."

"What? How do you know?" I don't want to get my hopes up, but that fire lights in my chest again.

"Because." Ruby takes a bite of her sandwich before continuing. She starts counting on her fingers. "You had the cartwheel night. The meaningful looks. Then, he was mad at you when you broke up with Andy. Like, why did he care, really? Then, he was ignoring you. Now, he's not only saying hi, but he's walking with you in the hallway?! Sounds like a love story progression to me," she says, waving her hand dismissively.

"Hmmm." I munch on a Cheeto, lost in thought. It's kind of confusing. After Andy, Matt was mad at me, then he was ignoring me, and now we're talking? That doesn't mean he likes me.

But, clearly, something is happening, so it also doesn't mean that he *doesn't* like me…

Ruby points a long finger at me. "Exactly," she says, as if she knows what I'm thinking.

FRIDAY, MARCH 4TH

10:01 A.M.

SPANISH

Matt and I have walked down the hallway together every day since Tuesday. On Wednesday, he told me about the cake his mom made for his birthday. (Yellow cake with chocolate frosting. His little sister covered it in sprinkles.) Yesterday, he asked me if I had any siblings. (We both have younger sisters, and he has an older sister.) Today, we talked about our weekend plans.

"I have a soccer tournament all weekend, which is cool I guess, but I have to get up early on Saturday and Sunday," Matt said, moving closer to me to avoid two large boys barrelling down the hallway, PE uniforms slung over their shoulders.

Matt's shoulder briefly bumped against mine. Touching him, even if it wasn't on purpose, lit a fire inside my body. Everything warmed, from my cheeks, to the spot on my shoulder where we touched, all the way down to my toes.

"Yeah, that kind of sucks," I told him, pretending like his shoulder touching mine had no effect whatsoever on me. My brain felt fuzzy, though, like everything was happening so fast around me, and it couldn't keep up. Somehow, I managed to conjure up some words. "I'm hanging out with Ruby and my friend Cher tomorrow. We're going to the mall. I think I want to get a soft pretzel."

Matt laughed. "Oh, yeah. A soft pretzel with cheese from the mall is the best."

"Right?" I laughed, too, trying to continue wading through the static in my brain. "Ruby's always trying to say cinnamon raisin pretzels are superior." I shook my head. "I don't know what's wrong with that girl sometimes."

Matt laughed again, this time turning his face and smiling. "You're funny," he said. His smile slipped as we reached the English hallway. He hesitated, and our eyes locked for half a second. But in that half a second, I was frozen to the ground and everything around me got quiet.

Matt cleared his throat, breaking me out of my trance. He glanced down at his shoes and then back up at me. "See ya," he said before turning down the hall.

I took a deep breath, my mind finally clearing a bit, and made my way to Spanish, where I'm sitting now. I'm supposed to be conjugating verbs, but I can't stop replaying Matt's laugh in my head.

Something is happening.

SATURDAY, MARCH 5TH
4:07 P.M.
MALL FOOD COURT

"Okay, it's time. We need to discuss Emma and Matt and the hallway," Ruby announces over the din of conversation in the food court. Smells of pizza, fried rice, pretzels, popcorn, cookies, and a hundred other things mingle in the air.

Ruby licks the last of her ice cream off her spoon and raises her eyebrows at me. Cher wipes her hands on a napkin and nods. We filled her in on everything with nightly updates throughout the week.

I blush and pluck another piece of my pretzel off. "It's not that big of a deal," I say, even though it feels like a big deal.

"Yes it is, Emma," Cher says.

Ruby points her spoon at me and gives me a smirk that says, *I told you*.

I roll my eyes, very aware of the way my heart is racing. Ruby and Cher both stare at me. "What do you think it means?" I ask quietly.

"He liiiikessss you," Ruby says slowly, as if she's explaining something to a toddler.

"I don't know…" I don't want to get my hopes up.

"Don't be stupid. If he didn't like you, he wouldn't be walking you to class," Cher says.

"He's not walking me to class," I remind them. "We walk together to our respective classes, which happen to be close to each other."

"Whatever. Still, he would've kept ignoring you if he didn't have a reason to talk to you," Cher says, raising an eyebrow at me. She turns to Ruby for backup.

"And the reason is he likes you," Ruby says. She scoops some more ice cream onto her spoon. "Man, I wish my morning classes were closer to you so I could see this go down. I think you need a second set of eyes to confirm what's happening."

I nod. "That would help."

Ruby sits up straighter in her chair and points a long, slender finger in the air. "I have an idea," she says with a mischievous smile.

"Uh-oh," Cher says.

CHAPTER 36

Maybe Ruby was right.

MONDAY, MARCH 7TH

7:53 A.M.

MY LOCKER

"Let's review the plan," Ruby says as I reach for my pencil case on the top shelf of my locker. "Step one: go to class. Step two: with ten minutes left in class, I ask Ms. Frank for a pass to the nurse, pretending I have a stomach ache." She pauses and grips her stomach, as if in pain. "Step three: walk very slowly to the nurse and ask for a tampon—"

I interrupt her. "When did you start using tampons?" I've still only ever used pads. I'm scared to use a tampon. Will it hurt? How do I know it's in far enough? Or how do I know if it's in too far?

"Yeah," Ruby says, slightly impatient. "I had to use one when my mom and I stayed at that resort over winter break. I couldn't *not* go swimming while we were there. It's actually way better than a pad. Plus, you'll have to use one soon. We have swimming in PE this semester." She waves her hand in front of her face. "But let's not lose sight of the plan here."

I can't believe Ruby didn't tell me she started using tampons. I feel like such a baby. Also, let's pray I don't have my period during the swimming unit. How mortifying. What if someone saw the string?

Ruby continues with the plan while these thoughts are buzzing around in my brain. "Step four: go to the bathroom near the art room and wait for the bell to ring. Maybe stop at the vending machine for a snack," she adds, lightly scratching her chin. She shakes her head. "Step five: when the bell rings, walk to the art room and 'bump into' you and Matt." She winks. "Step six: observe."

We both nod, agreeing the plan is solid. The warning bell rings.

"Shoot," Ruby whispers, and without another word, she sprints down the hall to first period.

I follow behind her, walking at my normal pace. My chest feels tight. Why? I can go about my usual day. Ruby's the one doing the heavy lifting. I take a deep breath as I walk to English, trying to shake off the jitters I feel.

9:46 A.M.
HALLWAY

Matt and I are barely out of the art room when Ruby, who was clearly waiting for us, steps into our path.

"Oh my God, Emma! I forgot you had art second period. What's going on? Can I walk with you guys?" she asks quickly and loudly.

"Hey, Rubs," I say, widening my eyes at her and internally screaming, *Take it down a notch!* Ruby sticks her tongue out at me.

I glance at Matt but can't read his expression. His mouth pinches at the corner before he clicks his tongue and says, "I've got to go. Forgot something in my locker."

Ruby opens her mouth to say something, but before she can, he's gone. My stomach lurches with disappointment.

"I assume that is not how things usually go," Ruby says with a wince.

I shake my head. I don't feel like talking.

Why did Matt run away like that?

11:57 A.M.
LUNCH

"Maybe he doesn't like me," I squeak out. I glance around to be sure no one is listening, but everyone is too engrossed in their own lunchtime conversations to care about my pitiful one.

The group of sophomores who sit at one end of our table are arguing about who should have won the Battle of the Bands at the rec center over the weekend. The girls who sit at the other end are gathered around a phone, intently watching a makeup tutorial, the volume so loud I'm sure they can't hear me anyway.

Ruby munches on some chips. When she finishes chewing, she places the bag on the table, folds her hands, and looks me right in the eye.

"I've been thinking about it all morning," she says. "I'm not going to lie, at first I was kind of thinking the same thing."

My heart plummets into the pit of my stomach. I examine my hands, my throat tight.

"But," Ruby continues, "the more I think about it, the more I think it actually shows that he *does* like you."

I pick my head up. I don't say anything, but my brain is firing on all cylinders. What? How? Why?

Ruby puts her fingers at her temples like it's giving her a headache. "I know. I don't think I heard a thing Mr. Milo said in biology." She pauses. "God, I'm so glad I don't like boys." She quirks an eyebrow, and I giggle.

Feeling a little lighter, I prod Ruby. "Explain."

She takes a deep breath and raises her face to the ceiling. She huffs and returns her gaze to me. "Okay, so, you dated Andy," she starts slowly. "Andy's best friend is Matt." She waits for me to react.

I raise my eyebrows and roll my hands over each other, encouraging her to get to the point.

"Yeah, yeah, yeah," she says, waving me off. "I'll get there. The buildup is what matters."

"Ugh, fine," I complain.

"So, you and Andy. Andy and Matt. Everything is peachy. You and Andy are in love—"

"Not in love," I correct her.

"Whatever. You and Andy are in like. But you and Matt have a few moments, like the cartwheel. Perhaps feelings start swirling between you and Matt. Maybe he notices. Maybe he pretends it's not happening, like you did."

My heart jumps as I think back to Matt throwing me over his shoulder.

"*Then*," Ruby continues dramatically, "you and Andy break up. Andy is heartbroken. Matt, as his best friend, comforts him." She pauses, moving her hand down an imaginary timeline. "You and Andy get back together." Ruby rolls her eyes, and I glare back. "And then you break up again. Andy is devastated, again. Matt has to comfort him, *again*."

"Okay, I get it," I say, annoyed. "I broke Andy's heart twice."

Ruby ignores me. "But Matt is confused. He knows his nether region perks up when you're around—"

"Ruby!" I gasp.

She grins but continues. "But he also has to be there for his friend, so he channels those sparks into anger."

I nod slowly, thinking about Matt telling me to stop messing with Andy, and the cold shoulder he gave me at the beginning of the semester.

"Then—and this is the good part," she says pointing at me, "Andy gets a new girlfriend. He's not so heartbroken over you anymore. Matt stops feeling as guilty that seeing you in art every day gives him a thrill. He starts to warm up to you. Then you start chatting and walking to class together."

I nod again, waiting for the big reveal.

"Then you smooch," she finishes casually. She picks her bag of chips back up, grabs a few, and puts them in her mouth, all the while waiting for my reaction.

"That's it? Also, we have not kissed."

"Obviously," she says, waving her chip bag around, "but it's coming."

"What about that recap brought you to the realization that he likes me?"

"Oh, duh!" Ruby smacks her forehead. "I forgot the most important bit."

I sigh in frustration. Lunch is going to be over by the time she gets to the point.

"He's getting friendly, walking you to class, admiring your beautiful smile, blah, blah, blah. Then I show up today, and he must have figured out I was trying to do some sleuthing."

"I wonder what gave you away."

Ruby narrows her eyes but flicks away my sarcasm. "He realizes he likes you. And you like him. And that I know both of these things. And as a result, *you* probably know both of these things. But you're still Andy's ex-girlfriend, and he shouldn't like you. But he does. And he doesn't know what to do. And all of that came to him in the fifteen seconds I saw him after class, and his little boy brain couldn't handle it, so he ran."

I stare at Ruby, silent. Her big, brown eyes sparkle as she watches me process this information.

I want to believe it, but I don't know if I do. It's so easy for me to forget the Andy of it all. I let myself grasp at the hope Ruby's theory offers.

"So what do I do, oh Wise One?" I ask.

At the name, Ruby does a triumphant hair flip, but her smile falters half a second later. "No idea. My brain got this far and then basically imploded." She puts her hand to the side of her head and makes an explosion sound.

My mind swirls with disappointment, guilt, excitement, hope—I can barely distinguish any of the feelings. I take a deep breath, then slouch forward, resting my head on my arms.

I wish Cher was here. She would know what to do. Do I believe Ruby's theory? Do I give up? Either way, what do I do next?

I groan loudly. "Why does it have to be this hard?"

Ruby pauses her munching to simply say, "Andy." I lift my head, and she shrugs.

3:19 P.M.
MY LOCKER

Ruby, Alejandra, and I are at my locker. I'm reaching in to grab my backpack when Ruby interrupts Alejandra's complaint about the spring band concert.

"Hey! Matt! Hi!"

I freeze. My heart leaps into my throat. My arms feel both light and heavy at the same time. I pull my head out of my locker, and there he is, a few feet away. Matt hikes his backpack up on his left shoulder as he slowly approaches us.

I don't say anything. What's he doing here?

"Uh, hey," he says, raising his hand in a half-hearted wave. We lock eyes, only for a second, but my entire body blazes. Before I can gather myself enough to say anything, he's reaching his arm out. There's something in his hand. And he's giving it to me?

I grab it from him, and my fingers graze his, my heart dropping into the depths of my chest and then back up again like I'm on a rollercoaster. It's a small piece of paper, like it was torn from the corner of a notebook, folded in half.

"It's, uh, just something I drew while I was bored in geography today. I know you have a cat, so… I thought you might like it."

My fingers tremble as I open the paper. I hope Matt doesn't notice. When I see what's on it, my breath catches. It's the cutest little doodle of a kitty I've ever seen. It's drawn in pencil, so the cat is gray, like Albus, and it has a little smirk under its tiny nose, like it knows something I don't. Its paw is raised in a wave.

"Oh," comes out of my mouth involuntarily. My brain is going a thousand miles a minute, but I also feel like I'm stuck in mud, like my brain is moving too fast and the rest of my body is unable to keep up, or move at all.

I don't think I even manage to smile before Matt says, "Okay, well, see ya." He steps around the three of us and heads quickly down the hall. I stare after him, my hand still holding up the doodle, as he walks out of the building.

Alejandra tries to pick her story back up as if something momentous did not just happen.

"Interesting..." Ruby says, interrupting her girlfriend again. Alejandra turns her head between Ruby and me a couple times.

"What? Did I miss something? Neither of you are listening to me." She rolls her eyes. Ruby reaches an arm out and pulls her in to kiss her on the cheek quickly, then runs a hand over her face as she shushes Alejandra.

I'm still silent. My body is still hot. My mind is both racing and totally blank. I cannot form a complete thought, except...

Maybe Ruby was right.

CHAPTER 37

I didn't even look at him.

MONDAY, MARCH 7TH

9:38 PM

IN BED

My brain still hasn't recovered from today's events. I couldn't focus on my homework at all. I did it, but I have no idea if any of it makes sense. I barely said a word during dinner. Which worked out because Marie did not shut up about Ally wearing a low pony to school today.

I can't stop thinking about Matt.

I pick up the small paper sitting on my nightstand and unfold it for the thousandth time tonight. I stare at the kitty, smirking as if it has all the answers but can't tell me.

Did Matt draw this *for* me? Or he happened to draw a cat and *then* thought of me? I guess either way, he was thinking about me. And that has to be good, right?

I fold the paper back up and put it under my pillow. I lie back gently and stare at the ceiling. I sit up again and lift my pillow. *That's weird*, I scold myself, and I put the doodle back on my nightstand, next to the lamp. I turn the light off and roll over.

9:40 P.M.

What do I do tomorrow? Do I say something? Do I act like nothing happened?

Did anything *actually* happen, or am I letting myself buy into Ruby's theory? It was just a doodle.

9:50 P.M.

But it was a doodle he made. For me.

I reach over, feeling for the paper in the darkness, just to make sure it's still there.

10:01 P.M.

Even if Ruby is right, what happens now? Today doesn't change the fact that Matt is still Andy's best friend.

11:12 P.M.

But he specifically came to my locker to give me the doodle. That has to mean something.

Cher agreed. The three of us were on the phone for over an hour and a half tonight, dissecting the day's events. Cher was immediately on board with Ruby's theory and said the doodle proves it.

11:14 P.M.

Is Marie bringing back the colonial pony? Should I wear one?

TUESDAY, MARCH 8TH

8:54 A.M.

ART

My heart has been pounding since the bell rang at the end of first period, but it immediately sinks as I walk into the art classroom. Matt's chair is empty. He always beats me to class.

I slouch in my seat, crossing my arms. I don't know why, but I'm suddenly annoyed. I can't be bothered to go get my project before class starts. Instead, I sulk.

When the bell rings, I sigh, disappointed. I decided this morning that I would wait and see what Matt did or said and go from there, but I guess I'm not getting any answers. I sigh again and slide further down in my seat.

9:06 A.M.

Ms. Lesh gives directions for the day. "We're continuing our work on cross-hatching. If you haven't already, please grab your project and your item. I'll be making the rounds to provide feedback and guidance as you work."

The door opens, and everyone turns to see who it is. I freeze, and a jolt goes through me when Matt's eyes immediately land on me. They whip away quickly, though, as he walks to the front of the room to give Ms. Lesh his pass.

He has to walk past my table to get to his own. The girl sitting in front of me has one piece of hair still wavy that she must have missed when she straightened it. I stare at the lone wave, pretending not to watch Matt approaching out of the corner of my eye.

He takes his seat behind me. I didn't say anything. I didn't even look at him. But I'm still disappointed. What was I expecting? For him to drop to his knees and declare his love for me?

"Hey," he says, low and quiet, from behind me. My heart skips.

"Hey," I say, turning over my shoulder.

He doesn't say anything else, but he stares at me for an extra second before pulling his paper closer to him. I bite my lip as I turn back around, fighting a smile. Why am I smiling? What did that mean? Did it mean anything?

9:45 A.M.

At the end of class, I take my time packing my stuff up, trying to gauge what Matt is going to do. He glances at the door, then back at me.

"How's your project going?" he asks. He lingers at his table, shifting his weight on his feet. He's wearing a dark gray T-shirt today instead of his usual hoodie. His arms are lean but not gangly. A muscle flexes as he adjusts his books, and my mind flashes to him throwing me over his shoulder.

I sigh and roll my eyes, cool and casual, even though my brain and my heart are racing each other to see who can go the fastest, and my armpits are literally sweating even though I was freezing during class. I try to ignore everything happening in my body and not stare at his.

"Fine, I guess. I don't think I'm ever going to draw a coffee cup again, but..." I shrug, picking my books up and turning to the door. Matt turns with me.

My brain shouts, *SOMETHING IS HAPPENING.* While my heart shouts, *HE DOES LIKE YOU.*

"Ohhhh," he says, putting a hand to his forehead. His hair is getting longer, and a couple curls get in the way of his warm, brown eyes. I'm so distracted by this, I almost don't hear him say, "*That's* what you're drawing. I thought maybe you were working on a blob."

It takes me a second to register that he's teasing me.

"Hey!" I say, lightly pushing him on the arm. "I'm *very* talented."

He raises his eyebrows, and we both burst into laughter. His lopsided grin spreads across his face, and my heart soars.

"Okay," I admit. "I'm not."

We continue to laugh as we walk down the hallway. Together.

Chapter 38

You need to woman-up and do it.

"I think he likes me," I announce to the room.

"Who?" Alejandra asks as she taps on the iPad. "Girl of My Heart" by Celsius plays while she curates a playlist for our evening. Ruby is behind her, braiding Alejandra's long, dark hair into two fancy French braids. Cher sits at my desk, scrolling through something on my laptop, and I'm lying on my bed.

I sit up and grab Piggy, holding him in front of me like a security blanket. I look at Alejandra like she's lost her mind.

Ruby and I are thinking the same thing because she leans over Alejandra's shoulder and says, "Who? Alejandra! You are a smart, smart lady. Who do you think Emma's talking about?" She clicks her tongue and returns to her braiding as she says to me, "I told you." The corners of her lips turn up into a satisfied smirk.

Cher comes to sit on the bed with me. She fiddles with her new bangs and bounces on the edge before scooting back against the wall. She nods. "Yeah, I think so, too."

Every night this week, I sent Ruby and Cher my Matt updates—whether we walked to class together (yes, every day), what we talked about (drawing, music, the superior lunch snacks), and if he walked past my locker at the end of the day (yes, *twice*, and he even stopped to say hi as he passed yesterday).

Cher looks at me evenly. "I think it's time to do something."

"What do you mean? Do what?" I furrow my brow. What is she scheming?

"He's not going to make any moves because of Andy, but you clearly like each other. If he's not going to do anything, I think you should." Cher shrugs, examining her nails. "It's the twenty-first century. You don't have to wait for a boy to make the first move."

"You don't need a boy at all, if you ask me," Ruby says, leaning forward again, this time to kiss Alejandra on the cheek. Alejandra glances quickly at Cher and me before smiling up at Ruby.

"Let's slide into his DMs," Cher says, getting back to the point.

My stomach clenches. "I don't know..." While I agree with Cher that I don't *need* a boy to make the first move, I would like it if he did. What if he *doesn't* like me? What if I come on too strong, or say something embarrassing? What if he says he's not interested? What if he says nothing at all? I don't want to ruin what we have now. I can't go back to the silent treatment.

I don't say any of this out loud.

"Cher's right," Ruby says. "Matt isn't going to pounce because of Andy. You need to woman-up and do it. I believe in you."

Out my bedroom window, the sky is mostly dark but hanging on to some purple and even a few small pink streaks. I rub Piggy's leg for reassurance. I take a deep breath and sigh, trying to calm the jitters throughout my body. I turn back to my friends.

"Okay, fine."

Ruby hops up and starts cheering, Cher bounces on the bed next to me, waving her arms in the air, and Alejandra simply smiles up at me.

I lie back on the pillows behind me and stare at the ceiling. I guess I'm doing this.

8:40 P.M.

"No. Too aloof," Cher says, grabbing my phone out of my hand and rereading what we've written so far. The four of us sit in a row on my bed with our backs up against the wall, Alejandra next to my pillows, then Ruby, me, and Cher at the end.

We've been working on this message for ages, trying to get it perfectly right. We're drafting it in the Notes app so we don't accidentally send it early. Can you imagine? My stomach turns at the thought.

"Can we take a break?" Ruby asks. She rubs her stomach. "I'm starving. I neeeed a snack." She slithers out from between Alejandra and me and off the bed.

I nod in agreement. "I need a break, too. Let's make a pizza."

Ruby pulls her fist down in front of her in a celebratory gesture. Then she puts her hands out. "Wait, no sausage, though. Alejandra doesn't like it."

Cher snorts from behind me, still on the bed. We all ignore her.

"Same," I assure Alejandra.

"Not the same," Alejandra says, giving Cher a sidelong glance.

After a second, Ruby's mouth drops open. I'm still not getting it.

"You dirty girls," Ruby says, pointing at Alejandra and Cher laughing on the bed.

My cheeks warm. What am I missing?

Ruby turns back to me and, seeing my confusion, says, "Get it? Sausage?" I stare at her blankly. "Alejandra and I don't like *sausage...*"

It finally dawns on me. Sausage. Like, boys. Ruby and Alejandra don't like boys.

"Oh my God!" I shout. I push Ruby back onto the bed. We're all laughing, and it feels so good. Maybe I don't need Matt, or any boy for that matter. Maybe I just need to laugh with my friends.

10:02 P.M.

Alejandra had to be home at 10:00, and almost as soon as she leaves, Ruby makes an announcement.

"I have news." She turns the music down on the speaker and sits on the corner of my bed. Cher and I give her our full attention. Ruby pauses, smiling down at her knees while she twists one of her braids around her finger.

She takes a deep breath and says, "Alejandra and I have done more than kissing lately." She looks up at us through her lashes, biting her lip.

"Ooooh! What does that mean?" I ask.

Ruby covers her face with her hands for a second, then takes a deep breath. "I don't know why I'm feeling so twirly talking about this." She giggles and shakes her head.

"Second or third base?" Cher interrupts.

"What exactly *is* third base?" Ruby asks.

Cher thinks for a second. I look back and forth between them. I have no idea.

"I think it's anything below the belt before sex," Cher says.

"That's a wide range of possibilities," Ruby says.

"If you're not going to get to the point, I also have news," Cher says with an eye roll. She doesn't wait for us to respond before continuing. "Jacob and I have gone to third base. Hands only. Just me." She says it confidently, but her cheeks flush.

"Same!" Ruby shouts. "Except, both of us."

"What?" I gasp. "Oh my God. When? Tell me everything! What's it like? Were you scared? Did it feel good? I have so many questions."

Cher and Ruby look at each other and giggle. Now I blush. But I also lean forward. I need answers!

1:01 A.M.
IN BED

Ruby and Cher filled me in on *everything*. It was very informative, actually.

It's kind of crazy. They've both been to third base, and I'm over here trying to figure out if a boy even likes me. I can barely get to first.

1:12 A.M.

Honestly, I don't think I'm ready to go to third base anyway. The idea terrifies me. Will I ever feel comfortable enough around someone else to do that?

1:16 A.M.

I think the message for Matt is pretty good, but I didn't send it. I'm not ready. My chest constricts just thinking about it. I'll wait a couple more days so I can be sure he *actually* likes me. It's too risky right now.

1:39 A.M.

Sometimes I feel like I'm being left behind. Like Ruby and Cher are both moving forward and growing up so much faster than me—without me. Like I'm their dorky friend who had the cringey boyfriend who felt her up one time but now doesn't have anyone.

It's like I'm standing under the spotlight on a stage, alone, with the audience staring at me, whispering and snickering.

Who is that girl? Why is she here? Why is she standing like that? Why doesn't she do something?

She can't. She's scared.

CHAPTER 39

Has he read it?

FRIDAY, MARCH 24TH

7:02 P.M.

CHER'S LIVING ROOM

"It's been two weeks. You have to send it. What are you waiting for?" Cher demands. One hand is on her hip while she uses the other to get the movie set up. It's only the two of us tonight. Ruby and Alejandra went to see a play with Alejandra's mom and cousin. Something about newspapers, I think.

My face warms, but I don't say anything. I tuck my phone under my thigh so Cher doesn't try to snatch it from my hands and do something crazy.

Cher points the remote at me. "Silence is not an answer," she says. Then she shudders. "Ew, that sounded like my mom." I giggle because she's not wrong.

Cher turns her body fully toward me now. "Seriously. Why haven't you sent it yet?"

I shrug. Cher rolls her eyes and sits next to me on the couch. She takes a deep breath.

Her voice is softer when she says, "If you don't send it, you'll never find out. Even if he doesn't like you, wouldn't you rather know?"

"No," I say immediately. God, how mortifying. Cher wouldn't understand. She's smart and beautiful and confident. Boys like her. Why wouldn't they? Look at her and Jacob—they started dating, like, the first week of school.

"Oh come on, Emma," Cher says quickly. She's losing patience with me. "Don't be such a baby." She stands up to get snacks from the kitchen, leaving me alone with my cheeks on fire, my eyes prickling, and my heart racing. Cher's words hurt.

But maybe she's right.

I take a deep, shuddering breath. I open my phone and read the message. I gulp. My fingers hover over the screen.

And then I send it.

7:12 P.M.

Cher comes back into the room and starts to say, "Emma, I'm—" but stops in front of the couch. "Why are you lying like that?"

My legs are sprawled out in front of me, my arms are stretched out to the side, and my head is thrown back. After I hit send, I flung my body back onto the couch and haven't moved since.

"I sent it," I say without moving.

Cher's face is blank for half a second, then her eyes go wide. "No, you didn't… you did not… did you, really?"

I nod, still frozen on the couch.

She squeals and runs over, placing the bowl of popcorn and chocolate-covered pretzels on the end table haphazardly. "Oh my God, oh my God, oh my God! Emma! I'm so proud of you!" She claps her hands together. "Sit up. Come on, you look weird."

I drag my body upright. I can't believe I did it. My heart continues to slam against my chest.

"Ruby is going to be so mad she missed this," Cher says excitedly, grabbing a pretzel from behind her. She sits criss-cross applesauce on the couch, facing me.

"Did he respond?" I hand Cher my phone because I'm too scared to look for myself.

Cher types in my code and glances at the screen. Her face falls a little before she says, "No."

A knot forms in my stomach, and I clench my jaw. My mouth feels dry as I ask the next question.

"Has he read it?"

She pauses, her green eyes locked on mine. "Yeah…" she says with a grimace.

8:47 P.M.

Cher's fingers fly furiously across her phone screen. I'm sure she's texting Ruby, giving her a minute-by-minute update.

"Are you sure you don't want to spend the night?" Cher asks, pausing to look up at me. Her eyebrows are furrowed, and her mouth is pressed into a thin line.

"Yeah," I mutter. Mom is on her way to come get me. I just want to go home and crawl into my bed and not talk to anyone ever again.

CHAPTER 40

Seen 11h ago.

SATURDAY, MARCH 25TH

6:03 A.M.

IN BED

Why am I awake so early? I open my eyes and snatch my phone off the night-stand. No new notifications. The glimmer of hope that Matt had responded while I was sleeping is extinguished, and I drop my head back onto the pillow with a heavy thump. I open the message and reread it for the thousandth time.

Heyyyy,

I was telling my friends the story about doing cartwheels after the football game at the beginning of the year. Do you remember that? You tried to throw me in a garbage can, you jerk!

I guess you made up for it, though, with the cat drawing. Seriously,

I love that little guy. He actually looks a lot like my cat!

Anyways, I've had fun walking to class with you the past couple weeks. I like talking to you. I know things were a little weird for a while after the Andy breakups, but it's nice to have someone to talk to after I'm forced to think about lines and shading and my horrible art skills for an hour.

I guess what I'm really trying to say is... I like you. And I know it's weird because I dated your best friend. But I think you might like me, too.

I hope this doesn't make things weird again. I'm sorry. Actually I'm not sorry. I like you. And I hope you like me, too.

And underneath it, taunting me, is "Seen 11h ago."

I slam the phone face down onto my nightstand and roll over, pulling the covers over my head. Maybe if I go back to sleep, I'll wake up and discover this was all just a bad dream, that I never listened to my stupid, beautiful friends who don't understand that sometimes boys don't actually like you, and never sent that dumb message telling Matt all about my embarrassing, cringey feelings.

Why did I think this might work? Of course it didn't. Matt doesn't like me. I'm so stupid.

9:58 A.M.

A stream of light dances over my face and wakes me from my fitful sleep. I groan.

Mom pulls back the other half of my curtains and says, "Emma, are you ever getting up?"

"No," I say, rolling over toward the wall.

She pulls my comforter off, and I curl up into the fetal position, trying to ignore her.

She starts talking about all the things she wants me to do today. "You need to change your sheets. When was the last time we washed these?"

I put my pillow over my head, pretending I can still sleep.

Mom stops talking and sits on the edge of the bed. She's silent. My shoulders relax, and I warily lift the pillow up to peek at her over my shoulder. She's staring at me.

"Hi," she says with a small wave.

I put the pillow back over my head.

She gently shakes my shoulder. "Hey, what's going on? You're always a grump in the morning, but this is a new level."

I internally roll my eyes. It makes me even grumpier when she calls me grumpy.

"Emma." She says my name with a more serious tone. I sigh and then be-grudgingly sit up, leaning back against the wall.

Mom doesn't say anything. I don't say anything.

"I can do this all day," she says.

"No you can't," I counter.

She snorts and shakes her head before turning her sea glass eyes—the ones exactly like mine—back to me. She quirks an eyebrow. She wants me to dish, but I'm too tired. The idea of telling her about Matt and the message and my embarrassment feels like too much right now. The backs of my eyes feel tight, but I resolve that I'm not going to cry.

Mom is looking at me now like she can see the thoughts racing through my brain. Her eyes are soft, and it hurts my heart a little, knowing that she cares so much about me.

I muster up as much fake energy as I can and give her (what I hope is) a reassuring smile.

"It's nothing," I lie. "Stayed up too late watching movies."

Mom stares at me for a beat too long. She knows I'm lying. She puts her hand on my leg and squeezes.

"Okay. Come downstairs when you're ready. Marie and Dad made waffles."

I nod, the strain behind my eyes building. Mom leaves the room with one last glance over her shoulder and a half smile. She closes the door and tears immediately start streaming down my face.

Why does it make me so sad that she cares? Why does the idea of Marie and Dad making waffles also make me want to cry?

I flatten my pillow and lie back, slamming my head against it a few times.

Why doesn't Matt like me?

10:20 A.M.

After a few more minutes of wallowing, I drag my booty out of bed. My arms feel heavy as I run my hands through my hair. I grab a hair tie and pull it back into a low pony. I can see the appeal now. It's so easy, and it gets my hair out of my face.

I shuffle into the bathroom to brush my teeth and wash my face. Watery, red eyes stare back at me in the mirror. My neck is splotchy, too. I finish brushing my teeth and take a deep breath, letting it out in a huff. I splash cold water on my face, hoping it will help with the evidence of my crying.

10:31 A.M.
KITCHEN

Marie eyes me as I cross the kitchen to refill my water cup. She's at the table, munching on a waffle. I sit across from her, grabbing a plate and a couple waffles from the pile on the table. They smell so good. I drown them in syrup and start shoveling bites into my mouth. I'm suddenly ravenous.

Breaking my focus from the waffles, Mom says quietly, "Nice pony." She stirs her coffee and glances up from whatever she's reading on her iPad, her eyebrows raised and her mouth twisted like she's trying not to laugh.

I reach back and run my hand over my hair. Marie clocks it and smirks. She's wearing a low pony, too. I shrug and return to my waffles, but out of the corner of my eye, I see Mom wink at Marie. Marie giggles and gets up to put her dishes in the sink. She's humming as she crosses the room but pauses in the doorway.

"I have things to do this morning. Please don't disturb me, Emma," Marie says. I'm about to retort, but I don't have the energy. She prances out of the room and up the stairs.

"What do you have on the docket today, kiddo?" Dad asks, taking a couple gulps of milk from his glass. Gross. I hate milk.

"Homework, I guess," I mumble.

Dad nods but doesn't say anything else. I finish my waffles and get up to put my plate in the sink. Neither of my parents say anything. It's the kind of quiet that feels heavy, and I know they're going to talk about me as soon as I leave the room. I turn over my shoulder before heading up the stairs. They're leaning in toward each other, whispering.

Called it.

8:32 P.M.
BEDROOM

Nothing all day from Matt. Every time I think about him reading that message and choosing not to respond, my insides twist.

Ruby and Cher are trying to cheer me up on the phone. Ruby's face takes up the entire frame in an unflattering angle as she lays in bed. She has her purple silk bonnet and fuzzy pink teddy bear pajamas on, and she has a giant frog stuffie under her arm. Cher has her phone angled perfectly at her desk, so we can see her smooth, glowy skin and the beige loungewear set she's wearing. She pulls one of her legs up onto her chair. I'm sitting up in bed, trying not to have a double chin and look like a bald alien with my low pony.

"I can't believe I listened to you two," I whine for the hundredth time. I watch myself in the small frame at the bottom. The low pony is not doing me any favors, so I pull it out. I regret it instantly as my hair falls around my face. I push it behind my ears, but the hair sitting on my neck makes me feel squirmy, so I put the phone down for a second to reassemble my new favorite hairstyle.

"There was no way we could have known it would go like this," Ruby says. I glare at her in response. "Okay, fine. We knew it was a possibility, but I. Am. Shocked." She puts her hand to her chest. "I really thought he liked you."

"I still do," Cher says. "Just because he hasn't responded doesn't mean he doesn't like you." She puts her chin in her hand, and her eyes shift down. She's watching herself, too.

"It seems like a pretty clear indicator to me that he does not," I argue.

Cher rolls her eyes.

"Look on the bright side: it's spring break, so you don't have to see him on Monday," Ruby says. This provides a very small sense of relief.

But I will eventually have to see him. How am I supposed to face him when we go back to school? Is he going to ignore me again? Do I ignore him since he left me on read? What do I say? What do I do?

I lean my head back against the wall and groan. Ruby and Cher are both silent, staring at me with pity in their eyes.

9:02 P.M.
IN BED

I can't believe this is happening to me.

Actually, I can. Of course it's happening to me. Everyone else gets to be in love, and I'm over here crying in my bed.

I may as well resign myself to the fact that I'm going to be alone forever. I already have a cat. Maybe Mom and Dad will let me get another one so I can start working on becoming a cat lady.

I'll die alone in my apartment, with no one to care except my cats. And Ruby, probably. Cher might desert me once I get a bunch of cats. She hates cats.

9:28 P.M.

I can't stop myself from checking my messages again.

Nothing. Obviously.

What was I thinking, sending this stupid declaration of my feelings? It's so embarrassing. I pull my covers over my face to protect myself from my own actions.

9:50 P.M.

I'd actually started to believe he liked me. I mean, walking to class together, teasing me about art, the cat doodle, even the way his eyes linger on me sometimes. Did I really read all of that wrong? Did Ruby and Cher read it wrong, too?

9:54 P.M.

Is it because of Andy? HE HAS A NEW GIRLFRIEND.

A tear rolls down my cheek. I brush it away. No. I'm done crying about this. *It's fine. I don't care. I don't need him,* I lie to myself.

9:58 P.M.

Ugggghhhh. This sucks.

CHAPTER 41

Not feeling very chatty lately, eh?

THURSDAY, MARCH 30TH

12:11 P.M.

WALKING DOWN THE STREET

Ruby, Alejandra, Cher, Jacob, Jacob's friend Alec, and I meander down the street. Jacob and Alec picked us up from Ruby's house, and now we're on our way to the park to hang out.

The weather is so crappy, though. The sky is gray and dreary, and it's cold. All of us girls are wearing jackets. Ruby and Alejandra each have a hat and scarf on—which is probably a little extreme, but I have a hat on, too. Cher let me borrow her slouchy beanie hat. The boys, though, are in hoodies and basketball shorts. They have to be freezing.

I'm pretty sure Cher told Jacob to bring Alec for me. She and Ruby have been trying to distract me from Matt all week. I guess it's sort of working. Alec is cute. He's tall and kind of lanky. His brown hair is buzzed on the sides and longer on top. His eyes are greenish. He's very animated, constantly using his hands to emphasize whatever point he's making. And he's definitely paying attention to me, which feels especially nice after being ignored for six days.

He walks backward in front of us now. Jacob is to his left, peeling the bark off a stick as he walks.

"And then, the ship implodes and everyone dies," Alec says solemnly. He clasps his hands together briefly, then throws them up into a "what are you going to do?" kind of gesture.

"That sounds like a really depressing movie," Ruby says.

"It was," Alec says, "but it was also awesome." He pauses and his gaze settles on me. "What's your favorite movie, Emma?" He holds a finger up. "Wait, let me guess." He rubs his chin. "Celsius: Boy Band of the Century." He pulls his arm back and points at me.

I giggle, and Cher bumps her shoulder against mine. Maybe I could get over Matt this way.

12:20 P.M.
THE PARK

The park is empty when we get there. Alec flies across the wood chips to the monkey bars, swinging across them with ease. A little brown bird flits about in a puddle of rainwater at the base of a slide, and a swing sways slowly in the wind. I glance over at the picnic tables near the basketball court and flash back to being there with Connor last year.

All the feelings from that night rush back to me. Lonely. Embarrassed. Sad. Not only had I pushed Connor off of me and effectively ruined whatever pitiful relationship we had, but I was also fighting with both Ruby and Cher. It sucked.

I think about how far I've come since that moment. Yeah, it sucks that Matt doesn't like me. But I have the two best friends in the world, we're hanging out with cute boys, and Mom is taking me shopping next week because my bras don't fit right anymore.

A sliver of the sun pokes out from behind the clouds, and I reach out and wrap my arms around Ruby and Cher, hugging them to me. Ruby asks no questions, throwing her free arm around my shoulder, her left hand still holding Alejandra's.

"What are you doing?" Cher asks, stiffening slightly.

"I'm just... thankful for you both. Thanks for being there for me. I love you," I say. Ruby squeezes my shoulder.

"Okay, love you, too," Cher says, sliding out from under my arm. "But that's enough of that for me."

Ruby and I share a glance, giggling. Cher jogs to catch up to the boys but smiles back at us. My heart is full. It's the first time since last week I'm not feeling an active ache inside of me.

Jacob puts his arm around Cher, and Ruby and I exchange another look.

"Hypocrite!" Ruby shouts. Cher turns over her shoulder and sticks her tongue out. We all laugh.

Finally, we make it to the end of the park where the big, brown pavilion stands. Underneath it are some picnic tables and a gross, metal garbage can in the corner. The ceiling is covered in declarations of love and hate and phone numbers scrawled in permanent marker. The girls climb on top of the picnic tables, and I sit between Cher and Alejandra.

Alec comes over to stand in front of me. He pokes my knee as he tells us a story about his cousin falling off his water skies last summer. Alejandra bumps her leg against mine. She raises an eyebrow and smiles. I'm glad she's here, too. I can't believe I thought she was trying to steal my best friend.

We hear voices approaching behind us and turn to see who it is. My heart stops. Alejandra's head whips toward me. Cher reaches over and grabs the top of my leg.

There are three boys walking over. Andy, Jeremiah, and Matt.

12:30 P.M.

My mouth is dry, my hands are sweating, and my heart races uncontrollably. I honestly might throw up.

Why are they coming over here? What do I do?

I stare at the ground in front of me, my eyes unfocused, and try to remember how to act like a normal human.

Jeremiah's voice rings through my ears.

"Ruuuubyyyy!" he bellows. Ruby hops off the table as Jeremiah runs over. They high-five over their heads and then behind their backs.

"What's happening my friends?" Jeremiah asks, taking a step back. Andy walks right over to Jacob and Alec, bouncing a basketball to Jacob. Do they know each other?

Matt follows Andy a few steps behind. He's looking at the ground, but when he glances up, our eyes meet. We both look away like we've been caught doing something we shouldn't. My face is on fire, and I can barely breathe. I stare down at my knees.

Cher wraps an arm around my waist, Alejandra scooches closer, and Ruby comes to stand in front of me, putting a hand on my knee protectively. Her eyes search mine, and I know she's asking if I'm okay. I give her the smallest of shrugs.

Andy smiles brightly over at the girls and me. His nose is red, but at least he has long pants on. Jeremiah and Matt are both wearing shorts, like Jacob and Alec.

Andy lifts his hand, pointing to the other boys. "I play travel soccer with these two goons." He leans in then, and the three of them all kind of hit each other's hands and make a noise that sounds like the grumbling of a hungry troll's belly. Why can't boys be normal?

I risk another peek at Matt. I can't help myself. He's standing off to the side a bit, not fully entering what has become a circle, with the girls on the picnic table, the boys facing us, and Ruby kind of in the middle.

"Hi, Matt," Ruby calls out. He picks his head up and gives a small wave. "Not feeling very chatty lately, eh?" She stares right at him. Without thinking, I kick her.

"Ruby!" I hiss. "Don't." Ruby rolls her eyes, then climbs back onto the table next to Alejandra.

There's an awkward silence. Jacob and Alec look around the group wildly, probably trying to figure out where the weird energy is coming from.

After several long seconds, Jeremiah asks, "Anyone want to play basketball?" Jacob, Alec, and even Ruby and Alejandra all start toward the courts with Jeremiah and Andy. Matt follows slowly, his back to us and his hood covering his face.

Cher and I stand up. My legs feel like jelly.

"Do you want to go over there?" she asks, facing me.

"Yeah, I guess."

"We don't have to," she says, squeezing my arm.

"It's fine," I tell her. "Am I red?" I ask.

Cher clicks her tongue. "Uh, yeah. A little."

Matt stops walking. He pauses and then turns around. He pauses again.

I freeze. I can hear blood rushing in my ears.

Matt sort of kicks at the wood chips, spinning around. He puts his hands in his hoodie pocket... and starts walking back toward Cher and me.

I grab Cher's hand. "He's coming," I whisper.

"Huh?" Cher glances over her shoulder and smirks. "He's coming to talk to you. I knew it."

I can't focus on Cher right now. All I can focus on is keeping my body from betraying me. I swallow hard and try to regain control of my shaky limbs. It's not working.

"Uh, hey," Matt says as he walks up.

I don't say anything. I stare at the grass.

"Hi," Cher says, confident enough for the both of us.

"Um..." He hesitates. I want to look at him, but I can't bring myself to do it. Then he says my name. "Emma, could I, uh... could I talk to you?"

I drag my eyes up from the ground. Matt's face is blank. His mouth is in a straight line, no sign of his lopsided smile. My throat tightens around the lump sitting there. Matt looks off to his left, like he's watching for something, clearly avoiding eye contact with me. That's when I know.

He's going to tell me he doesn't like me.

CHAPTER 42

Obviously?

"You okay?" Cher asks quietly.

"Yeah," I squeak out.

She raises her eyebrows and gives Matt a scathing once-over before walking off to the basketball courts where everyone else is. Over her shoulder, she gives me a small smile and a nod. I know she's trying to tell me, *You got this*, but I really don't feel like I do.

Matt's eyes are on the ground, his hands still buried in the pocket of his hoodie. The silence between us feels heavy. And loud. Can silence feel loud? Why isn't Matt saying anything? It's making me even more nervous. I breathe in through my nose deeply, trying to catch my breath, even though I'm literally not even moving.

Matt clears his throat, then says, "Uh, do you want to walk?"

I shrug. "Sure." I hope he doesn't hear the shakiness in my voice.

He stomps through the grass over to the sidewalk, and I follow half a step behind him. He pauses, not quite looking at me, waiting for me to fall into step with him.

He still isn't saying anything. This is torture. Can we please get this over with?

I clear my throat, unsure what else to do. I'm not going to speak first.

Matt takes a deep breath. Probably preparing to let me down. A dozen scenarios race through my brain in the half-second before he opens his mouth, all of them with the same ending: *I don't like you.*

"So, um, I got your message," he finally says.

I nod, unable to speak. My entire body feels like it's been set on fire, and I'm honestly amazed I can put one foot in front of the next because I'm so mortified. That stupid message.

I continue staring at the ground as we walk. Out of the corner of my eye, I watch Matt pull his hood forward. He stops. We're about half a block from the park now, and the basketball courts are hidden behind the activity center next to it.

We're alone. I hope he lets me down easy. And then I can cry alone, behind the building where no one can see me.

He sighs, pulling his hood down now and turning to face me.

Oh God. Here it comes. My brain reminds me to breathe, but it feels too hard. I can't look at Matt while he does this. It's too embarrassing. Instead, I watch the tree branches up ahead sway in the wind, little buds starting to grow on them. I take a deep breath, this time through my mouth, and appreciate the chill that cools my currently overheating body.

Matt kind of grunts and puts his hands on either side of his head.

"*ListenIdolikeyou*," he spits out. But I'm not sure I heard him correctly because he said it so fast and so quietly.

"What?" I ask, knowing he can hear the shakiness in my voice now. But he has to repeat himself. I must have heard him wrong.

He sighs, turning to me and digging his hands deep into his hoodie pocket again.

"I like you," he says more slowly. "Obviously," he adds as an afterthought.

I freeze, goosebumps popping up all over my arms, but it's not from the wind.

"Can you say something?" Matt asks. His warm brown eyes search mine as I finally look at his face.

I stifle a laugh and bite my lip, thinking. I don't know what to say. I don't even know what to feel. Am I relieved? Am I excited? Am I annoyed? I think all of it.

"Obviously?" I demand.

"Yeah, obviously."

"You completely ignored my message for six days. You left me on read. Not even a like." Heat rises through my body. I think I'm mad.

"I know," he mumbles. "I'm sorry."

I roll my eyes.

"I didn't know what to say," he adds.

I scoff, gazing into the distance to our left. Matt shifts his weight from foot to foot a few times, slightly rocking side to side.

"It's complicated," he tries to explain. "You know, because of Andy. You said so yourself in the message."

"Yeah, I know," I concede.

"He's my best friend."

"I know."

"But, I really like you," Matt says, and there's a shakiness in his voice for the first time. He takes a step closer, hesitating for a second before grabbing my hand.

My heart beats faster than ever before, but it feels like everything else slows down around me. My mouth is suddenly dry, but my armpits are sweating like I had to run the mile in PE. There's an electric energy pulsing through my veins from the place where his hand touches mine.

I take a step closer to him. The air around us feels like it's buzzing. Matt takes a shaky breath, and he leans in closer. I can feel his body heat. My heart drops into the pit of my stomach and flies back up to sit in my throat, all the while thumping so hard, you could probably see it on the outside of my chest.

Is he going to kiss me? Oh my God. He's going to kiss me. It's happening. He leans in even closer now, our bodies almost touching. I close my eyes, waiting for it...

Until my mouth meets his shoulder. He wasn't leaning in for a kiss. It was a hug. We break apart immediately.

"Oh my God." I start babbling uncontrollably. "I'm sorry—I thought—I didn't realize—"

But I don't think Matt hears me because he's also talking. "Oh, you thought—I'm sorry—I, uh—"

This is the most embarrassing thing that has ever happened to me in my life. More embarrassing than the time I had a zit on my nose and had to present in front of the class last year. More embarrassing than the time Mom picked me up from school wearing faded Mickey Mouse pajamas. Even more embarrassing than the first time we had to change for PE, and I was wearing white granny panties. My face is so hot, I'm afraid it might sear the skin off. But even that wouldn't be more embarrassing than this.

"Screw it," Matt says and takes two steps forward. He reaches his arms out and pulls me closer to him and puts his mouth right on top of mine.

And the world lights up. This is what they mean when they talk about fireworks. My heart thumps in my chest, warmth spreads from the tips of my toes all the way up to my mouth, which is kissing Matt. Sparks literally fly in front of my closed eyes. I lean into the kiss and let it take over my body.

I don't know how long we stand there kissing, but eventually, we break apart, both breathing heavily. We look at each other and burst into laughter.

I like Matt more than I've ever liked anyone. I never felt that way kissing Connor last year, and I never felt that way kissing Andy either time he was my boyfriend. I've never felt this way ever before in my life. Every inch of my body tingles.

"I told you," Matt says once we catch our breath.

"Told me what?"

"That I like you," he says matter-of-factly.

"You could have made that clear sooner," I say, pushing his shoulder.

I want to kiss him again. He regains his balance, and I step closer to him, leaning my head back slightly. Matt understands and leans in, too. His kiss is quick this time, but gentle. I smile against his lips, feeling giddy.

He holds onto my hand as he steps back. He clears his throat, and my heart, which was whirring not unpleasantly in my chest, freezes.

"What?" I ask sharply.

Matt lets out a noise that is half-laugh, half-sigh.

"What?" I ask again, dropping his hand from mine.

He raises his face to the sky, closing his eyes and taking a deep breath. He lets it out, and his brown eyes lock on mine again.

"I like you. A lot." His lopsided smile appears on his face, but it's fleeting. "But..."

A knot immediately forms in my stomach, and I have to swallow the lump in my throat. I take a step back.

"Andy," he finishes. I hold my breath, waiting for more. "I have to tell him," he says quietly.

"Did you tell him about the message?" I ask.

Matt shakes his head no, his curly hair swaying with it.

"Have you mentioned me at all to him?"

Matt bites his lip, again shaking his head. Part of me wants to be mad. But watching him bite his lip makes me want to kiss him again. Heat rushes through my body, but I try to shake it off. Now is not the time.

"He has a girlfriend," I remind Matt, but he doesn't look convinced.

He stares off into the distance for a couple seconds. His mouth quirks up, and he inclines his head slightly, like he's having a silent argument with himself and conceding to the opposing voice.

"Maybe..." he starts, stepping back into my space and grabbing my hand again. His voice is quiet but deeper than usual. "Maybe, let's not say anything yet." I furrow my brow. "Not that it's a secret. Just, until I can talk to him. Later. Today." Relief floods through my veins. "Promise," he says, swaying our hands lightly.

"Okay," I say, barely above a whisper. We're standing toe to toe now, so close that I have to look up at him. All I want is for him to lean down and kiss me again. He doesn't. But it's almost better. I can feel the anticipation in every part of my body. Even in my toes. My elbow. My ear.

"So..." He hesitates for a second, rubbing his thumb in circles on my hand. His eyes dart to the ground before he continues. "Does that mean you'll be my girlfriend? I mean, that didn't come out right. Uh, I want to—um, yeah. I guess that's it. Will you be my girlfriend?"

"Yeah... Obviously." I roll my eyes for effect and try to contain the joy that bursts from my heart, but a smile spreads all the way across my face.

Matt laughs, shaking his head. Then he pulls me close and kisses me, and once again, the world explodes around us. I finally got my fireworks.

But it doesn't last long.

"Woah. What the hell?"

Matt and I turn. Andy is there.

What's next for Emma?

Need to know what happens next? Pick up right where we left off in *We'll Never Be Friends... and Other Girlhood Mishaps.*

If you want behind the scenes looks, sneak peeks, and early access to my next book, be sure to sign up for my newsletter at **rebeccagarnerauthor.com** or follow me on social media **@rebeccagarner_author**.

If you loved this book, please leave a review on Amazon and/ Goodreads!

Acknowledgements

I've written the book—shouldn't the hard part be over? I don't know why the thank-yous feel so hard to write. Maybe because there are so many people to thank, so many people I could not have done this without, so many small moments of encouragement that lifted me up when I needed it.

Thank you to my editor, Whitney McGruder, for loving Emma and the girls before anyone else and helping me make this story the best it could be.

To my earliest readers, Kelly, MJ, and Sisel. Thank you for helping shape this story into what it is today, and for telling me there were too many J names.

Thank you to my writing group, for helping me write the hardest part of the book (nope, not the acknowledgements)—the blurb—and for inviting me to be part of such a special space. You all inspire me to be a better writer.

Thank you to my beta readers, Lindsey, Deborah, Kelly (again), Mel, and Lily. You all helped make this story more authentic and a little less cringey, which Emma especially thanks you for.

And to the readers, thank you for picking up Emma's story and for making my dreams come true. I'm sorry about the cliff-hanger.

To my parents, thank you for giving me the life that inspired Emma's and for always being first in line to support me.

To my sister, Rachel, thank you for inspiring the nation with your own colonial pony. Everyone loves Marie, but I love you more.

Thank you to Lucy and Cameron for being the lights of my life. I hope someday you're proud of what your mama has done (and maybe a little embarrassed).

And the biggest thank you to Stephen for, well, everything. You give me fireworks every day.

A final shoutout to everyone who ordered a copy of the book before it was even done. Thank you for believing in me and in Emma's story. I couldn't do it without you.

www.ingramcontent.com/pod-product-compliance
Lightning Source LLC
Chambersburg PA
CBHW022113310726
48972CB00007B/2013